2 × 6/12 LT 9/11

RIVAL TO THE QUEEN

Also by Carolly Erickson

RIVAL
to the
QUEEN

Carolly Erickson

ST. MARTIN'S PRESS

NEW YORK

This is a work of fiction. All of the characters, organizations, and events portrayed in this novel are either products of the author's imagination or are used fictitiously.

www.stmartins.com

Library of Congress Cataloging-in-Publication Data

Erickson, Carolly, 1943–
    Rival to the queen / Carolly Erickson. — 1st ed.
        p. cm.
    ISBN 978-0-312-37974-2
    1. Leicester, Lettice Dudley, Countess of, 1543–1634—Fiction.   2. Elizabeth I,
Queen of England, 1533–1603—Fiction.   3. Leicester, Robert Dudley, earl of,
1532?–1588—Fiction.   4. Nobility—Great Britain—Fiction.   5. Queens—Great
Britain—Fiction.   I. Title.
    PS3605.R53R58 2010
    813'.6—dc22

                                                                    2010025197

First Edition: October 2010

10 9 8 7 6 5 4 3 2 1

To Charles Spicer
with heartfelt thanks

ONE

FLAMES crackled and rose into the heavy air as my father's servants piled more bundles of brushwood on the fire. Smoke rose grey-black out of the flickering orange tongues, the heat from the rising fire making my younger brother Frank draw back, fearful that we too might be singed or burned, even as the stench of burning flesh made us put our hands over our noses and recoil from its acrid, noxious reek.

I did not step back, I held my ground even as I heard Jocelyn's agonizing cries. I held my breath and shut my eyes and prayed, please God, make it rain. Please God, put the fire out.

It was a lowering and cold morning. The overcast sky was growing darker by the minute, and I had felt a few drops of rain. I thought, it wouldn't take much rain to douse this fire. Please, let it come now!

A large strong hand clamped onto my shoulder—I could sense its roughness through the sleeve of my gown—and I felt myself pulled backwards.

"Get back, Lettie! Can't you see the fire is spreading? Stand back there, beside your brother!"

"But father," I pleaded, my voice nearly lost amid the roar of the flames and the sharp snapping of twigs and branches, "it's Jocelyn. Our Jocelyn. I am praying that the Lord will send rain and save him!"

I looked up into my father's anguished face and saw at once the ravages of pain on his stern features. His voice was hoarse as he bent down and whispered "I'm praying for him too. Now do as I tell you!"

The fire was growing hotter. I was sweating, my flushed face was burning though the day was cold and once again I felt a spatter of raindrops on one cheek. I moved back to join my brother, who was weeping, sniffling loudly, and took his hand. At first he had tried his best to be manly, to resist the strong tug of emotion that we all felt. But Jocelyn had been his tutor, our tutor. He taught us our letters, and our writing hand, and, later, gave us our lessons in Greek and Latin. I had studied with him for seven years, Frank for nearly six. We loved him.

And now we were being forced to watch him die.

He was being burned for heresy. For professing the Protestant faith, as we did. For refusing to obey Queen Mary's command that all her subjects attend mass and revere the pope and renounce the church of Luther, the church her father Henry VIII and her late brother Edward VI had officially embraced, in sharp opposition to the age-old Roman belief.

Many felt as Jocelyn did, but most hid their convictions, and attended mass despite them. My father, who was always a practical man, did as Queen Mary ordered and told us to do the same.

"What we do outwardly does not matter," he told us. "It's what we believe in our hearts that makes us members of the true faith. The Lord sees what is in our hearts, and protects and favors us."

But Jocelyn, who was very brave, and very learned, a scholar from Magdalen College and a student of the ancient texts of the church, was not satisfied. To pretend allegiance to the pope and the mass was wrong, he said. To disguise the truth. And so he had spoken out against the queen and her Catholic mass, and had been seized and thrown into a dungeon. And now, on this day, he was condemned to die.

I had watched him, looking thin and gaunt, as they made him walk across the damp grass to where the reeds and split branches were being piled knee-deep. In the center of the pile was a three-legged stool, and he had been made to stand up on it. But before he did so he reached down to pick up some of the reeds and kissed them reverently.

"See how he blesses the reeds! See how he embraces his martyrdom!" I heard people in the crowd exclaim. "Surely he will be with the Lord in paradise!" But they kept their voices low, for they did not want to be put in prison or forced to submit to punishment, and we were all aware that there were guards and soldiers everywhere, listening for blasphemous words against the church of Rome.

Then the torch had been put to the twigs and branches, and the fire had blazed up, and Jocelyn, praying loudly for the queen who had condemned him and for my father and the servants who had built the fire, had at last been overcome by pain and began screaming.

I heard my father, in anguish, call out to Jocelyn, asking his forgiveness. But the only response was a loud wail of agony, and hearing it, I saw my proud, stern father shed tears.

Young as I was, only sixteen on the day Jocelyn was condemned to die, I realized that my father was being punished alongside our tutor. Queen Mary was making him suffer. She knew well that he had been a faithful servant of the crown ever since he was a very young man, serving in King Henry's privy chamber and, after the old king's death, serving King Edward as an envoy and councilor. He was unwaveringly faithful to the monarchy—but he did not, in his heart, profess the old religion, and she resented him for this. She was vengeful, everyone said so. Now she was taking vengeance against my father by forcing him to carry out the sentence of death against the young man she knew he was fond of, Jocelyn Palmer.

All of a sudden a strong wind blew up, I felt it lift my skirts and draw its raw breath against my neck. I let go of Frank's hand for a moment as he pulled away from me, escaping the glowing sparks that blew toward us.

The wind was putting the fire out. I dared to look at Jocelyn. His hair was burnt away as was most of his clothing, and the skin of his face was scorched and blackened, but his lips were moving.

He was singing, a hymn tune. His voice was scratchy but I recognized the tune. Others joined in the singing as the fire died to embers.

"Dear Jesus, Son of David, have mercy upon me," Jocelyn cried out. "Let it end!"

Soldiers approached my father and spoke to him, standing so near to him that I could not hear what they were saying. I looked up at the darkening sky. Surely it would rain soon, a hard rain. The sign of God's mercy.

Then my father was giving orders and fresh loads of brushwood and branches were being brought and the fire rekindled. But not before a burly guard had reached up to strap two swollen sheep's bladders around Jocelyn's waist.

"No," I cried to my father. "Spare him! Let him live!"

Once again my father grasped my arm, bending down so he could speak to me, and to me alone.

"I must do as the queen commands. Otherwise we all face Jocelyn's peril. But there is one last mercy I can show him. The bladders are filled with gunpowder. When the fire reaches them, they will explode, and he will die. He will be spared much agony."

Torches were put to the wood and the fire began to blaze up, though I could feel drops of rain falling now, the rain I had prayed for, and smoke rose with the fire, black, choking smoke that was blown into our faces, and with it, the stink of Jocelyn's flesh. I thought then, I cannot bear this.

I felt my gorge rise. I doubled over. My legs felt heavy, and it was hard to breathe. Minutes passed. All around me I could hear people weeping and sighing and coughing from the thickening smoke. I glanced at Frank. He had closed his eyes and bowed his head. His fists were clenched at his sides.

With a bright flash and a loud crack the bladders of gunpowder exploded, but there was to be no mercy for Jocelyn. The blasts went outward, tearing away part of one of his arms but leaving his blackened torso intact.

How I found the courage to look at Jocelyn then, in his last extremity, I will never understand. His legs were burnt, blood seeped from the fingers of one arm and his eyes were charred sockets. Yet his swollen tongue moved within what was left of his gums, and I knew that he prayed.

"Lord Jesus," I heard my father say in a broken voice, "receive his spirit!"

Then with another loud crack the skies opened and rain began to pour down in thick sheets, flooding the grass and quenching the fire and turning the ground to thick squelching mud underfoot.

It was the rain I had prayed for, but it came too late. What was left of Jocelyn's body hung limp and lifeless, the flesh of his face—a face I had loved—so burned away that I could not have said whose face it was.

I felt Frank reach for my hand and we clung to each other, standing there in the drenching rain, until the crowd scattered and my father gave the order to wrap the body in a burial cloth and take it away.

TWO

WE left England shortly after Jocelyn died. We had no choice, father said, and mother agreed. England was no longer a safe place for the Knollys family.

It was not just that my father, Francis Knollys, could not bring himself to preside over any more cruel executions of fellow Protestants—or of Catholics either, for that matter—for he was, deep down, a tenderhearted man. Or that Queen Mary was growing more and more vengeful, ordering more and more men and women to their deaths because they would not conform to her Catholic beliefs. Or that some said she was mad, crazed by anger and sorrow over her inability to give birth to a living child to succeed her on the throne.

It was more than all these things, a deep-rooted taint of blood that made us vulnerable to the queen's wrath. For we were related to Queen Mary's half-sister Princess Elizabeth, and Elizabeth, just then, was imprisoned in the Tower of London, accused of treason.

My beautiful mother Catherine was Princess Elizabeth's aunt, and I and my brother and sister were the princess's cousins. Queen Mary believed that everyone related to her half-sister was suspect, and probably dangerous to her throne and to the peace of the realm, and certainly immoral.

My mother had explained our family history to my sister Cecelia and Frank and me when we were quite young. It all began, she said, early in the reign of our famous King Henry VIII, many years before we were born.

"You see, our late King Henry, when he was married to Queen Catherine, his Spanish wife, needed a son to inherit his throne. But all Queen Catherine's baby boys died, and nearly all the baby girls too, all except for Mary, who is now queen.

"If only Queen Catherine had died!" she went on, a little wistfully. "Everything would have been so much easier. But she did not die, she just went on having more and more babies, and they kept on dying. The poor king thought that God was cursing him, and maybe He was. So in time King Henry honored other women and let them become the mothers of his children. One of those women was my mother, your grandmother Mary Boleyn."

Our grandmother Mary Boleyn had died when I was a very small child, far too young to remember her, but I had seen portraits of her, painted when she was young. A lovely girl, with light brown hair and blue eyes. An innocent girl, or so one would have thought from the look of the portraits. Yet I knew from what my mother said that she had the reputation of being far from innocent.

"She had a husband, William Carey," mother was saying. "Yet she also had the king's love. And his was the stronger." The last words were almost whispered, as though mother were confiding to us a precious secret.

"So you are the king's daughter!" I cried. "And we are all his royal grandchildren!"

My mother smiled, an enigmatic smile.

"Some people say that, but only my mother knew for certain. And she would never say. I think the king made her swear to keep everything about our birth a secret. Certainly King Henry always favored me, and your uncle Henry too."

Our mother's brother Henry was a frequent visitor to our family home at Rotherfield Greys. He was a tall, muscular man, an exceptional horseman and fine athlete. Yes, I thought. Uncle Henry could very well be the son of the late King Henry, who had had the reputation of being able to match or exceed any man at his court for height and strength and was a champion riding at the tilt.

"So you are a princess, and Uncle Henry is a prince," I said. "You should be granted royal honors."

My brother and sister nodded enthusiastically. "You should, mother," they urged.

But mother only laughed. "I am no princess—at least I was never acknowledged as such. I am plain Catherine Carey, daughter of Mary Boleyn Carey and Will Carey of the privy chamber. And brother Henry is of the same lineage—officially. In truth I do not know who my father was, the king or my legal father Will Carey, who died when I was very small. Or possibly some other man, for my mother was said to have other lovers. I have no desire to make exalted claims to the throne, or to be a rival to Queen Mary."

"Yet you look like him," I insisted. "You have reddish hair and blue eyes and are very fair, just as he was." I knew only too well what King Henry had looked like, all the royal palaces were full of his portraits, and there was a sculpture of his head and shoulders in a place of honor in our family home.

At this my mother nodded, but then she went on, in quite another tone.

"Whoever my true father was, there is a far darker aspect to our family story. It concerns your grandmother Mary's sister Anne."

We all knew of Anne. The witch. The harlot. The evil woman who had cast a spell on King Henry and used her magic to force him to divorce good Queen Catherine and marry her instead. The wicked queen who had been beheaded.

I had heard the servants gossip about Queen Anne for as long as I could remember. They often crossed themselves—in the Catholic fashion—when they spoke of her, as if to ward off her potent evil that lingered on, even though she had been dead for many years. My parents never spoke of her at all—at least not in my hearing—so mother's mention of her made me pay particular attention to her words.

"My aunt Queen Anne Boleyn never liked my mother. They were very different. Mother was a soft and comforting sort of woman, who liked to laugh and dance and had a sunny nature. She loved to eat and drank more wine than was good for her."

Hearing this I glanced at my sister, and caught her eye. We quickly looked away again, but each of us knew what the other was thinking: our mother also drank more wine than was good for her.

"My aunt Anne was a shrewd woman," mother was saying. "I liked to think that she saw the world through narrowed eyes. She thought Mary was a fool—though in truth I think it was Anne who was, in the end, the more foolish. My mother was happy most of the time, while Anne, for all her shrewdness, never was. At least I never saw her when her face was lit with happiness."

Smiling, she reached down and cupped my face in her two hands, then Cecelia's. "That is what I wish for you girls," she said. "That your pretty faces will be lit with happiness, all your lives long."

"Did you watch Queen Anne die?" Frank asked mother, "like we had to watch Jocelyn die?"

"No. Brother Henry and I were away, living in the country. We were in disgrace, as were all the Boleyns. As we still are. But it was Anne who mattered. Anne and her brother George and all those in their households. Oh, that was a horrible time. Everyone I knew was frightened, and my mother most of all."

"Was Queen Anne really a witch?" Frank asked.

Mother looked thoughtful. "It was said that she practiced alchemy. Mother told me about a room she had, where she kept potions and powders. The servants thought she was turning lead into gold, though if she did, she never gave any to us. She may have made poisons. But as to witchcraft—" She broke off, shaking her head and looking dubious. "It was said the king loved her with an uncommon hunger. But I think it was the hunger of great lust, and not of witchery. In any case," she concluded, "Queen Mary never forgave her stepmother Queen Anne for being so alluring to the king that he divorced her mother. Mary hates all Boleyns, and no doubt she always will."

Mother's words were much in my thoughts as our family boarded the *Anne Gallant* at Dover, leaving Queen Mary's Catholic England and bound for the safety of Protestant Frankfurt, where my father had acquaintances who he said would take us in. I held my head high, convinced, as I was, that I had the royal blood of the Tudors in my veins. And I remembered what my mother had said, that it was far better to be happy than shrewd, and above all to be wary of the wrath of kings and queens.

THREE

WHETHER it was because of my newfound certainty that I was of royal ancestry or simply because, at sixteen, I was coming into my years of promised beauty, I was much admired when we arrived at our new home in Frankfurt.

I had been a beautiful child, everyone had always agreed on that, though my father had frowned on all talk of my loveliness and said "You'll make her too full of herself" or "Too much praise makes the devil's playground" when my mother and others spoke admiringly of how pleasing my looks were. My younger sister Cecelia, my father's favorite, tended to burst into tears and leave the room when I was the center of attention; this made him vexed at me, though it was hardly my fault that my hair was the rare red-gold of autumn leaves and my skin as flawless and as translucent as the finest ivory. (Cecelia's hair was a mousy brown and her skin, while smooth, tended to be the color of sand. But she had very good teeth, as I often reminded her.)

We were lodged in the grand house of Jacob Morff, a member of the Consistory and an elder of the Lutheran church, the dominant influence and authority in Frankfurt. The four-storey gabled house was near the Old Bridge, where a few Catholic sisters continued to operate a foundling home and to take in unwanted infants. We heard the babies crying at all hours, in fact it seemed to mother and me that their numbers were growing with each passing day. But beyond this nuisance all was comfortable in the Morff household, and we were shown a courteous if impersonal hospitality.

It was the custom for Protestants to shelter one another, for as our numbers grew we were persecuted mercilessly, and there were many English Protestants coming to the continent, fleeing Queen Mary and her burnings, when I was a girl. Herr Morff had several English families living in his large house, though he was not a genial host, rather he kept a grave distance, as though unsure what to make of us foreigners. In time I was to understand why.

At first I quite enjoyed myself in our new town, a large and bustling place, its narrow streets crowded with horses and carts and peddlers on foot. The sprawling marketplace was bursting with commerce, except on Sundays, when all business transactions were forbidden by the Consistory as were all amusements. The ancient cathedral with its tall spire towered over all other city structures, and the massive stone bridges that spanned the Main river, the thick brick walls that surrounded the town and the weighty, many-storied houses centuries old gave the entire place an air of solidity, if not of grandeur. London was older than Frankfurt, father said, but Frankfurt was richer—and much more moral, now that the Consistory governed all.

That it was a moral place we knew from the abundance of hymn-singing that went on, not only in church, where the services were long and tedious (though no one was allowed to complain about this out loud), but in the streets and squares. When we went out in the afternoons, we often walked or rode past group after group of townspeople who had gathered to sing hymns or other pious songs.

"We must join in," father said. "We must not appear strangers in their midst." So we learned to sing "How lovely shines the morning star" and "My trust in Thee can nothing shake" and "From depths of woe I cry to Thee" in our English-accented German and we tried our best to imitate father's expression as he sang, his heavy-lidded eyes sad, his lined, narrow face full of a dark longing.

We did our best to look and act pious, but true religious feeling cannot be feigned, and in truth we were young and full of pent-up energy and had few outlets for our restless physical vigor. Hymn-singing was not the activity we needed.

But the elders made and enforced strict rules about what we could and could not do. We were not allowed to swim, lest it lead to "promiscuous bathing" with men and women, boys and girls all joining in together. Long walks were forbidden, because they made the blood flow more rapidly and heightened the passions. Athletic feats promoted pride in the body, and the body was the prime portal of sin. Dancing, which led to frivolity and flirtation, was condemned with especial rigor.

One Sunday there was a scuffle in the square near the Old Bridge, in front of a tavern called the White Lion. I had often seen men quarreling and fighting in our village of Rotherfield Greys and on our visits to London but until that afternoon I had never seen men attacking one another in hymn-singing Frankfurt. Then I noticed that at the center of the brawl was Jacob Morff's sturdy, blond son Nicklaus, a boy I liked for his jokes and a way he had of imitating the cleaning women in the

Morff household. These maids walked with their knees together, taking short steps and always looking down at the floorboards, never at each other or objects in the room or other people. They were not shy, nor furtive, merely inconspicuous to an extreme degree. Nicklaus Morff, despite his girth and strong young muscles, could squeeze himself down and assume the appearance and carriage of one of these maids, pressing his knees together and walking in a way that made me laugh out loud, and Cecelia too if she was nearby.

Now, however, Nicklaus was pounding the head of another boy onto the rounded stones of the square, and shouting "No, you won't! You can't!" as the cluster of squabbling men and boys grew larger, drawing a crowd.

"Stop this at once!"

It was the voice of a big man I had seen once or twice at Jacob Morff's house, a senior member of the Consistory who, as he began to speak, seemed to cleave a path through the crowd until he stood amid the fighters, pulling them apart and shouting at them. Several other older men joined the leader in putting a halt to the violence. The brawlers, disheveled and dirty, several of them bloody, stood stiff-limbed and scowling. I heard Nicklaus swear angrily under his breath at the boy he had been scuffling with.

"Each of you, take note! This is your warning. If you are seen lifting your hands against each other again, you will be publicly denounced by name. Come out, saith the Lord, lest the body be cankered by its weakest members. Now, speak! What is the cause of this rioting and drunkenness?"

At first no one spoke. Then a man was thrust forward by some of the others.

"It is the White Lion, Elder Roeder. It is to be closed!"

"That is correct. There are to be no more taverns in this city from now on. Only Christian eating houses. With a Bible on every table. The Consistory has ordained it."

A loud moan of outrage arose from the crowd.

"Silence!"

But the moan of protest went on, and there were shouts of "Beer! Beer!" and a few people began singing a drinking song.

Elder Roeder drew from his long black gown a tablet and a charcoal-tipped stick, and began writing down names. Meanwhile I saw, somewhat to my amazement, that Bibles were being flung out of the door of the White Lion, landing on the cobblestones and raising small puffs of dust. I thought to myself, are these the same citizens of Frankfurt who meet to sing hymns in the streets? Or are there two Frankfurts, the city of the pious and the city of the others, who do not sing hymns and who drink in taverns and, most likely, engage in promiscuous bathing and athletics and card-playing and dancing.

"Sacrilege!" shouted the elder, and he wrote more furiously on his tablet. "You are all denounced! You will all appear before the Consistory!"

"Well, if we must," shouted Nicklaus Morff, "then we must. But we can all get drunk first!"

And before anyone could stop him he darted into the White Lion, and a good many of those in the crowd followed him in, leaving Elder Roeder to his writing and shouted threats.

Father led us all away before we too could find our names recorded on his tablet. But the elder's angry shouts followed us as we made our way along the river, past the bridge and the foundling home, and began to hear, as well, the strains of a raucous drinking song.

FOUR

NICKLAUS Morff began to intrigue me. Not because of his looks, which were quite ordinary—heavy-lidded, pale blue eyes, a broad unlined brow, a nose too wide and shapeless for handsomeness and thin lips, nearly always creased into a grin—but because he and his friends dared to defy the iron grip of the Consistory and were showing the rest of us a path toward a freer and more adventuresome life.

The strictures of the governing elders did not frighten him, though he suffered his share of beatings for defying the rules and was eventually expelled from the congregation, much to his father's disgust. He had a group of friends, mostly Catholic boys, I assumed, for I never saw any of them in our Protestant church, who loitered near the Old Bridge waiting for him after dark and then went with him to the public gardens where, according to Elder Roeder, wickedness kept its kingdom.

I watched from the window of the small bedroom Cecelia and I shared on an upper floor in the Morff house as the boys clustered near the torchlit bridge abutment and leaned against the stonework, laughing and poking each other and occasionally looking up toward me.

"Put out that candle," Cecelia whispered one night when I was watching the boys. "Don't you know those boys can see you?"

I did know, and I did not snuff out the candle. I wanted them to see me. I wanted to be down among them, laughing and joking and flirting.

"Those godless worthless boys!" Cecelia was saying. "Worse than Nicklaus, at least Nicklaus has been baptized."

Cecelia, I knew, was quite infatuated with Nicklaus. I could tell by the way she kept her eyes on him whenever he was in the room, and the way she tried to inch closer to him. Once I had seen her brush up against him as they passed through a doorway and I noticed that she never again wore the pair of blue sleeves she had been wearing that day. I supposed she had made a shrine of them, a shrine to her infatuation, and the thought made me laugh.

As for Nicklaus, he kept his eyes on me. There was no question about which of us had attracted his interest. He had not yet spoken to me, he had only smiled at me rather shyly once or twice, though he was not shy with anyone else. But I knew who it was that he liked, and it wasn't my sister.

"They are not godless. They are Catholics. And all Catholics are baptized when they are babies."

Cecelia sniffed. "Elder Roeder says they go to the public gardens, where the bad women wait for them. And they drink and fornicate there."

"If the White Lion had not been shut down, they would not be forced to go to far worse places to get their beer."

There were footsteps outside our door, and in a moment the door was opened and our mother came in.

"It's past time you were in bed, girls. Letitia, put that candle out!"

"She's watching the boys by the bridge. She does it every night." Cecelia's tone was querulous, but also plaintive.

"She knows the rules. She will obey them."

I carried the candle from the window ledge to my bedside, and slipped into bed beside Cecelia, snuffing the candle out. Mother pulled the thick counterpane up to cover us both, bent down to kiss us, then left.

I waited until I heard Cecelia's breathing become slow and even. Then I got out of bed, careful not to wake my sleeping sister, and went to the window again.

The sky had grown darker. The stars were out, and the flickering lights on the bridge shone on the rippling surface of the river. A light rain was beginning to fall, but the boys, still waiting where I had last seen them, seemed not to care. Before long I saw Nicklaus run out of the house and join his friends, who whooped with joy at his approach. Together they all set off half-running, half-leaping across the bridge, in the direction of the public gardens.

The city was in furor over the arrival of the Anabaptists.

They swarmed into Frankfurt like bees, colonizing and swarming and gathering in large numbers in the weavers' districts and wherever the ragged people lived.

They were a religious group, my father said, but they were not like us. Nor were they like the Catholics. They had no churches but preached in cellars or out in the open air. Poor people flocked to hear them preach, for they deluded the poor by speaking of a pure and simple belief in following the path of Jesus. They did not talk of sin, but rather of leaving the world behind and seeking a sweeter home. Of making this world into a better one.

The Anabaptists did great harm, according to my father and the elders, who preached against them every Sunday and during the week as well. They threatened to destroy the true faith— our Protestant faith. They ignored sin, and the wages of sin. They were like a horde of locusts swooping down on crops and destroying them, the elders said, only the crops were the Christians, we Protestant Christians whose task it was to destroy in turn every Anabaptist who crossed our path.

"Death to the Anabaptists!" the Consistory declared. Soon we began seeing evidence that the crusade against the invaders was having its effect.

In the square near the White Lion—now renamed the Soldiers of Christ eating house—six Anabaptists were burned at the stake. Others were rounded up by the town authorities and taken to the dungeons and garroted, their corpses piled in the gutters. Severed heads rotted on the Old Bridge, hanging from the tall lantern posts, open-mouthed and swaying ghoulishly. Worst of all, so it seemed to me, Anabaptist women, many of them mothers, were denounced and condemned, and then brought to the riverside quite near the Morff house. On orders from the elders, the women were bound with ropes, their arms pinned to their sides, their legs tied together. Then their feet were cut off, and they were thrown into the river to drown.

We could not help being aware of these horrifying executions, though I did my best to avoid witnessing them.

Each evening Jacob Morff led his entire household, including our family, in prayer, and thanked the Lord that the crusade against the wicked Anabaptists was resulting in so many deaths. I had to join in these prayers, but I could not contemplate what was being done without feeling a crushing weight of pain. I had nightmares about the executions, especially the drownings of the women and the sight of their small children, abandoned and weeping, along the river's edge. I told my father about these nightmares, and he said that I must think of these Anabaptist enemies of Christ not as humans, but as monstrous beings sent to test our faith. That would help me surmount my feelings of pity, he said.

"But it is not just pity I feel, father. It is horror."

"Then thinking of them as monsters will prevent you from feeling horror. These are times that go beyond our understanding, Letitia. Only God understands. And he leads the elders of our congregation. Where he leads, we must obey."

I could not help but argue. "Is he leading Queen Mary in England?" I asked.

He paused, and when he answered, his voice was quiet. "She believes that he is."

"Then I don't understand, father. And I need to."

He shrugged. His shoulders sagged, as they always did when he had lost an argument, especially when he argued with my mother.

"I don't either. I just pray. And I am thankful that God has let me endure, and keep my family safe."

I saw then that he was indeed bewildered and saddened by all the cruelty made necessary by faith, just as I was, though he had to believe that what the Consistory was doing was right and necessary and even holy.

The burnings and beheadings and drownings continued in Frankfurt for months, and still the Anabaptist scourge did not abate. I kept imagining that in time I would become hardened to these acts, that my feelings would grow coarsened or even numb. But that did not happen. Instead I felt myself becoming even more sensitive to the horrors around me, and it became my prayer that I might find a way to live with them. To endure them.

Late one afternoon as the shadows were lengthening and the

river was turning from the deep grey-blue of noon to the muted ashen grey of evening, an Anabaptist woman was brought to the riverside near the Morff house to be drowned.

Usually, when this happened, I went down into the cellars and hid there for an hour or two until I could be certain the execution was over. But on this afternoon I felt a different impulse. I stayed by the bedroom window and forced myself to watch.

The woman who was being led to her death, a plump, apple-cheeked woman wearing a sacklike shapeless gown, was young and blond. The executioner had cut her hair very short. She was pale, but her hands and arms were brown, the hands and arms of a peasant who worked in the fields during the warm months and who was accustomed to a life without comforts. There was no one with her. No one, that is, who appeared to be a relative or friend. But she carried a small bundle, hugging it close to her heart. It had to be a child.

The execution proceeded. The presiding elder bowed his head and said a prayer, then gave the order for the woman's arms and legs to be bound. I did not see what happened to the bundle she carried, so swiftly were the orders given and so suddenly was the woman thrown to the ground. A long gleaming knife was lifted, and with two sure strokes her feet were severed at the ankle. Blood gushed out, spewing not flowing, staining the grey rocks at the river's edge. Then two men seized the woman's upper arms and lifted her, and threw her into the water. I saw her open mouth but could not hear her scream. The current was swift. It carried her toward the center of the river where her body turned and bobbed, lifted and sucked under by the force of the waters, and then was lost.

As darkness gathered the men who had taken part in the execution pulled their cloaks around them and hurried away. In a moment the site was empty, though the rocks were still stained

red and I thought I could see a small scrap of dark cloth lying at
the water's edge.

And then, for some reason, I thought I heard a faint cry.

At first I wasn't certain I was hearing it, so weak was the
sound, so hard to distinguish from the customary sounds of the
street. But it persisted, or I thought it did.

I continued to hear the sound as I went down to the riverside.
It seemed to be coming from under the bridge, where thick tall
grasses covered the rocks and there was a stench of rotting food
and slops from the butchers' stalls.

Making my way with difficulty, parting the undergrowth, I
heard the cry more and more distinctly. It was a baby's cry.

"Do you hear that?"

Light shone on the grasses and suddenly Nicklaus was beside
me, holding a lantern aloft.

"Yes. A baby. It must be the baby the condemned woman was
holding when they brought her here. Someone tried to save it."

"Or just tossed it aside."

As if in response to our voices the crying grew louder and
more sustained.

We continued to search, side by side, until we came upon the
tiny child, naked and shivering, lying in a patch of weeds.

"He needs a blanket," Nicklaus said. "Here." He handed me
the lantern, then pulled off his thick shirt and wrapped it
around the infant, lifting it up and starting to make his way out
from under the bridge, toward the roadway that ran in front of
his father's house. The sound of the child's crying grew more
muffled.

"My father would never allow this baby in his house, if he
knew where it came from."

"The foundling home," I said. "We'll take it there. Surely the
nuns will accept it."

"They will turn it into a little Catholic," Nicklaus said with a wry smile. "But at least it will live. That is the important thing."

We smiled at each other, then walked together the short distance to the convent. An empty basket sat beneath an eave of the religious house day and night, ready to receive any infant brought to the nuns for care. We placed the baby in the basket and rang the bell that hung from the wall nearby. Almost at once the flat metal wheel on which the basket sat began to turn, bringing the small contribution within the walls of the convent.

"Good night, little one," I whispered. "May the Lord protect you."

I heard Nicklaus whisper an amen as invisible hands reached for the whimpering infant. We stood beside the wall until we could no longer hear any sound. Then we went back to the Morff house, and though we did not speak, we were both aware that we shared a secret. That night, when Jacob Morff led the household in prayer, I did not join in thanking the Lord for the deaths of the wicked Anabaptists. Rather I said a prayer for the motherless baby, and for the nuns, in thanks that they were willing to take in all the lost and unwanted little ones from the great city of Frankfurt, knowing nothing of them save that they were in need.

FIVE

"Y OU were seen."

Elder Roeder glared at me accusingly.

"Pardon me?"

"You were seen. You and Nicklaus Morff. Putting your baby into the basket of the foundling home."

"Yes—and why not? Is there a reason why a charitable act such as saving a child's life should be kept hidden?"

"You make your sin worse by adding effrontery to it!"

His voice had risen, he was shrill. Others in the congregation were listening.

It was the hour when believers gathered for the public chastising of sinners, when the elders denounced transgressions and the worst of those who broke church law were excluded permanently from the community.

My father stepped forward from among the group. "If my daughter is at fault in any way, I will correct her."

The elder now glared at father. "It is the Consistory that corrects!" He turned once again to me, and looked me up and down.

"Young girls hide evil beneath their skirts," he said with contempt. "Do you deny that you and Nicklaus Morff placed an infant in the basket of the foundling home?"

"I deny nothing. We saved a baby and gave it to the nuns to prevent it from dying. We acted charitably."

"Charitably! You acted wickedly! You committed fornication, and produced a bastard, then made your sin worse by hiding the proof of your wickedness among the sisters to raise according to their abominable rites!"

"But that is not true!" I cried out. "Nicklaus!" I looked around me, at the faces of the congregants, hoping to see Nicklaus. But he was not there, nor was his father, or anyone else I recognized from the Morff household.

"Where is Nicklaus?" I asked. "He will join me in saying what really happened."

"Nicklaus Morff is a brawler and a liar who sins nightly in the public gardens." I saw, to my dismay, that a number of people were nodding in agreement at the elder's words. A murmuring had begun. A hostile murmuring. My heart sank.

Elder Roeder was unfolding a piece of writing.

"The congregation is informed," he read, "that the sinner Letitia Knollys was seen holding trysts with Nicklaus Morff and other young men at night, near the Old Bridge. That she has often left her bed at midnight to join her lover. And that on the night of the full moon she was seen going under the bridge, and her lover with her, and some time later they came out from under the bridge with a newborn child." At these words a gasp went up from those standing nearest me, and I felt my cheeks grow hot.

There had been a full moon on the night the Anabaptist woman was killed, I remembered.

"But there was no sin!" I burst out. "It was an act of mercy!"

"How the wicked deceive themselves," I heard someone in the congregation mutter.

"The baby was the son of Anabaptists," I went on, but as soon as I said the word "Anabaptists," there were cries of horror.

Elder Roeder glared at me once again.

"You admit, then, that in addition to fornication you are guilty of consorting with the worst of sinners, those who preach error and turn the faithful from the true path!"

I saw then that it was hopeless. I stood condemned unheard, no one believed or trusted me except Nicklaus, who knew the truth, and he was nowhere to be seen.

Summoning all my courage, and remembering, as I did in times of distress, that I had royal blood in my veins, I stood as tall as I could (Elder Roeder being much taller) and shouted in my loudest voice, "Who is the informer that accuses me?"

The room fell silent. The elder folded the paper he held, and put it back into a pocket of his robe. Then, looking out across the sea of faces, he said, "Stand forth!"

There was a rustling of skirts and a shuffling of feet. From the back of the room a young woman came through the crowd. At first I could see only her cap, but as she came closer I was able to see her face and realized who it was.

"Cecelia Knollys, do you swear that the words you have written and delivered to this congregation are truthful?"

"I do."

She did not look at me, or at our father, or indeed at anyone but the stern-faced elder. Before I could accuse her of lying, or

27

spit out the vengeful words that rose to my throat, the Consistory pronounced its judgment.

I was banned from the congregation, and not only I, but our entire family. We were ordered to leave the Morff house, and the town of Frankfurt, by sunset on the following day, or face the wrath of the congregation and its implacable God.

SIX

AS fate would have it, Queen Mary died very near the time our family was expelled from Frankfurt. Her Protestant half-sister, our relative Elizabeth, became queen. The persecutions were at an end. It was safe for our family to return to England once again.

I was still very angry with Cecelia for denouncing me to the Frankfurt congregation, and accusing me of a sin I did not commit. I did my best to explain to my family what really happened on the night Nicklaus Morff and I took the baby to the foundling home, and to point out, among other flaws in Cecelia's story, that I had certainly not been carrying Nicklaus's child for nine months, concealing the very large round ball of a growing child beneath my gown. I hoped that I was believed, and redeemed in their eyes.

In any case our joy at returning home served to soften my anger somewhat, and when we received an official summons to court from the queen herself—the greatest of honors, as my father was quick to point out—our petty family squabbles were temporarily laid aside as we prepared to take our places in the royal household.

"The new queen is eager to raise up all her Boleyn relations," my father said, having brought mother and me and Cecelia together in his private closet, where he kept his important papers and wrote at his untidy wide oaken desk. "She is sensitive about her birth, and about her late mother's reputation. Say nothing about it! Do not mention the name of Anne Boleyn! If she mentions her mother by name, just smile and nod and look agreeable."

He looked at me, taking me in, head to toe, with a critical glance.

"Lettie, the queen is very sensitive about her beauty," he began, only to be interrupted by mother, who laughed.

"But she has none," mother said. "Her face is pinched and narrow, her skin has no glow, and is such an odd color—too sallow—and her eyes! Small, with no lashes (not like our Lettie here, whose eyelashes are so long and thick they need no darkening or lengthening), and such sparse light eyebrows! No man would look at her twice, if she were not the queen."

"Catherine, such sentiments are best kept to yourself," father upbraided her, then turned back to me. "Lettie, as I was saying, you will need to be shamefaced and modest, and not flaunt your charms. Perhaps if you make an effort to compliment Her Majesty on her looks, that would help."

"Indeed!" mother said. "She is so vain! She requires constant praise. Have you ever wondered," she said to father, "why she keeps so many looking-glasses and hand mirrors in her rooms? Why she cannot stop looking at herself?"

"No," my father said curtly. "And neither should you, Catherine.

The ways of majesty are not our ways, and we ought not to seek to understand them."

Mother scoffed at this, but fell silent. I thought I saw, in listening to my father talk about the queen, why it was that he had been a valued royal servant and official for so long, first to the boy-king Edward and then to Queen Mary, before we left for Frankfurt. He was genuinely, unflinchingly loyal, respectful, reverent toward the anointed monarch, whoever he or she was.

It was no wonder that, when we presented ourselves at the palace, we discovered that the queen had appointed father Vice-Chamberlain of the royal household, Captain of the Halberdiers and, before long, a member of her privy council.

Mother was appointed Mother of the Maids and Cecelia and I were given posts as maids of honor, along with a dozen or so other girls, of various shapes and sizes and dispositions. Over the first few days of our time at court I observed the other maids. Some were haughty, some sweetly submissive. All were eager to make the most of their good fortune in being appointed to such an exalted position. And all were very eager to be married to wealthy men, with grand titles and wide lands. Their marriage prospects— along with those of the queen—were their favorite topic of conversation.

We maids of honor were quartered in rooms adjacent to the queen's bedchamber, so that we would be available at all hours if needed. We were crowded together, sharing beds as nearly all those in the royal household did and with very little space for our clothes and other possessions. Everything we did and said was public, every cross look or unguarded expression was noted and reported to our mother in her role as Mother of the Maids.

When Cecelia and I were first brought into the queen's presence, and formally presented to her, we curtseyed low and bent our heads as we had been taught to do. At length she raised us up with a gesture of one white hand.

She stood before us, tall and slim, her rather sharp gaze resting on me with particular interest. I remembered my father's warning and made an effort to look shamefaced and modest (though it was against my nature), and not to call attention to myself or give myself airs.

There was a long silence.

"Is that a wen on your forehead?" she asked me at length.

"I know of none, Your Majesty," I said. "Though my skin has not Your Majesty's perfection, nor its glow—"

"Are you flattering me, girl? Have you been told to flatter me, because you are so comely yourself? It is a common enough tactic, I fear, and a foolishly obvious one. Still, I do believe I glimpse a wen."

She reached for the small hand mirror that hung from her girdle, detached it and handed it to me.

"Look for yourself."

I obeyed, but saw no mole or spot or flaw on my forehead.

"I shall have to call my father's surgeon," I suggested, handing back the mirror.

"Do so," was her sharp retort. "A wen is the mark of a whore."

"I do hate women with whiny voices," the queen went on after a moment. "Yours is annoying. Come here, closer to the window, into the light."

I did as she asked, and went to stand where the sunlight fell directly on me. She looked at me again, then nodded to herself.

"Yes. You have the Boleyn beauty—and I sense something of the Boleyn fire as well. Not so your lumpy sister," she added rudely. "It never ceases to amaze me, how sisters can be so unalike! My sister Mary and I—" she began, then broke off.

I wanted to say, but Queen Mary was only your half-sister, but bit my tongue.

Meanwhile Cecelia, always ill at ease when my looks and attractions were being discussed, shook out her kirtle and petticoat noisily. She had put on weight, she was the plumpest of the maids and at the sound of her rustling skirts the queen looked at her scathingly.

"Have that gown let out," she said. "It fits you too tightly. Or throw it away, and order another."

I held my breath, hoping that Cecelia would have the good sense not to make a tart reply. We had both been cautioned, by the other maids, that the queen was subject to sudden fits of anger, and that her anger could be terrible.

"Yes, Your Majesty," was all my sister said, and I sighed with relief. I felt the queen's eyes on me again. "Now, come and dress me. I've changed my mind about the sleeves. Not the ivory silk, I'll wear the prune velvet with the gilt embroidery."

And she made her way into her dressing closet and sat before the wide pier glass, looking at her reflection, taking no further notice of me or of Cecelia. But during the next hour, as her hair was arranged and her eyebrows darkened, as the layers of under-garments and petticoats, stomacher and sleeves and ruff were put on and fastened in place, I saw that she was glancing at us in the pier glass as well as scrutinizing her own image. When she looked at me she was thoughtful, when she looked at Cecelia, she was scornful.

You are of little worth, that look conveyed. Something to be thrown away, like your gown.

SEVEN

MY father was ardently eager to find me a husband.

In his mind I was a "forward virgin" who would continue to bring dishonor to the family until I was wedded to a husband who would control me and stifle my waywardness.

Mother agreed that it would be very desirable to find husbands for both me and Cecelia, though in this as in all things she was good-humoredly relaxed, apparently nonchalant.

"There is plenty of time," she told father in languid tones when he brought up the subject of our marriages, which he constantly did. "They are still quite young."

"But Lettie's reputation is bad, and likely to become worse. We must find husbands for them both before—before—"

"Before one of them finds herself with child—and we know which one that is likely to be—and the problem worsens. We can only trust that, should the worst happen, the man will act as a gentleman must, and marry her. And if he does not, I will bring the matter to the queen's attention, and she will force him to."

Mother was not overly concerned about our futures, and I envied her her calm, though being more my father's daughter I understood his worries and felt a good deal of empathy for him, hounded as he was by too much responsibility.

Father went to Ireland about this time, sent there by the queen to curb the expenses of her Lord Deputy who was overspending his budget in his futile attempt to control the wild Irish. While there he wrote to us, to say that he was negotiating a match for me, with a lord who had extensive lands in Ireland and who lived there most of the year.

I held my breath; I did not want to marry in Ireland, or live there. Fortunately we received word not long afterwards that the bargaining over my hand had fallen through. And not only that, but father had become ill, and was returning home.

"Bog fever," the tirewomen remarked to one another, nodding their heads and giving each other ominous looks. "It never fails. They go to Ireland, and come home with bog fever."

I had little time, in those crowded early days of my service to the queen, to think of my own future, or even to sit by my ill father's bedside while he recovered. As a maid of honor I was expected to wake at dawn and dress quickly in the grey gown that was the indicator of my office, then attend chapel, consume a bit of bread and a bowl of ale in the queen's chamber and then attend Her Majesty and carry out my assigned tasks, which occupied me for the rest of the morning. After midday dinner we maids spent our afternoons among the gentlewomen of the court, standing by while the queen touched those of her subjects afflicted with "the king's evil," the malady that only the royal touch could cure, or met with ambassadors, or stitched at embroidery or sewed silk edging on ruffs or sleeves. When the weather was fine and the queen's temper favorable we went riding, or played at shuttlecock, or the most frivolous of the maids invented frolics and we carried them out—sometimes to the queen's amusement, sometimes arousing her ire.

After supper the gentlemen came to join us, and then came the hour of "eyes and sighs" when heart spoke to heart across the room or across the chessboard, the musicians striking up a coranto or a galliard and the men choosing partners from among us to skip and slide, leap and hop until we were dripping from our exertions and had to call for a tankard of small beer to ease our thirsty throats.

Often it was after midnight when we went wearily to our final task, that of making certain the ushers and grooms had prepared the queen's bed for her nightly rest, that great high bed with its many coverlets and hangings, the whole topped with a gilded coronet and seven plumes of eagles' feathers.

Once the queen had gone to her rest, we too sought our shared lumpy beds, our bare feet freezing on the cold wooden floors with nothing but the rushes to warm them, the stink of the rushes lightened by a scattering of wormwood (which helped to kill the fleas) and by the infusions of rose and orange-flowers that sweetened the air.

Cecelia, only too aware that the queen had taken a dislike to her, and that my father was putting most of his efforts into finding a husband for me, her own future union a secondary concern, was burning as usual with suppressed rage. She took vengeance in small ways, putting camphor in the queen's scent bottles, setting the queen's treasured Nuremberg watch with its delicate crystal case on the very edge of a table (I saw her place it there carefully) so that it would be certain to be swept to the floor by the next gown that passed by, and broken. She left one of the aviary doors open, so that all the songbirds would have escaped had I not been watching, to close it securely.

I thought that these vengeful pranks had gone unnoticed until, one morning, we were dressing the queen, and she was having her many wigs brought in, as she often did, to choose one to match her gown. She couldn't make up her mind among them, and became irritated.

Her irritation grew, as the French wigmaker brought forth one wig after another and offered them to her. She shook her head and stamped her feet. In the end her anger came to rest on one of the younger tirewomen, a mere girl, who had not been long in her service.

"Stupid child! Not the chestnut, the tawny one! Not that tawny one, the darker one, the one with the bone lace!"

The girl reached for the wig, fumbled, dropping it, leaving a heap of untidy curls.

Elizabeth stood and slapped her. She shrieked, at which Cecelia swore, and reached for the heavy silver-backed mirror that lay on the royal dressing-table. The queen grabbed Cecelia's hand, wrenched the mirror from it and flung it at the girl. It struck her on the forehead. Blood dripped from her temple. Almost at once, an usher stepped forward and, taking the girl by the arm, hurried her out of the room. The wigmaker remained.

"There!" the queen shouted. "There is just the color I want!" She pointed to Cecelia's mousy waves, and tore off her headdress so that her hair fell down her back untidily. Cecelia was gasping, shaking her head, still reeling from what she had just witnessed.

Cecelia's hair was far from being the dark tawny shade of the wig the queen had chosen and the girl had dropped. It was not a shade that matched Elizabeth's gown, it was not thick or shiny, it had no beauty whatever. My hair was much closer to the shade she seemed to want—and would have been more flattering.

But no one, I'm sure, thought of that at the time, and in fact all was happening very quickly. Cecelia swore, but her oath was drowned out by the queen's shouting.

"I will have that hair. Shave it off at once! Make me a wig of it!"

There was a shocked silence in the room.

"Surely Your Majesty—" my mother began timidly, but at a look from Elizabeth she broke off.

"I said, I will have that hair. And immediately!"

"But Your Majesty," the Frenchman objected, "it will take me some time to make a wig. Even if I had the hair removed and before me now, combed and ready, it would take me several days—"

"Then I will wait several days. And when it is finished, it had better be the most beautiful wig ever made!"

Cecelia, broken, was crying. She started to run from the room, but mother caught her and held her.

"Be brave!" she said. "Submit! It is the bravest thing you can do!"

And she did.

That night, as she lay beside me, her shorn head covered in swathes of cloth, her eyes swollen and her breathing ragged, I forgave her everything from the past, because she had done what I never would have had the courage to do. She had submitted to the queen's vengeance, not for any noble purpose, but because it was the best and most practical course to take. And because mother, who had a great deal of common sense, told her to do it. She followed her mind, not her feelings. She followed good advice.

So this is what it means to grow up, I thought. To lay childhood and girlhood aside, and become a wise maid. A wise maid, prepared to accept whatever life offers—or forces upon me. To go through the narrow portal that separates the world of hopes and dreams from the grim world of real life, and to know, with sorrow, that that portal is closed forever.

EIGHT

*T*HE first time I saw Robert Dudley he was laughing very loudly and joyfully and carrying a squealing, squirming piglet into the queen's large, sumptuously decorated throne room.

Everyone watched Elizabeth, to see what her reaction would be—and then she burst into laughter and the rest of us joined in.

Lord Robert took his place to the right of the queen, a magnificent, tall figure, handsome and debonair, seeming not to care a whit that his costly blue velvet doublet with its gleaming golden stars was being scratched and dirtied by the little pig or that my father, who scorned trivial jests in the throne room, was shaking his head in disapproval.

I could not look at anyone else.

He was smiling, I remember, not only with his bow-shaped lips but with his deep blue, expressive eyes, and it was not the practiced, artificial smile of the seasoned courtier but the genuine smile of a man pleased with himself and his life. A man at ease with himself, who had subdued his demons and his fears and was master of his situation.

And a man only too aware of how potent an effect he had on others, especially women, and most especially the queen.

His jest having run its course, he handed the squirming piglet to a groom and proceeded to talk in a low conversational voice to Elizabeth. I watched as they conversed. The looks that passed between them were eloquent. I could plainly see that they were the most intimate of friends.

At one point he bent down to whisper something in Elizabeth's ear, making her smile and glance up at him with a look that was almost trusting—and the queen, I believed, trusted no one completely.

It was said that they were lovers, though as everyone at court knew, Lord Robert was married, and had been since he was eighteen, to the daughter of Sir John Robsart.

"She never comes to court," I was told by the shrewd, rotund Mistress Clinkerte, who quickly became my most reliable informant at court. The all-knowing Mistress Clinkerte had been one of Elizabeth's rockers, or nursemaids, when she was a baby, and had served her ever since, through all the many changes in her status and circumstances. She had even served the Princess Elizabeth when she was imprisoned in the Tower during her half-sister's reign, and had stories to tell about that tense and dangerous time. When I became a maid of honor Mistress Clinkerte was the queen's principal tirewoman, surprisingly spry despite her girth—and her age, which was near to fifty summers.

"Lord Robert's wife never comes to court," she told me. "She knows better. They say she bides her time, at one country house or another, just waiting for the queen to marry. Like as not she will marry, though she swears she won't. She'll have to, won't she? No woman can be queen on her own. Look what happened with her sister! She tried to reign without a husband, and was an unhappy failure."

"And then she married, and things got a lot worse," I put in. "They say everyone hated King Philip, and he was cruel to her."

"That was her punishment for burning all those poor people," Mistress Clinkerte insisted. "She went wrong, and she got her comeuppance."

"Tell me about Lord Robert's wife," I said, bringing the tire-woman back to the subject that interested me. "Is she beautiful? Is she rich? Does she have lovers?"

Mistress Clinkerte lowered her voice. "Amy Dudley, Amy Robsart that was, is an heiress, her father has lands and a fortune, and heaven knows Lord Robert needed to marry an heiress, for his family—you know they were all in terrible disgrace, and went to prison and had all their lands and money taken away—left him with nothing of his own. He does like money! He spends and spends, and when he has spent it all, he borrows.

"Is she beautiful?" Mistress Clinkerte went on. "No. Her face is quite ordinary, and one shoulder is higher than the other, and her bosom is not raised nor her waist reed-slim like the queen's. She knows her value, I'll say that for her. Lord Robert was not the only one hoping to win her hand. But she would never come to court, and the queen would never invite her. As to whether she has lovers, I've never heard of any. Then again, no one really cares what she does."

Lord Robert was everywhere, it seemed, fulfilling his highly public duties as Master of the Horse, riding beside the queen when she went out hunting, leading the dancing when she called the musicians into her chamber, ordering the Yule-games at Christmastide, entertaining us all at banquets with merry tales and jests and darker stories of his time in battle (he had fought valorously, it was said, at the Battle of St. Quentin, alongside King Philip's Spaniards).

Lord Robert rode out, adorned splendidly in a velvet coat and chains of gold, at the head of his large troop of yeomen, when the queen went through the streets to be received by the Lord Mayor. He gave receptions at his grand house in the Strand, Leicester House, and entertained the queen at his country houses as well, though I never heard of his wife being present at any of those entertainments.

When Elizabeth boasted that all the men of the court were dyeing their beards to match her hair, Lord Robert was one of the first to display his newly dyed, curling beard, and when she remarked that her favorite scent was musk, he ordered all his gloves perfumed with musk (and, it was rumored, his codpieces as well). He talked at length and knowledgeably about many things, from the latest voyages of exploration in the distant waters and lands of the New World to the price of pigeon pie to the latest reports of the queen's envoys in Scotland and France. Many men talked endlessly and were endlessly dull; Lord Robert was endlessly entertaining.

I could not look at, or listen to, anyone else.

And I discovered, by chance, that the queen shared my fascination.

Late one afternoon, when Elizabeth and most of the maids of honor were taking their ease on the terrace, watching a lazy game of croquet, I was sent back to the royal bedchamber to get a shawl, which had been left lying on the bed. I found it, and then noticed, with great interest, that on a low bench beside the bed was one of the queen's beautifully printed books, open to a page where she had been writing in the wide margin before being interrupted. A quill and inkpot and other writing implements had been laid aside, evidently in haste. No doubt she had meant to close the book but had been called away by something urgent. Or perhaps she had left it open so that the ink might dry.

I knew her script, spidery and large, the letters well formed and easy to read.

I was tempted. I could not resist the temptation. I read.

"A year since he became mine, and I his. A year of mad delight. No one can know, though many guess. He has offered to free himself—"

There the words stopped. What could they mean? They certainly seemed revealing enough, to one who had been at court even the short few months that I had been there.

Gently I touched the ink. It was dry.

Hearing footsteps in the passage, I busied myself opening cupboards, pretending to look for something. The footsteps passed on.

I returned to the bedside and hovered over the open book. I turned back the pages and found that there were many entries in the margins, all in the same spidery hand. Four lines of verse caught my eye:

> He hath my heart, and always shall
> In memory perpetual.
> One soul are we, one mind, one life
> But I can never be his wife.

Lord Robert and the queen, the queen and Lord Robert. She loved him, just as I thought. And he, for his part, had at least "offered to free himself."

Did Mistress Clinkerte know about the book, and its secrets, I wondered. Or had I stumbled upon something so very private, so very close to the queen's heart, that not even the all-knowing tirewoman was aware of it? Words so secret that no one but

Elizabeth herself—and now me, a maid of honor and her kinswoman—knew of them?

I took up the shawl and began to walk toward the doorway, intent on returning to where the court was gathered. But then I turned back, and went to where the book lay open by the bed. Gently I closed it, leaving the writing things undisturbed, and hoping that no other inquisitive eyes would be drawn to its revealing pages.

NINE

BY far the most disconcerting thing about the boy my father brought to meet me in my second year at the royal court was that he was not very intelligent. He was manly enough, to be sure, and not bad-looking, though his dark hair was already beginning to recede from his low forehead, but his eyes! His dark eyes had almost nothing behind them, no spark of mental life, no glint of humor, no indication at all that when he looked out at the world, he saw anything in it but things. Not ideas, not forces, not absurdities or even dangers. Just things, heavy and lifeless, most of them, to be moved or hoarded, stored or polished or kicked or knocked into shape.

I am one of those things, I thought as I watched him. In me he sees flesh—ripe, young female flesh—to be used and enjoyed. To breed sons upon. To decorate his halls and run his household. To wait for him when he goes off on the queen's business, and welcome him back on his return.

I saw it all, there in his lusterless dark brown eyes.

And in my father's much more lively eyes I saw satisfaction, for in this boy, this Walter Devereux, he believed he had found me a husband.

What gave him even more satisfaction was that he believed he had found a husband for Cecelia as well. Walter had a second cousin, Sir Roger Wilbraham, a widower in need of a wife to care for his children and look after him as he aged. Sir Roger was not a young man, and Cecelia would be his third wife. But at least he was willing to consider her—especially if father was able to use his influence to make Sir Roger a Justice of the Peace, with all the income that important office brought with it.

Father was rubbing his hands together when I entered the room on that memorable afternoon—always a sign that he was pleased. Then I took one look at the boy standing next to him, the boy who could only be Walter Devereux. And I saw his eyes, and I thought, no. Please no.

I glanced at mother, sitting demurely off to one side, chatting with another woman who I took to be Walter's mother. She would not meet my glance. A bad sign. My brother Frank was not present, I looked around in vain for someone—anyone—to share my initial impression of the vapid Walter. But there was no one.

He came closer to me and stared. Father introduced us. Walter bowed and I bent my knee in a curtseyed acknowledgment. He was silent. What a dullard, I was thinking. Where did father find this boy? His next words answered my unspoken question.

"Young Walter went along with me to Ireland, Lettie. He was of the greatest help to me there."

"And how did you enjoy Ireland?" I asked the boy, more out of politeness than curiosity.

47

"It looked a lot like Wales," was his succinct reply. "Lots of greenery."

What could I say to a boy who reduced Ireland to "lots of greenery"? To be sure, I had never been to Ireland, but I had heard a lot about it from my father. And I had the impression it was a grand, sweeping land, boggy in parts, quite magnificent if one overlooked the hostile natives.

I tried another subject.

"Are you drawn to greenery then? Do you enjoy cultivating your gardens?"

But Walter only shrugged. "The gardeners do that. It's what my father employs them for."

I was ready to plead illness and leave—I could think of no other plausible reason to avoid further talk with this dolt—when I heard my mother's soothing voice. She had gotten up and come over to us, and was speaking to Walter.

"Your mother was just telling me that hunting is your passion. Especially boar-hunting."

At once Walter's face lit up. "Yes, indeed it is. I have taken many boars, and red deer and fallow, and foxes, and hares, though coursing is not really to my taste—"

He turned to my father and continued his sudden spate of words.

"Have you attempted going after boar with the crossbow? I have several, made for me by a master armorer, with special hunting bolts. You see, the main thing, in going after boar, is not to penetrate the flesh too deeply. Boar-spears are adequate, or even a plain woodknife if there is nothing else at hand—"

"One of my men stabbed an Irishman with a boar-spear," my father was saying. "It was—too great a success, if I may put it so." He looked sour.

"No doubt the man deserved it," was Walter's blunt reply.

"But to get back to the hunt, you must let me take you to Framlingham Park, or better still, to Umberleigh, the game are plentiful there. I have had the finest venison—flavored with currants, of course, otherwise it would hardly be fit to eat—after my hunts at Umberleigh."

At last he smiled. Walter smiled, and then there was a bit of light in his eyes. It was something. It was enough to keep me from pleading illness and leaving the room.

"Surely Master Devereux is not come among us solely to discuss hunting," my mother was saying somewhat tactlessly, taking my arm on one side and Walter's on the other and leading us toward a bench with soft cushions. "Unless it be hunting for a lady to share his future. Or is my speech too forward?"

She paused, a charming smile on her face, and looked at my father, then at Walter's mother, and last of all at me.

"We must leave it to Walter to answer for himself," my father said.

And in time he did.

But his proposal was a very long time coming, for Walter was nothing if not thorough, and he took his time and gave much thought to asking me to share his future.

And in that space of time, over many months, my admiration for Lord Robert grew.

Every time Walter came to visit me, or took me along on one of his country walks, or dined with my family, I could not help but compare him with Lord Robert, who was so much more handsome, more clever, more amusing—and, I must admit it, wealthier also. He not only had his wife's fortune to spend, but from the start of her reign Queen Elizabeth had been enriching him with the salaries of official posts, the income from lands, and other perquisites of office. I hope I am not greedy but I have to confess that Lord Robert's increasing wealth made him seem even more desirable—though had he lost every penny he would still have been the most desirable man at court.

One afternoon I was told I would be riding out with the queen and Lord Robert and I hurried to put on my riding clothes. Three other maids of honor were to go along also, the four of us forming a sort of escort for the unmarried queen. It was the day before her twenty-seventh birthday, and the royal household was in a state of urgent preparation for the celebration. She would be twenty-seven, I was a bare nineteen. I remember thinking how old she seemed to me on that day, how mature. Twenty-seven might as well have been forty-seven to me then, except that, as I knew from long observation, women were old by forty-seven—if they lived that long—and starting to wither and turn inward with pains and illnesses.

The day was overcast, the sun trying in vain to come out from behind a darkening bank of cloud. It had rained the day before, and the ground was muddy. A light wind was blowing the yellowing leaves off the trees.

Lord Robert rode with ease on his costly mount, keeping his seat without fail despite the rough going, while the queen, a bold rider but not a skilled one, fell frequently, only to cry "No hurt! No hurt!" and get back on her horse with the aid of a patient groom, her skirts and shoes dark with sticky mud but her good humor unabated.

I noticed that Lord Robert smiled whenever the queen fell and remounted, her grit and determination pleased him. He tempered the pace of his fine horse to hers, he joked with her as they rode along, he chased her when she challenged him to a race—always careful, I noted, not to catch her or overtake her.

It must have taken skill to hold his fiery, impatient mount back, I thought. Skill and patience.

We came to where a narrow bridge crossed a pool—too narrow a bridge to allow the horses to pass across it.

"Wait for us," the queen called out in a casual tone before dismounting and starting off on foot across the bridge. Lord Robert dismounted and accompanied her, taking her hand as they walked slowly along. The four of us attendants got down off our horses and sat on a thick cloth the groom spread out for us, glad for the wine and bread and fruit he had brought along for our refreshment and glad too for the glimmer of sunshine that began to warm us as we began to eat. We were poor chaperones just then, preoccupied as we were with our meal. But I did glance at the bridge, and the two figures who crossed it and disappeared, arms entwined, into the thick woods beyond. And I could not help thinking, as I attempted to peer into the dark of the forest, of the words I had read in the margins of the queen's bedside book.

"A year of mad delight," she had written. "He hath my heart, and always shall . . ." They were lovers, how could they not be? I wished them all happiness (for who does not wish happiness for those who have joined their hearts?), and I envied the queen the devotion of the handsome and devoted Lord Robert. Yet her private words revealed a regret beneath her delight. "I can never be his wife," she had written. It was her wish, her deepest wish, to be Lord Robert's wife—or so it seemed to me then. And fate had denied her that wish. Her delight must ever be tinged with sorrow.

A shadow fell across the grove as once again clouds veiled the sun. We ate and drank our fill, as we waited for the queen to take her pleasure in the woods, the other maids smirking and winking as the minutes lengthened into hours. Then it began to rain, and we sought what shelter we could, until at last Elizabeth and Lord Robert returned to us and we all trooped quietly and wetly home.

TEN

THE startling news arrived on the day after the queen's birthday. Lord Robert's wife was dead. She died, it was said, from a fall down a staircase.

"Pushed down a staircase," was the universal whisper. "She didn't fall. Somebody pushed her. And we all know who it was."

"King Robert's Jig" was all the servants could whistle in the corridors. Jokes multiplied, most of them far too vulgar to repeat, though they made me laugh, and Cecelia too. It was nervous laughter, laughter born as much out of fear as out of ridicule.

And besides, there were doubts.

Amy Dudley had died in Oxfordshire, and Lord Robert had been far away at Greenwich, overseeing the elaborate birthday celebrations for the queen. We knew he had been there, at the palace, active and at the center of things, giving orders, spreading cheer. We had seen him with our own eyes. He could not have been in Oxfordshire, pushing his wife down the stairs.

"Then he had one of his henchmen do it," was the whispered response. "Or one of the servants."

"But the servants were all out for the day," it was said in response. "Lady Amy sent them all away."

"So one of them sneaked back in, and pushed her. And Lord Robert paid him well to do it."

On and on the scandalous gossip went, spreading from the palace up to London and from there throughout the realm and to the realms beyond, where Lord Robert was spoken of as "King Robert" or "the king that is to be." I heard no one contradict the presumption that Amy had died at her husband's hands, either directly or through others he hired.

"That man ought to be locked in the Tower," my father announced solemnly at dinner. "Just like he was when he was a boy, with all his treasonous family." Everyone at court knew Lord Robert's dark history, how his father John Dudley, Duke of Northumberland, and Robert himself and all four of his brothers had been imprisoned in the Tower of London following the duke's attempt to dethrone Queen Mary and put Lady Jane Grey in her place. All the Dudleys bore the taint of treason; Lord Robert had worked hard to overcome it. Now he never would.

Walter Devereux was dining with us, as he often did, and nodded when he heard my father's remark, his dark eyes full of accusation. When he spoke I heard a new tone in his voice.

"I have heard that Lord Robert is laying in a good stock of arms at Charney Bassett, and in the caves at Midvale Ridge. He has many men under arms. He is planning rebellion, just as his father did. He will marry the queen and take over the kingdom."

"With her encouragement," I heard my mother say under her breath.

My father looked straight ahead and said, very distinctly, "I hope I did not hear any treasonous words uttered at this table."

Mother looked down at her plate and said nothing more.

Though I had never warmed to her, and did not look on her with any degree of fondness, I was concerned about Elizabeth for she appeared to be under great strain after learning that Lord Robert's wife was dead. She was very pale, indeed alarmingly pale, and her long white fingers trembled when she suffered an attack of nerves—something that happened often in those gossip-filled days. Time and again she called for Mistress Clinkerte—whom she trusted above all others, except perhaps Lord Robert—and asked for a cordial, to steady herself. And Mistress Clinkerte, expressionless and close-mouthed, brought her what she asked for, making no comment, even when the queen drank several cordials in the course of an hour and became tipsy—or, as more often happened, quarrelsome.

The queen was preoccupied just then with ordering a new bed. ("Large enough for two," was my mother's pointed comment, made when not in my father's hearing. "And why not?" she added. "Lord Robert is in her bedchamber day and night, and sometimes very early in the morning, before she is even dressed, so that he has to hand her her shift!")

The bed the queen was having made was carved from aged cedarwood, painted and gilded in rich detail and with a heavy tester and valence sewn in cloth of silver. There was to be a headpiece of crimson satin, with tall fluffy ostrich feathers strewn with shining bits of gold foil. But she fretted over the bedcurtains for the new construction.

"There are no finer bedcurtains than those at Cumnor Place," she announced loudly in the midst of conferring with her seamstresses. "I will have no others. Lady Dudley no longer has need of them. I will have them here, to trim my new bed." Her eyes rested on me. "You, Lettie, must go to Cumnor with Mistress Clinkerte and fetch them."

"Surely Your Majesty could send one of Lord Robert's servants," I suggested. "It would look more seemly."

The queen glared at me and did not reply. "You will leave for Cumnor on the morrow," she said presently, and I did not demur, though I could sense the smiles and hear the titters the queen's request for Amy Dudley's bedcurtains brought forth from the others in the royal bedchamber.

Eventually even I joined in the private laughter, to be sure. The queen's brazen request was so daring, and so transparent, that it was very amusing. The curtains from the dead Amy Dudley's bed, to be brought to the royal palace, and installed there along with Amy's husband! It was an idea the queen's fool might have suggested, to make us all laugh. Instead it was a genuine royal command.

I thought, not for the first time, what a strange woman the queen was.

And yet I resisted joining in the easy laughs and jibes, and dreaded going to Cumnor to fetch the bedcurtains. Deep down, I did not want all the scandalous gossip to be true. I had developed a strong partiality for Lord Robert. I did not want to believe that he was capable of having his wife killed. But rumor has a powerful voice, and I could hardly ignore all that was being said. I remembered the queen's stolen rendezvous with Lord Robert in the forest, and all the nights he had been in her bedchamber until long after midnight, sometimes alone with her, sometimes joined there by William Cecil, Lord Robert's strongest rival in the royal council and most cunning competitor.

William Cecil, I thought, turning the situation over in my

mind. William Cecil must surely have rejoiced at Amy Dudley's death, for the suspicions surrounding it were doing great harm to his rival Lord Robert. Everyone I talked to at court was saying that Lord Robert would never recover from the suspicion of murdering his wife. His rising favorable repute was destroyed forever. Could it have been Cecil who connived to have Amy Dudley killed? It was not impossible, I thought.

The queen knew the answer, surely she did. That was why she was so pale and nervous. She knew the truth. And there was one other, I suspected, who might know. The all-knowing Mistress Clinkerte.

As my trunk was being packed for the trip to Cumnor Place, I vowed that I would ask her. And recalling how she liked to talk, and had told me things in confidence in the past, I hoped that she would tell me, in the course of our journey, what she knew of this greatest secret of all.

ELEVEN

DO you think he was the one?" I asked Mistress
Clinkerte after we had ridden along the Oxford Road
in silence for some miles. Her broad, wrinkled face was hard,
the small eyes unyielding of emotion. I had no doubt she knew
the meaning of my question.

Sighing, she looked away.

"I read her book," I went on. "The book she keeps by her bed.
Where she writes her secrets."

Now her face showed alarm.

"You should not have done that."

"She wrote in it that they loved each other. And that he had
offered to free himself. Was that what he meant, that he
was willing to free himself by removing his wife, so that
they could marry?" After a time I added, "Was his wife's death
the queen's birthday gift? She died on the queen's birthday,
didn't she? Or the day after?"

Mistress Clinkerte nodded. After a time she leaned closer to me and whispered, "You say too much."

I held my peace for the rest of the journey, except to remark on things of no consequence. I did not mention the queen, or Lord Robert, or the late Amy Dudley, again.

Not until we had arrived at Cumnor Place, and had been shown by the steward of the household to the apartment provided for our use, did Mistress Clinkerte say anything further about the vital question I had raised. When we were alone, she led me to a window embrasure and said what she had to say.

"People gossip about how the deed was Lord Robert's doing. But whether it was or not, she will never marry him—or any other."

"But she must. No queen can rule alone. Lord Cecil, the royal council, my father—they all urge her to marry. And soon."

She nodded. "But the aim of marriage is to have sons. Sons to inherit her throne. She cannot bear sons. Or daughters either."

"Why not?"

"Because she is not as other women."

I thought I knew what Mistress Clinkerte meant—that the queen had an illness, or was in some way flawed or deformed, or (heaven forbid!) was cursed. Yet we who lived alongside her, dressed her, supervised the gathering of her laundry, the making of her bed, the storing of her underclothes—we were surely in the best position to know her bodily conditions. Next to her physicians, that is.

"You say she is not as other women, yet her monthly cloths are red with blood," I said bluntly. "Surely she can bear children."

Mistress Clinkerte drew me closer to her face, so that I could smell the strong odor of the herbs she habitually chewed.

"It is not her blood," she whispered. "It is the blood of others."

"What others?"

"That is for her tirewomen to know."

So the queen was only pretending to undergo her monthly courses, as all women do until they age and begin to wither. Or nearly all women.

"Does Lord Robert know the truth?" I asked when I had pondered my informant's startling words.

Mistress Clinkerte raised her eyebrows and shrugged.

"I know only this—that the queen does not want to be a wife who is ridiculed and despised for her barrenness. Knowing that she would be barren if she married, she will not marry."

"And yet—she must have an heir."

"She will have to choose one, in time."

Mistress Clinkerte's revelations were disturbing, but equally disturbing was the scene spread out before us in the courtyard below the window where we stood, and the increasing noise that drowned out her low voice.

Carts were rumbling into the courtyard, loaded with stacks of arms, heavy oak barrels, ropes and harness, boxes and baskets. Soldiers and servants were unloading them and taking the supplies into the storehouses and other buildings adjacent to the house. Armed men rode in and out through the arched gate of the manor, I saw soldiers lounging in the doorway of the saddlery and guardsmen playing dice against the stable walls. Cumnor Place was an armed camp, full of men of war, coming and going, many looking purposeful, as if on urgent errands or obeying urgent commands.

There was much shouting and bustle, much confusion. Was anyone in command?

I remembered what Walter Devereux had said about Lord Robert, that he was accumulating arms and plotting rebellion. Was this why the queen had been so pale and nervous in recent days? Was she afraid of Lord Robert and his men? Was she his pawn?

I remembered what my father had told me before I left for Cumnor Place, standing before me and looking grave, as he so often did, putting his hands on my shoulders and looking into my eyes.

"Letitia," he had said, "whatever you may hear or see, and whatever Walter Devereux may say, know this: I do not believe the kingdom is tottering. There are too many of us holding it up! The throne is secure."

It was a relief to turn from such serious matters to the business we had been sent to the manor to accomplish, on the queen's behalf. The steward escorted Mistress Clinkerte and me to Amy Dudley's bedchamber. On the way we passed along several corridors and went up a short flight of stairs. On each of the steps, off to the side, was a small heap of wilted flowers. As soon as I glimpsed the flowers I knew this must be the fatal staircase, the scene of Amy's accident or murder, and I could not help but catch my breath.

The steward opened the bedchamber door and we stepped inside.

The first thing we noticed was an old woman, cringing, as if to ward off a blow, standing against the far wall of the room.

"Pirto!" the steward called out, "these are the ladies from the palace. Sent by the queen. Do you understand?" It was odd to hear Mistress Clinkerte referred to as a lady. The steward meant to flatter her, I supposed. Or possibly he genuinely mistook her for one, despite the coarse fabric and poor cut of her gown, her lack of jewels, the old-fashioned style of her headpiece. All the indications that, to a courtier, would have given away her modest status in the hierarchy of royal servants, and her low birth, at first glance.

The old woman nodded, at the same time seeming to shrink down, as if trying to make herself even smaller.

"They have come about the bedcurtains. See that they are given whatever they want." To us he said, "This is Pirto, the late Lady Dudley's maid. She was devoted to her late mistress."

He left us then, and I went over toward the great high bed. Hanging around it, foot and sides, were some of the richest, most elaborate bedcurtains I had ever seen. Tapestry work in brilliant colors portrayed mythological scenes. I recognized the rape of Leda, Venus and Adonis embracing, Psyche bending over Cupid, holding her lamp low to reveal his beauty. The stitching was exquisite. No wonder the queen wanted these bedcurtains to install on her own new cedarwood bed—though there was no escaping the bald meaning of her seizing them.

"Pirto," I said, addressing the maid, "will you please take down these hangings and have them packed safely for our return journey to London?"

But the only response was a loud sniffing.

"Please," she managed to whisper, "please don't let them take me."

I looked at her more closely. She was frightened to death. "No one is going to take you anywhere. We have only come for these curtains." Seeing that she went on sniveling, I added, in a softer voice, "It was you who left the flowers on the staircase, wasn't it?"

She nodded, then looked at me for the first time. There was great sorrow in her old eyes, red-rimmed and ringed with deep wrinkles. Sorrow—and fear.

"The soldiers—all the soldiers—they will take me to a dungeon—"

Mistress Clinkerte strode firmly toward the weeping old woman and slapped her.

"Stop indulging yourself and do as you are told!"

But the only response was a fresh outburst of weeping.

"Where are the baskets?" Mistress Clinkerte asked impatiently. "I'll pack the bedcurtains myself."

"The soldiers—the soldiers—" the old woman kept repeating. "My mistress—where are they taking her? Where will they take me?"

Mistress Clinkerte was yanking down the beautiful bedcurtains and attempting to fold them, stiff and heavy as they were, into a pile on the bed. Meanwhile Pirto had gone to a tall cupboard and was opening it, her hands trembling as she fumbled with the latch. She brought out a metal box decorated with scrollwork and with the initials AD in a gilded design. Taking a ring of keys from her pocket, she chose one and fitted it to the lock, then opened the box.

I watched as she laid the box down on a chest and began taking the contents out.

"These are my lady's keepsakes," she said in a reverent voice. "Her precious things."

"Lord Robert should have them."

"He cares nothing for her things. Or even for her poor broken body." Pirto's voice was low but full of anger. "Do you know where they have laid her? In a plain wooden box, behind the alehouse. The churchwarden had her laid there, and the vicar said a prayer over her and that was all."

"Surely there will be a churchyard burial at some later date. This loss has come as a shock. No one was prepared for it. And Lord Robert is much occupied with the queen's affairs. She relies on him very much. He cannot be away from court."

The maid looked at me sharply, accusingly. As if I had uttered some slander about her late mistress.

"Lady Dudley was the one who needed him. Who relied on

him—and he was never here." Her face crumpled into a tearful mass. "I was the only one who was here. I am the only one who knows—"

"Who knows what?" Mistress Clinkerte asked curtly, looking up from attending to the bedcurtains. "What is it that you know?"

But instead of answering, Pirto held up one of the things she had removed from the box. A miniature portrait, so small I could not tell whose face it represented. She held it up to the light, and contemplated the tiny image, smiling through her tears. At the same time I saw her surreptitiously take a folded piece of paper from the box and, turning aside from us, conceal it in a pocket of her apron.

"I know what happened the day she died," she said, raising her head to look at me—this time with a look of defiance. "And I am going to tell the coroner, at the inquest."

TWELVE

THE bare, whitewashed courtroom was filling with noisy spectators who elbowed one another as they fought for space on the hard wooden benches provided for them, quarreling loudly and reeking of ale. The coroner's inquest concerning the death of Lady Amy Dudley, late of Cumnor Place, was to convene at four o'clock and the taverns had been open since noon. Few of the village residents had failed to partake of the local ale as they waited impatiently for the inquiry to begin. Still fewer were in any doubt about the outcome.

"He's bought them all, every last man," went the whispered verdict of the villagers as they frowned at the members of the coroner's jury, a nervous group of men hastily assembled in recent days, as the steward at Cumnor Place told us. "Lord Robert's sent his men up from London to pay them off, the foreman too. They say he's already wed the queen, in secret, and will be crowned himself just as soon as ever he can be."

The foreman, a short, raddled fellow who fussed with his vest and did not meet the eyes of the watching spectators, looked distinctly uncomfortable as he shifted from one booted foot to the other.

"Bribed," was the common opinion. "All of them, bribed to say Lord Dudley had nothing to do with it."

A chill wind swept through the unheated room as the coroner entered, his pursed lips in his round, cherubic face fixed in a sardonic half-grin, his small eyes looking out contemptuously over the quarrelsome men attempting to secure seats on the benches. He commanded no respect, but all those in the room rose and grew quiet as another man came in, a tall figure in a long red gown and fur-lined hood, august and magisterial in his manner as he took his seat on a dais behind the coroner and looked out across the room with the quiet, impartial authority of a man accustomed to being obeyed.

"That's Rouge Cross Puirsuivant, sent from the royal court. To represent the queen."

"As if the queen could be an impartial member of *this* jury," said someone and the spectators burst into laughter.

"Be seated," the coroner called out, and the benches creaked as the crowd sat down, muttering and murmuring, a few still laughing over the jibe at the queen.

"In the matter of the death of Lady Amy Dudley, this court being duly assembled, shall hear the testimony of several witnesses," the coroner began, droning on through the remainder of the afternoon, as witness after witness gave his or her evidence. Mistress Clinkerte and I, seated toward the back of the room, listened as the witnesses described Amy's last afternoon, how she insisted that all the servants leave the house and attend the local fair, how she became angry when a few of them insisted on staying with her, eventually driving them away, how on that afternoon—as on many afternoons—her state of mind was very low, and she was in tears and bereft, complaining of her lot, taking medicines to relieve the strong pains she suffered, and praying to be delivered from desperation.

"Would you repeat those words?" the coroner asked the doctor, who had been describing Amy's depressed spirits.

"I said, she prayed to be delivered from desperation."

"That very afternoon, you heard her pray for this deliverance."

"Yes. Or I heard words with that meaning."

"I require you to be precise."

"As well as I can recall, she stood before her cross, that hung above her bed, and—"

"But there was no cross above her bed," I said, rising from my bench. "Mistress Clinkerte and I were in her bedchamber only this morning, removing the bedcurtains, and we saw no cross there, only the hangings with their depiction of pagan scenes."

The coroner looked at me, his eyes narrowing. Rouge Puirsuivant also regarded me with calm interest.

"Are you certain of this?"

"Yes."

"Surely you do not mean to imply that the lady was not a Christian?"

"No, Your Honor. Merely that the doctor's recollection must be inaccurate, because there is no cross above Lady Dudley's bed."

Rouge Puirsuivant spoke. "Was nothing in the room touched or altered, from the hour Lady Dudley died until the bedcurtains were removed today?" he asked the coroner gravely.

"Nothing."

The onlookers, who had been alternately fidgeting and dozing with boredom during the testimony of the previous witnesses, sparked to life. I felt many pairs of eyes on me.

The doctor was glaring at me, exasperated. "Possibly she made the sign of the cross then," he said through clenched teeth.

Now it was Pirto who spoke up. She had been sitting among the witnesses, awaiting her turn to tell what she knew.

"It was never my lady's habit to cross herself in the Roman fashion," she said curtly, and sat down again.

"What difference does it make?" the doctor cried out, tense and irritable. "All that matters is what she said."

But I could tell that Rouge Puirsuivant did not trust the doctor's words. He pressed him further, making him more and more nervous. He began to hem and haw and contradict himself, until it was evident to us all that he was not being truthful.

"Now Dr. Huick," the coroner put in, speaking in his most serious tones, "I am going to put to you a question of the gravest importance, and you must answer as an honest man, or I assure you, you will suffer for your dishonesty." He cleared his throat. "Has anyone paid you, either in money or in favors, to deceive this court, to give the false impression that the Lady Dudley was in such a state of suffering that she put an end to her life?"

To my surprise, the doctor looked angry.

"Of course not!" he snapped. "I am a man of means."

The laughter that greeted this response could not be suppressed. The doctor, flustered, and not realizing the impact of his words, threw up his hands.

But the coroner pressed him again, once the noise in the room had died down.

"Are you in fact deceiving this court by your evidence?"

The doctor did his best to recover his composure before he spoke. "I am telling you what I recall, Your Honor."

Now Rouge Puirsuivant resumed his questioning.

"When, exactly, were you in Lady Dudley's apartments on the day she died?"

"After she had eaten her midday meal."

"Who was it that served her that meal, if all the servants were ordered to go to the fair?"

"I served her," Pirto said, from the bench where she sat. "I never left her."

"And were you present when the doctor came in to see her?" the puirsuivant asked.

"Begging your pardon, Your Honor, but on my word as a Christian woman, the doctor did not visit my mistress that afternoon."

"Of course I did! The woman is lying!" the physician burst out. His red face was covered in sweat, and his voice trembled.

"Put your hand on the Bible and swear that you tell the truth," said Rouge Puirsuivant. A Bible was brought to the front of the room and presented to the witness.

"I swear," said the doctor as he placed one beringed hand on the heavy book, "that I heard Lady Dudley pray to be delivered from desperation."

"Was she on her knees when she prayed this prayer, or standing?"

Puirsuivant had come to stand next to the shaking doctor, his tall charismatic form clearly intimidating the shorter, younger man.

"Standing, as I have said."

"She always knelt to pray," Pirto said, with granite in her tone.

The room grew silent.

"Perhaps, doctor, you are mistaken in your recollection. Let us hear from the maid, who was with her mistress on the fatal afternoon."

"Lady Dudley was a strange woman of mind," the doctor cried out. "She was not in her right senses. She had no wish to live."

But at a nod from Rouge Puirsuivant two guards had taken the physician's arms and were leading him out of the courtroom, still shouting, his words lost in the moaning of the wind.

Meanwhile Pirto, holding the miniature she had taken from the box of Amy's treasures, went to stand in front of the court, facing the jury. And at a nod from the coroner she began to speak.

THIRTEEN

AT Pirto's first words the onlookers bent forward on their benches, straining to listen. Unlike the doctor, she was composed. She conveyed a quiet assurance—the opposite of her demeanor when Mistress Clinkerte and I were introduced to her the previous day. The seriousness of the occasion did not intimidate her, indeed it seemed to bring out a newfound confidence in her. I watched her, and listened to her, with growing attention.

"My lady was a good and virtuous lady," she began. "She prayed daily on her knees. She read her Bible. Her faith made her strong. She always knew her worth. She was proud of her family, and her wealth. Yet she was a sweet lady, with the face of an angel—"

"Like no angel I ever saw," Mistress Clinkerte whispered to me through clenched teeth. "She had a long sharp nose and eyes that could drill through walls. And there was nothing sweet about her."

Having never met Amy Dudley I did not know what to think of her, though I was inclined to imagine that Pirto was exaggerating her virtues. She was doing her best to protect her mistress, and her mistress's good character, even beyond the grave.

"On the afternoon of her accident, she was full of happiness. I had never seen her look more joyful.

"'Oh, Pirto,' she said to me, 'send everyone away! I have a special visitor coming. I want to keep her visit a secret, a secret from everyone, even my husband. There must be no servants in the house.'

"I did not know what the reason for this secrecy was, but I did what she asked. I sent everyone away. When her visitor arrived, I understood. It was the midwife from London. You see, my lady was with child."

A gasp of astonishment swept through the rapt crowd. "Ah!" I heard several women exclaim. I looked over at Mistress Clinkerte, who appeared dubious.

"She was not sad, or wanting to die," Pirto was saying. "Oh no! She was in a state of delight. She was looking forward to giving her husband a son to carry on his name."

"And to the best of your understanding, her husband did not know of her condition," the coroner said.

"No one knew. Only my lady, the midwife from London and myself. And I found out only that afternoon."

"I take it her physical appearance gave no hint of her approaching motherhood."

"No. She did not expect her child to be born until the spring."

The buzz of excited talk in the room increased. The stout, red-faced jury foreman shouted for order, but no one heeded him.

"And I want to say one more thing," Pirto went on, speaking to the coroner.

"Yes?"

The crowd grew quieter.

"I want to say, my mistress was very happy, because she believed that now her husband would stay home with her and not dishonor her any longer."

"Dishonor her in what way?" was the coroner's sharp question.

"By staying with the queen. Beside the queen."

Rouge Puirsuivant's deep voice boomed forth.

"You had better say precisely what you mean, and I advise you to choose your words with great care when speaking of our monarch."

Pirto raised her old head on her long wrinkled neck, and fixed her faded blue eyes on the tall, red-cloaked official.

"I speak a truth known to many. Lord Dudley is the queen's para—"

Before she could complete the word "paramour," the double doors of the courtroom were thrown open and crashed against the wall with a loud bang.

"Lord Dudley is what?"

Robert Dudley burst in, armed in glittering steel, a jewel-hilted sword at his waist, a look of outrage on his handsome features. He strode rapidly to the front of the room, agile and athletic despite the weight of his body armor, and confronted the cowering Pirto.

"Spit out your words, old woman! Lord Dudley is what?"

Chaos erupted in the room, while the tramp of boots told us all that Lord Robert's escort, dozens of guardsmen strong, had come in after him and were taking their place in forbidding formation surrounding the open doorway.

It was hard for me to see what was going on, for all around us men were shouting, some (the most drunk) guffawing, struggling to stand, pushing and shoving. I did manage to see that Pirto had tried to run from Lord Robert, but had fallen. With a single sweeping gesture Lord Robert scooped her up in his arms, as if she weighed nothing, and sat her down on a bench.

Rouge Puirsuivant shouted for silence, and eventually, after more unseemly scrambling in the room, and a good deal of swearing, a murmuring quiet fell.

Lord Robert stood over Pirto. "What were you saying, Pirto?"

She swallowed, and turned very pale, but managed to speak. "That you are the queen's para—"

"Paramount adviser, you were going to say? Or paragon? Or perhaps parasite? I have been called all these things, and worse. And the truth is, neither you nor anyone else but the queen herself knows all that I do for her, as her trusted servant and member of her royal council."

"If you please, Lord Dudley, we are here to inquire into the death of your wife," the coroner said bravely, refusing to be cowed by either the nobleman's power, or his strong presence or his equally strong emotion. I held my breath, thinking, he'll draw his sword and cut Pirto in half. He'll set his guardsmen on the coroner. He'll overturn the court.

"I am more concerned than anyone about my late wife's death," Lord Robert said curtly.

"Yet you were not aware that she was carrying your child."

"I do not believe it. Has her body been opened?"

"No, your lordship, it has not. But we have heard testimony from the maid Pirto that a midwife from London was summoned on the afternoon of Lady Dudley's death."

"Nonsense. Lady Dudley was barren." He glowered at Pirto. "What was the name of this midwife from London?"

"I was not told her name," Pirto said defiantly.

"Quick! Inquire of the grooms whether a woman was brought from London on the afternoon of my wife's death!"

Immediately several of the guardsmen were heard leaving the courtroom. But Pirto had already burst into tears, and put her head in her hands.

"There was no midwife, was there, Pirto. You invented the entire incident. My lady wife was not happy. She had not been happy for a very long time. She spoke often of how she could no longer bear the pain of living. I could not find a way to aid her, or comfort her. I sent for priests, ministers, doctors—but no one could help her, or cure her gloom, least of all me. In fact I seemed to deepen it. She was wretched—and I was wretched, living alongside her. Her constant despair was one of the reasons I was glad to be detained at the royal court."

Lord Robert's ringing words, words evidently wrenched from his heart, and spoken not in impatience, but from an anguished exasperation, hung in the air.

"I see," the coroner said quietly, and with finality. He paused, then continued. "And will you please tell the court, my lord, why you have come to Cumnor Place at this time? You were not summoned to appear at this inquest."

"I would have thought that obvious. I am here to take command of my men. The queen fears rebellion. Rebels are stirring, in the aftermath of my wife's death. It is being said that I was responsible for her death. That I mean to marry the queen and take over the kingdom. The queen is also being falsely slandered and blamed. Rebellious forces—Catholic forces, loyal to the pope and encouraged by King Philip—are taking this opportunity to muster in secret. The queen commands me to raise a thousand men and provide weaponry from my stores here in Oxfordshire. I am doing so, in all haste, as our enemies are even now marching toward London."

"Then we must detain you no longer," the coroner declared briskly. "I decree this inquest at an end, and order the jury to bring in a verdict of death by misadventure. The body of Lady Dudley will be laid to rest in the Church of Our Lady in Oxford a fortnight hence, with full honors due to her rank and that of her exalted lord."

FOURTEEN

I left the inquest feeling very impressed with Lord Robert. I found him to be convincing when he described his late wife's distraught state, and I believed him to be innocent of any involvement in her death, whatever the gossiping courtiers and servants might say.

Amy Dudley fell down the stairs, it was an accident. That was all. The coroner had said so, and the impressive Rouge Puirsuivant agreed.

I was even more convinced of Lord Robert's innocence when I went back to Amy's bedchamber to retrieve the bedcurtains, which had been placed in baskets for our journey back to the royal court.

When I went into the room I was surprised to see Lord Robert kneeling beside the bed, tearful, his hands folded, murmuring his goodbyes (or so I assumed) to his late wife. He was not dressed as he had been in the courtroom; he had untied his stiff metal leggings, breastplate and pauldrons and laid them on the bed. Kneeling there in his white linen shirt, so thin it was almost transparent, and soft clinging hose, without his armor, without even the wide slashed sleeves and voluminous coat he always wore when at court, he looked vulnerable in his near nakedness.

He looked vulnerable—yet strong. I could not help but admire his sinewy arms, broad back and muscular legs, though I stopped myself from admiring them for more than a brief moment. I wondered if he had noticed.

For he looked up as I came in, and began wiping the tears from his cheeks. I could tell from his expression that he felt bereft, and genuinely sorrowful. I thought, even though he was not in any way to blame for what happened to his wife, and had in fact tried to comfort her and get help for her, he felt regret—and perhaps more than a little remorse.

I was touched by the sight of him, and felt my heart go out to him.

"I'm sorry to disturb you, my lord," I said. "I did not realize anyone would be here. I only came to get the bedcurtains the queen has asked for."

He got to his feet and sat on the bed. He seemed quite unconcerned to be wearing only his thin shirt and hose. Sitting there, he looked very young, with the lanky, slightly awkward appearance of a boy rather than a grown man.

He looked at me.

"I cannot attend the funeral service, so I must say my farewells now, as best I can. Better here, at the bedside where she died, than at the shabby grave behind the alehouse where they buried her." We both knew why Lady Amy had been hastily interred in unconsecrated ground, but neither of us spoke of it. If she had deliberately thrown herself down the stairs, with the intent to take her own life, then she could have no grave in a churchyard. Suicides were not permitted to rest in consecrated ground. The vicar, aware of this delicate spiritual matter, had made the hasty decision to give her a temporary grave in an inconspicuous place on the manor grounds.

Lord Robert looked more closely at me, and smiled—a small, tentative smile.

"You are Francis Knollys's daughter. You haunt the queen's apartments, and flit in and out of her rooms, doing her bidding, with the other maids of honor."

"I am Letitia Knollys, your lordship."

"You are to be married to the Devereux heir, am I right?"

"It may be so. We are not yet betrothed."

"And I sense you are not eager to be."

I could not help but smile at this, yet I felt uncertain whether I should be discussing my future with the great Lord Robert.

He passed one large hand over his face, wiping away the last of his tears, and as he did so he let his muscles relax, and I saw the weariness that burdened him.

"Talk to me, Letitia Knollys. Help take my thoughts away from this dreary sad place."

I sighed, wondering what I ought to say. While I gathered my thoughts I drew a bench toward the bed and sat down, wishing Mistress Clinkerte or the steward or even Pirto were with us. But that would never do, not with Lord Robert in a state of undress.

I remembered something I had once been told, that Lord Robert had spent time in Italy in his youth. Surely that would be something we could speak about without awkwardness.

I asked him about his Italian travels, and he seemed to brighten a little as he told me of the charming countryside and delicious food of Tuscany, of a centuries-old villa where he had stayed, of his happy tramps through the hills and the good shooting to be had in the marshes farther to the south, near Rome.

I enjoyed listening to him, as we talked on; all my uncertainty fell away and it was as if I had known him a long time, as if our inequality in rank and position and his far wider experience of life did not matter very much.

"No doubt you have heard the rumor that I brought a poisoner back with me from Italy," he said at length, and all of a sudden a shadow fell between us, our pleasant conversation truncated. "They are said to be expert in poisons, the Italians," he remarked.

I started to reassure him, to say that I had heard nothing about any Italian poisoner in his household, but then I stopped myself. Of course I had heard the rumor. I had an urge to tell him only the truth.

"Many terrible things are said about you," I said, "but I assure you, in all candor, that I do not believe them. I do not believe you were at fault in your wife's death."

"Thank you."

There passed between us then, I remember, a look such as I had never before shared with any boy or man. A look of frank openness and trust, untainted by flirtation or calculation—at least on my part. Neither of us spoke. It was a comfortable silence.

Eventually I said, "I must take the bedcurtains now." I reached for the nearest of the baskets.

"Yes, of course you must. We must all dance to the queen's tune." His wry tone surprised me. He surprised me further by putting one large, warm hand on mine, stopping me from lifting the basket. He leaned closer to me and spoke in low tones.

"Pirto was lying about the midwife, you know. There was no

child. There could not have been. My wife and I had not lain together for a long time. Amy suspected she could not bear a child and had no taste for sleeping with me. She was angry with me. She refused to allow me to share her bed. This bed, with the bedcurtains I brought from Italy." Having delivered himself of this intense series of confidences, he sighed heavily, and released my hand.

I hesitated. I had confidences of my own to share.

"Lord Robert—"

"Yes?"

I paused again, unsure whether to follow my strong impulse or to hold back.

"What is it, girl?"

"Lord Robert, there is something I think you need to have. It rightly belongs to you. Pirto gave it to me after the inquest ended, and she made me promise never to show it to anyone. She wants so badly to be loyal to her mistress! But I think you need to have it."

I drew from my pocket the folded paper Pirto had taken from Lady Dudley's locked box and handed it to Lord Robert.

"I have not read this," I said. "Your wife left it with Pirto, to give to you."

He reached out and took the paper, unfolded it, and read it aloud, in a strained voice. "To my husband Lord Robert Dudley, I can no longer bear to walk this earth in torment. I have decided to free myself. Farewell, sweet Robin."

He looked up at me, as if dazed, then cried out "Thank God!" and jumped up off the bed, hastily beginning to put on his armor.

"Here," he said, handing me the note. "Destroy this. Pirto was right to want it kept secret. Anyone reading this would believe Amy was mad. Only madwomen destroy themselves."

"Or women who are merely sunk in misery."

"No, not that. Don't you see? Before you showed me this message I thought for certain it must have been an accident, her falling down those stairs, but now I see that she must have killed herself deliberately, not because she couldn't bear to live, but because she wanted me to be blamed for her death. It was her revenge. Her revenge!"

"But why?"

"She was jealous of the queen. And of my ambition. Above all, of my ambition. She thought that Elizabeth and I were planning to annul our marriage, Amy's and mine—and, I have to confess, Elizabeth did talk about it now and then. How we could get a church court to do it, to say that Amy was my distant cousin and that our marriage had never been a true one in the eyes of the church. But I never took that kind of talk seriously. Elizabeth is full of playful fancies of that sort, you know. Imaginings. None of it means anything."

"It did to Amy."

"Besides," he said as he pulled on the last of his armor and did his best to tie it firmly in place, fumbling a good deal, no doubt because he was accustomed to having a groom dress him, "I want Amy to have a Christian burial. Otherwise she would bring shame on the family."

On you, I thought. To bury her as a suicide would bring shame on you, and harm your ambitions.

At length he stood before me in his gleaming armor, restored to his impressive role as military captain.

"Let this be our secret, Letitia. This mad confession, written by a madwoman. I will not tell the queen about it."

"And I will tell no one, if you wish it. Certainly not Mistress Clinkerte, who is the guardian of all secrets."

"You and I, Lettie," he said, using the playful name my family gave me. Had he heard my father use it when addressing me? "You and I alone will know the truth, through all eternity," he intoned with mock solemnity.

His sudden levity made me frown. We were after all standing in the room of a woman who had killed herself, whether through an excess of despair or out of desire for revenge.

"I will not forget, either," I said, "what Pirto told me. That Amy did not die right away. That after her fall she lingered for hours, in agony, before she died. Whatever moved her to this terrible act, she suffered greatly for it."

"She paid for the sin of destroying herself," Robert said quietly.

And you paid too, I thought, and will go on paying. Amy had her revenge.

Lord Robert left Cumnor Place, leading his thousand men southward to London, to defend the capital and the queen. The preparations for Amy's funeral in Oxford went forward without hindrance, and Mistress Clinkerte and I returned to court.

But I took with me the note Amy had written, instead of destroying it as Lord Robert had asked me to do, and hid it away for safekeeping. I knew it could prove his innocence, if the ugly accusations against him persisted. And I felt that I wanted to protect him—and to protect the truth.

As I had promised, I told no one of the note's contents, in fact I said little about what had happened during my few days at Cumnor Place. But I thought about those disturbing days a great deal, and about Lord Robert, as he had looked when he knelt weeping at his late wife's bedside, his sun-browned skin visible beneath his thin shirt, his powerful calves outlined by his velvet hose. His fine dark blue eyes, now full of sorrow, now full of determination as he tied on his armor, now gravely and steadily watching me as we talked. And the sound of his voice, resonant and mellow and rich, saying "You and I, Lettie. You and I alone will know the truth, through all eternity." The words went round and round in my head for a long time after we parted, until their meaning was lost in the deep ensorcelling web of their sound.

FIFTEEN

AT first we thought she was merely tired, worn out from riding and hunting, and wearied, too, by all the agitation and unease surrounding Amy Dudley's death.

She was slow to get out of her great cedarwood bed in the morning, slow to draw the beautiful bedcurtains with their bright embroidered scenes of Leda and Apollo and Adonis. She complained of a headache and called weakly for Mistress Clinkerte to rub her sore back.

It was unlike the queen to indulge herself in this way, it seemed to me. As a rule when she was ill her bad temper worsened and she became more demanding, but she forced herself to get out of bed and do what was necessary, reading and signing papers and meeting with Lord Cecil and her council and keeping us all in dread of her displeasure.

This time, however, she seemed to give in to her ailment, to sink into lethargy under its weight, until by the third day we were very worried about her and prayers were being offered in all the churches for her recovery.

On that day Mistress Clinkerte was bending over the bed, trying to persuade the queen to eat some soup and gruel, when I heard her cry out in horror.

"Her mouth! Her mouth! Quick! Call the physicians!"

"What is it?" I asked, going up toward the bed.

"The spots! She has the spots! It is the pox!"

Instinctively I drew back. Everyone knew the signs of the dreaded pox, the spots that broke out in the sufferer's mouth and that soon spread in a loathsome tide all across the face and down the arms. I had seen the tiny red spots before, and had been warned to stay away, stay far away, lest I too become a victim of the deadly disease.

"Quick! Bathe her!" the physicians urged, ordering the servants to bring boiling water to fill the queen's big metal tub and insisting that she immerse herself in the hottest water she could stand—until she protested that she was being scalded alive. Once bathed, she was then led out into the palace garden, where a chilly autumnal wind was blowing the brilliant orange and yellow leaves off the trees. On her return she was coughing and sneezing, her face red and her breath coming in short gasps. Instead of curing the pox, the doctors had caused her to be afflicted with a rheum.

The physicians were sent away and the queen was put to bed, tended by Mistress Clinkerte and the gentle, soothing Mary Sidney, Lord Robert's pretty sister who was one of the bedchamber women.

"How is she?" Lord Robert asked me when he came to court. I was sitting in one of the outer chambers, trying to occupy myself with needlework but distracted by my worries. For my sister Cecelia had begun to complain of feeling ill and several of the other bedchamber women and maids of honor were showing signs of the pox, as was one of the physicians, Dr. Meadowcroft.

"She never leaves her bed," I told him, noting that he was wearing mourning garb, black cloak and doublet, hose and slippers. He was in mourning for his late wife, I thought—and then I wondered, was he also making sure to be properly dressed when the queen died? "Her thoughts are drifting," I added. Mistress Clinkerte had confided to me that the queen was lost in semi-coherent reminiscence much of the time.

Lord Robert shook his head.

"Am I to be so afflicted," he mused, half to himself, "as to be deprived of my wife and my beloved queen in so short a space of time? Who will reign once she is gone? Who will keep order?"

"Lord Robert!" My father came in, wringing his hands as he often did, deep lines of worry on his brow. "Lord Robert, she has been asking for you."

"To say her goodbyes, no doubt," was his response.

"There is no need to assume the worst," my father chided. "She has a toughness in her. She may well survive—but she must be encouraged, supported. She must not see you or anyone wearing mourning black. That would lower her spirits."

"Then I will not go in to her just yet," was Lord Robert's immediate reply. I detected relief in his tone. He was as much afraid of the pox as anyone. "I am concerned about the need to maintain order—if she should succumb."

"As is every man on the council. We have assembled the city militias. Their numbers will be sufficient."

"My troops and arms are assembled at St. Thomas Waterings. I shall keep them there in case of need."

"You shall disperse them immediately! We can have no private armies within a day's march of the capital!"

"I brought them there on the queen's orders."

"Have you a written request from the queen?" was my father's insistent question.

"You are well aware that the queen hardly bothers to put her requests in writing, not when the person she is requesting to act is standing right beside her!"

"Or lying beside her," I heard my father mutter.

Ignoring this remark, Lord Robert said, "Nevertheless I shall obtain what you seem to require. I shall return in a few hours, after I have made myself presentable to the sovereign, and ask her for the request in writing." And having made this announcement, he took his leave.

But Lord Robert did not return when he said he would, nor did he come to court the next day, or the next. Meanwhile the queen sank deeper into the arms of the pox, seemingly losing what was left of her will, refusing to eat and turning her face to the wall, her eyes blankly staring. The only sign of life left in her, the weeping Mistress Clinkerte reported, was one bony hand fingering a gold crucifix, her thumb rubbing the face of the Christ, her lips moving in a sibilant whisper.

We all were on the point of despair, even my father, and were preparing ourselves for the worst news to come from the queen's bedchamber.

Lord Robert appeared then, wearing not his mourning black but a doublet and hose of a subdued deep green color. He had come, it seemed, because his sister Mary had to be removed from court, having been stricken with the pox as were several others who had frequented the inner chamber of the queen. Young Dr. Meadowcroft had died, and Elizabeth's fool Graziella, and the bride of Lord Hazelton who had been married only a week, and one or two of the tirewomen. My sister Cecelia, whose case was not as severe as Lady Mary's, was taken to our family home at Rotherfield Greys to recover and Lord Robert hoped that if his sister was removed to the country she would survive.

He had no sooner accompanied Lady Mary to her coach than he returned to the royal apartments, bringing a priest with him.

"This is Father Lockton," he said to me. "I have brought him to anoint the queen with holy oil, to aid her recovery. Please accompany us to her bedchamber."

"But the physicians have forbidden us all from entering—"

"She asked to see me, didn't she?" Lord Robert snapped.

"That was several days ago, my lord. Her condition is much worsened—"

"All the more reason for us to be admitted, and for her to welcome priestly comfort."

I shook my head. "I cannot enter her apartments without permission."

Lord Robert bent down so that he spoke close to my ear.

"Lettie! We are friends, we share secrets! Let us be allies in this! Besides, it is only a matter of time before I am the one to give and withhold permission in these royal apartments!"

I did not know what to say to this.

"I am told the queen wishes to receive the blessing for the sick," Father Lockton said in a surprisingly high voice. "I am prepared to succor her." He smiled wanly. "Please, take me in to her."

Instead of doing as he asked I went out into the corridor, hoping to see one of the councilors or physicians there. But there were only three grooms playing dice, and one of the gentleman ushers who lounged against the wall, drifting off to sleep. I heard voices coming from other parts of the palace, but saw no one. Ever since the queen fell ill there had been fewer and fewer people to be found in or near her apartments.

"Lettie!" Lord Robert was calling me impatiently. "Where have you got to? I need you."

Why he needed me I couldn't imagine just then, though it became clear enough soon afterward. Worried that I was doing the wrong thing, and exasperated and flustered by Lord Robert's demands (it was hard for me to say no to him), I resigned myself to give in. Nodding my assent, I led Lord Robert and the priest into the queen's private domain.

There was a stench in the royal bedchamber, my blunt sister would have called it the stench of death. The painfully thin, pale woman in the broad cedarwood bed lay inert, apparently unaware of our entry into the room. But when she heard Lord Robert say, "Your Majesty," she blinked her tired eyes and turned her head. When she saw him her lips turned upward in a faint smile and she slowly held out her hand.

He grasped it and, bending down over the bed, raised it to his lips.

"I have brought Father Lockton to bless you," he said.

Fear came into her eyes. "Is it over then?" she murmured.

"No, dear. This is just in case."

There was no need to say "in case you die."

The priest invoked the blessing in his shrill voice, and I saw the queen smile again, this time from amusement, as she caught Lord Robert's eye.

"Now then," Lord Robert said briskly when the prayer had come to an end, "there is something else we need to do just in case." He turned to me.

"Lettie, find Clinkerte. She must be near by. No one else, mind. Only Clinkerte."

I went in search of Mistress Clinkerte and found her, wrapped in a cloak, napping on a pile of pillows in the antechamber. I shook her and said that she was needed.

Frightened and disheveled, she followed me into the bed-chamber.

"Now, Your Majesty," Lord Robert said once we were standing beside the bed, "in the presence of these two witnesses, Letitia Knollys and Mistress Clinkerte, Father Lockton can join us in marriage, so that if the Lord should call you to heaven, you will leave your kingdom in the best and strongest hands."

SIXTEEN

"NO!"

The queen's scratchy, muffled voice was indistinct but the word she spoke was clear enough.

"No! Not that!"

Using all her remaining strength, she struggled to sit up in her bed—Mistress Clinkerte supporting her as she did so—and I put a pillow behind her back.

"There will be none of that!" she said hoarsely.

Lord Robert waved the priest away and sat down on the bed. He reached for the queen's hand, which she had snatched away when he said he wanted Father Lockton to marry them. She withheld it.

"You are weak, dear. You are not thinking clearly. Let me make the decisions now."

"Never!" she muttered. "I am still queen here! Call my council!"

"But my dearest girl," Mistress Clinkerte said, weeping, "I don't want you to die a spinster!"

"Hush, old woman! Remember who I am, and who you are!"

The voice that came from the bed was so low I had to strain to hear it, but the queen's accents were sharp. Still, her frail body trembled as she spoke, and the stink of decay in the room seemed to increase. Even as I admired her toughness—the toughness my father had been so sure of in her—I could not help but wonder whether the effort to resist Lord Robert's wishes would put too great a strain on her weak body.

I watched her. Her head drooped, as she clutched at Mistress Clinkerte's supporting arm. Would she collapse?

"Letitia! Summon your father," I heard her say. "Bring the council here."

"Wait, Letitia," Lord Robert was saying. "Wait until Father Lockton has heard our marriage vows."

I hesitated, and in that moment I heard the queen emit a scratchy sound, a muffled shriek. "Though death possess every joint of me, I will not be forced to marry! Do as I command you!"

Without waiting to hear more I hurried out into the anteroom and the corridor beyond, calling my father's name and Lord Cecil's. The servants, alarmed, began rushing around in their turn, looking for the men who customarily attended the queen.

"Is she dead?" they called out to me.

"No!" I shouted. "She wants her councilors!"

I finally found my father, sitting at a long table with two of the militia commanders, eating bread and cheese and poring over a map.

"Come quickly, father! Lord Robert is trying to make the queen marry him! She wants you and the other council members!"

"By the beard of the Lord!" he burst out, getting up from the table in such haste that he overturned his tankard and hurrying out into the corridor. When we got back to the royal apartments we found that several of the other councilors were already in the royal bedchamber, and that a secretary sat in a corner of the room, writing, the scratch of his quill the only sound.

The queen, alarmingly pale and thin, had wrapped a length of red flannel around her shoulders. Lord Robert no longer sat on the bed but stood against the wall, to one side of the bed, looking, I thought, somewhat wilted.

"Take this down with care," she was saying to the secretary, who turned his head toward the bed and shut his eyes, straining to hear her, before turning once again to his paper and quill.

"I, Elizabeth, queen of this realm, declare that upon my death Lord Robert Dudley—" she paused to allow the secretary to write—"that upon my death Lord Robert Dudley shall become Lord Protector, with full and free powers to rule in my stead."

"But Your Majesty!" my father cried out.

"I should advise caution," Lord Cecil said at the same moment.

"Silence!" the queen croaked. "I have not finished. As Lord Protector," she went on, "he shall have an income of twenty thousand pounds a year from the royal treasury."

At this Lord Robert, who had been standing open-mouthed, knelt beside the bed and took the queen's hand.

"My good lady!" he managed to say through his tears. "My dearest, good lady!"

"Never mind, Robin, I may outlive you all," I heard her whisper to him.

"I doubt whether the treasury has enough coins to meet this requirement," was Cecil's acid response.

"Then let it be your charge to fill it!"

The secretary completed his writing, and blotted his paper. Gritting her teeth with the effort, the queen grasped the quill offered to her and signed her name to the paper, handing it to Lord Cecil.

"There! Now everyone is satisfied. And my back still aches. Let me sleep!"

She waved everyone out of the room except Mistress Clinkerte and myself, who helped her to lie down again, turned on her side, and obediently began rubbing her back.

SEVENTEEN

THE spots on the queen's face and neck and arms became pustules, then turned to sores with ugly red scabs.

But she did not die. Night after night she slept beside the fireplace, wrapped in layers of red flannel, while Dr. Burcot gave her potions to drink and braved her threats and obscenities.

I was with her much of the time. Many of her ladies and maids of honor had withdrawn from court because of illness—real or feigned—but my father insisted that I stay with her, even serving her in her bedchamber though he knew—we all knew—I was risking coming down with the pox as Cecelia had, or even dying from it.

I took heart from Mistress Clinkerte, who remained entirely free of the red spots despite remaining with the queen night and day. And I could not help but notice that Lord Robert too stayed well, as did my father and most of the other councilors.

Gradually, day by day, the queen began to recover her appetite and called for quinces and game pies.

"But Your Majesty cannot eat such delicacies! Not when you have the pox!" Dr. Burcot burst out—to which the queen responded "Get out! I will have no such dour words spoken here!"

By this time those of us in her household were beginning to believe that she was improving, and would soon be fully restored to health. She ate more and more, she got out of bed and walked—haltingly at first—around her bedchamber. Her voice grew stronger, and her limbs as well, until once again she was stubborn enough and energetic and forceful enough to vilify us all in her usual fashion.

"I can't bear ugly women!" she cried one afternoon as we maids of honor were dressing her. She called for a tankard of small beer and drank it with relish. While enjoying her beer, she scanned our faces. Her gaze came to rest on my poor ill-favored sister Cecelia, whose face bore the marks of the pox and whose hair—shorn to make the queen a wig she hardly ever wore— had not yet fully grown back. Cecelia always kept her head covered with a French hood or round cap, but her ears were prominent and her sparse short hair could not cover them, their outline was evident even under the tightest headgear.

"Why do that girl's ears stick out so?" the queen demanded to know.

No one knew what to reply.

"I cannot help it, Your Majesty," Cecelia said. "We cannot all be as beautiful as you."

The sarcasm in her tone was not lost on the queen, whose face was similarly marred by pits and scars (though they would fade in time) and who was only too aware that the marks made her unsightly. She picked up the near-empty tankard and threw it in Cecelia's direction. It shattered into a hundred pieces.

"Leave my court!" the queen shouted hoarsely. Cecelia, predictably, burst into tears and ran clumsily out of the room. Despite my father's efforts to mollify the furious Elizabeth, she remained adamant: Cecelia had to go. She retired once again to Rotherfield Greys where, according to mother, she sulked and pouted and wept, blaming the queen for her unfair fate and lamenting that her life was over.

As I have said, all the maids of honor were eager to be married—to the wealthiest, most highborn men their families could secure for them. I was no exception, I suppose, except that, as Lord Robert had guessed, I was not eager to become the wife of Walter Devereux, the man my father had chosen for me and clearly intended for me to marry.

"He'll be a titled lord one day," my younger brother Frank remarked speculatively one morning not long after the queen was restored to health and the court returned to its usual state. Frank, who had grown into a lanky, amusing boy, sharp-witted and acid-tongued, with a capacity for cool appraisal, was observing Walter as the latter went about his favorite task of helping our father draw up lists of foodstuffs needed for the court's summer visits, or progresses, to the great houses of the nobles.

Every June, when the weather turned warm, we had to pack up the queen's things (nearly a hundred chests for her gowns alone) and our own and set out in a huge caravan, traveling at the speed of snails, to stay at country houses. It was torturous, that slow crawling travel. The packing and unpacking. The making of fires in cold rooms, the fleas lurking in the ill-tended rushes, the waiting along the roadside when carts broke down or horses died or serving women unexpectedly went into labor.

I dreaded the coming of summer because of all the work and fuss, but Walter looked forward to it. Helping my father plan for the great progresses was something he enjoyed almost as much as hunting. He was a born listmaker, I liked to say.

"Someone has to make the lists, Lettie," was my mother's practical reply whenever she heard me call my future husband a listmaker. "Imagine a progress with no organizing! What a commotion that would create!"

It seemed to me that whenever the court traveled, there was always commotion, but I held my tongue. I had no wish to argue with my mother about Walter, I much preferred discussing him with Frank.

"No one can ride rough horse better, or stalk with a bow," was Frank's admiring comment on Walter's proficiency as a hunter. "I once saw him come back from a hunt with three couple of coneys and a mallard and a doe—all killed in a single afternoon. And then there is Chartley—" he broke off, giving me a significant look.

"Yes, Chartley." The Devereux family castle, said to be three hundred years old, had walls that were twelve feet thick and a great hall the size of a throne room. Its hundred or so rooms were small and cramped, and the wind whistled fiercely through the old stonework, or so Walter told me when describing his childhood. But he added that the park was beautiful and well stocked with game, and the castle was very impressive in its size and undeniable strength.

"A very solid piece of masonry, Chartley," Frank said. "Not unlike Walter himself. And don't forget that he will have other estates some day, when he inherits, along with chests of gold and silver and offices and titles and subsidies from the queen, who likes him. No doubt she will make him a Garter knight. And he is not bad-looking, would you say?"

I had to admit that Walter, with his broad chest and shoulders and manly strength, his dark hair and eyes, his brawn and vigor on horseback, was the sort of young man most girls would be proud to marry. But when I looked at him I saw that, young as he was, his hair had already begun to grow thin like his father's (his father was not at all a good-looking man), and his nose was too long for handsomeness, and his eyes were small and set close together, not large and widely spaced and beautiful like Robert's.

"He is highly moral, so they say," Frank continued drily, still talking about Walter. "He will make a fine Justice of the Peace. And I know of no bastards he has fathered—"

I yawned, making Frank laugh. "And he is the dullest man I have ever met!" My exclamation, I felt sure, could be heard throughout the royal apartments.

"I quite agree," Frank said. "And mother does too, though she would never admit it. You were made for excitement, Lettie. Walter Devereux is not the man for you."

He paused, shaking his head. "Will father not consider anyone else?"

"Apparently there is no one else," I had to admit. "Cecelia has spread the tale of my supposed immoral doings in Frankfurt throughout the court and the maids of honor have told it to all their relatives and acquaintances. Half the servants in the household have heard the stories, the other half soon will. My reputation is all but ruined. Who would marry me now? Cecelia blames me for her having been sent away from court. She is spiteful. As usual, she chooses to vent her spite on me, and as usual, father does nothing to silence her or punish her. Now I am said to be the most forward virgin in the court. Which means no virgin at all."

I looked at Frank with tears of vexation in my eyes.

"If only there were a court of law where unkind rumor could be tried and condemned!"

"Never mind," Frank said fondly. "You are certainly the prettiest forward virgin at court. I see how the men all admire you, the married ones as well as the unmarried ones. I'd marry you myself if I wasn't your brother—and about to go to sea."

Frank's news about his upcoming departure surprised and delighted me. He had achieved his ambition, he would be sailing in a few days. The elderly master of a small coastal freighter had offered to take him on as an apprentice, provided he worked hard to learn seamanship.

"The old man says if I take to it, he'll train me up to take his place one day," my brother told me, his pleasure clear from the light in his eyes. "He's getting on in years, and has no son, so there is no one for him to leave the boat to. Father disapproves, of course, but then, I'm not like you. I don't intend to let father govern my life."

Frank's last words stung, and even though he quickly saw that I was wounded by what he said and did what he could to soften his meaning, I continued to feel the sting after he went away and I was left to ponder the truth of his observation.

He was right, of course. I did intend to follow father's plan for me. It was what all girls did, why should I be different? But then, why shouldn't I go my own way? Why did I lack the strength to tell father I didn't want to marry Walter, I wanted to wait. To try to make a better choice.

For the fact was that since coming to know Lord Robert, I felt certain I was bound to be discontented with almost anyone else.

If I was honest with myself I had to admit that I admired him, as all the women of the court did. He was, quite simply, magnificent, his tall figure elegantly blazoned in splendid velvet doublets with gold slashings, his high hats with blue feathers (the style in that year, the year the queen nearly died of the pox and the rest of us were relieved that she did not), his flashing diamond-studded ruffs (Walter would never be seen in such things) and bejeweled belts and shoebuckles—each day a different gorgeous costume. Robert was the stuff of dreams to the women of the court.

Yet he belonged to the queen. That was evident. So he wasn't to be touched. No one approached him or flirted with him, except the boldest and least prudent girls and women, and they were soon sent off by the queen with a warning and an order never to return.

To be sure, we all saw clearly that Lord Robert had flaws. He was boastful. He was egotistical. He loved looking at himself in his finery in the royal looking-glasses. And there were still whispers about how Amy Dudley died, and his possibly being a murderer. (Such rumors never seem to die.)

But with it all, he was likable. Walter was not! Walter was the sort of man you wanted to shut away in a room somewhere far off while you danced and laughed and had a good time. The sort of man you might not be sorry to discover had been sent to another country, or had moved to the Orkney Islands, or—heaven help me, but I did think this—been lost at sea.

Amid these dire fantasies I was brought back to reality by my father, who came to me one day about six months after the queen's recovery and told me that he had chosen a day for my wedding to Walter. We were to be married, he said, in a month's time. The queen had agreed to grace our wedding ceremony with her presence.

"Oh, and Lettie, the best thing about it all is, Walter's second cousin Roger Wilbraham has agreed to marry Cecelia on the same day. Imagine! You with your bad reputation and Cecelia with her pockmarked face—and you will both have husbands! Thanks be to Providence, my girls will be married off at last!"

EIGHTEEN

WE were wed at court, in the queen's own private chapel, very early in the morning—so early, in fact, that the birds had barely begun to chirp. I was in my twenty-third year, Walter a little younger, though he did not like me to remind him of that.

It was a hasty ceremony, because the queen was impatient by nature and disliked weddings (probably they reminded her that she had never had one) and kept complaining to Lord Robert that our ceremony was making her late for her morning ride. Mistress Clinkerte had helped me dress in the lovely gown mother insisted on providing for me, a silken gown, bombasted in the latest fashion, the sleeves worked by a silkwoman in silver edging with rosebuds embroidered in white and pink. The ruff was of lace with a wire beneath it to make it stand out around my face. The petticoats were of soft Bruges linen. I had never had such finery before, and when mother saw me in my beautiful gown on my wedding morning she wept—in part because of all the ale she had drunk the night before, it must be said—and told me I had never looked more pleasing and that she hoped I would be a good wife to Walter.

Cecelia too had a costly gown, but there was no disguising her plump form and the contrast between us was remarked upon. Her fiancé, the stout, rather choleric Roger Wilbraham, a man of forty-five who had already buried three wives, did not appear to favor her, or even to take much notice of her; Walter had confided to me that the price of his cousin's consent to the marriage was the office of Collector of Fines and surveyor for Salisbury and the additional sinecure of Deputy Master of the King's Ships, two valuable perquisites that together would bring him at least fifty pounds a year. My father had been glad to arrange these appointments; thanks to him, Roger Wilbraham would be a comparatively rich man. Cecelia would have every comfort—except, perhaps, the comfort of knowing that Roger had married her out of love and not greed.

As soon as the ceremony was concluded and the queen hurried away to have her morning ride we sat down to a wedding breakfast of stuffed partridge and venison pasties, grapes and pears from a faraway hothouse, all washed down with good malmsey and muscatel. Walter informed us all that the venison came from one of his does, and proceeded to describe, at some length and in overmuch detail, the particular hunt at which the doe had been killed—which caused a silence to fall at the table.

"I have ordered some good hunters from Ireland," Lord Robert said presently, in an effort to revive the conversation. "Perhaps you would like to try them. The queen will have first choice, naturally, but those she rejects might suit you well." He paused, then added, "She does not spare her mounts—or her officials, for that matter."

This made us laugh, as it was meant to, though my father did not join in the amusement.

"Her favorite, Bay Gentle, was run off his legs last week and had to have a dressing for his forefeet."

"You have a new fine stud, do you not?" Walter asked. "A stallion from Turin?"

"Great Savoy, yes. I have high hopes for him."

Robert's brother Ambrose raised his glass in a toast. "To all stallions and new husbands, on this their wedding day!"

We drank a toast, but the mood at the table remained subdued—in part, I felt sure, because the hour was so early, and we were all a little drowsy, but there was a more obvious cause. Walter was droning on about his favorite pastime—hunting and horses—instead of admiring and cherishing me, and my new brother-in-law Roger Wilbraham, his red face stony, was wolfing down his food in the greatest haste and paying no attention whatever to the rest of us. Without waiting for the third course to be served Roger abruptly took his leave, bowing curtly to us all (and not even kissing his bride Cecelia on the cheek) and saying something about having to attend to his new duties.

Cecelia's lip quivered. I was afraid she would burst into tears. Instead she smiled bravely, for Lord Robert, who was signaling to the musicians to play a lively tune, held out his hand to her and led her in a dance. At once the mood began to lighten. Walter and I joined in the dancing, as did my father and mother and even Mistress Clinkerte, whose partner was the spry elderly equerry Whaffer who, it was said, had been a page at the court of Henry VIII as a boy.

We whirled and dipped in a country dance, and later there was a disguising, with Lord Robert and his brother dressed up as Knights of Pegasus seeking the Fortunate Isles. It was all foolishness, as disguisings invariably are, but foolishness was just what we needed. We laughed and applauded and I felt very grateful to Lord Robert for turning our melancholy wedding breakfast into a mirthful celebration.

The morning having been whiled away, we returned to our duties, Cecelia and I among the queen's ladies and Walter to his desk and his lists. I was very aware, however, that with each advancing hour my wedding night was approaching. I would be put to bed with Walter for the first time. We would become one flesh. We would enjoy what my father called the sins of the flesh. What would those sins—those pleasures—be like?

When at last the hour came and Mistress Clinkerte helped me to put on my black satin dressing-gown my stomach lurched and my heart was beating rapidly. Would I be pleasing to Walter? (All I had ever heard, all my life, was that girls and women had to be pleasing to men; no one ever mentioned the question of whether men might or might not be pleasing to the girls and women they married.) I looked at myself in the longest looking-glass in the candlelit bedchamber. The black dressing-gown clung to my shape in a flattering way, outlining my prominent breasts and slender waist, the widening at my hips, the long taper of my legs, which no man had ever seen bare, not even my father. My skin glowed golden, my curling auburn hair, which Mistress Clinkerte had brushed out so that its sheen gleamed like the satin of my gown, my bright blue eyes with their thick, upward-tilted lashes, my lips—inviting lips, as it seemed to me: all this held an undeniable loveliness.

Yes, I told myself. I would be pleasing to Walter.

Yet in that same moment an unsought wish flooded my thoughts. I wished with all my heart that this bodily loveliness of mine were going to be offered, not to Walter, but to Lord Robert.

An image came into my mind, of me, just as I was then, in nothing but my black dressing-gown, running from the bedchamber into Lord Robert's private quarters, giving myself to him, pleading with him to take my virginity.

What a fearful fancy! A wicked fancy, my father would surely call it if the thing were known to him. A thought put into my mind by the devil himself.

I blushed at the thought, and did my best to banish it from my mind. Yet when I was put to bed and Walter was brought in, in his nightshirt, his broad shoulders, thick neck and strong legs promising virility, his small eyes impatient with lust, a hound alert for the scent of prey, my heart sank at the sight of him. I smiled, I yielded to his touch (only a trifle unwillingly), I tried not to tense my body for the assault of him, an assault I knew must come, and that I could not avoid. But within, where my feelings were hid, I held back. Outwardly, I did what I knew I must, holding myself taut against the pain and bearing it without crying out, hearing Walter's grunts of satisfaction and taking them for pleasure. Perhaps foolishly, I waited to feel pleasure myself—for after all, if, as my father always said, lust is the devil's playground, then surely the pleasure of lust is the devil's lure.

But there was no pleasure in the wet stickiness between my thighs, or in the stink of blood that stained the bedlinens, or even in the memory of Walter's wet mouth on mine and his grasping hands clenched tightly around my waist as he thrust himself inside me. There was only a wound between my legs, and in my heart, and a man I did not love lying beside me, lost in the indifference of sleep.

NINETEEN

M Y beautiful daughter was born before we had been
married a year, and somewhat to our disappointment,
she was not the son Walter hoped for. She was a sunny, bouncy
child, wriggling and full of energy almost from the moment I
first held her in my arms. I chose her name, Penelope. Walter
said he didn't care what name I gave her, but that when our son
was born, he would be named Walter Devereux and would in
time inherit the lands and fortune he himself held.

My daughter consumed nearly all my attention for a time, and
I was surprised at how involving I found her to be. She gazed up
at me from her cradle, her wide blue eyes so clear and trusting,
and before long she began to smile, and then to sit up all by
herself, and would have crawled all across the floor if her nurse
had let her. I allowed her on our bed—though Walter disapproved,
when he was there to notice—and in warm weather, I went
along when she was taken outdoors, into the garden, and put

down briefly amid the flowers. She shrieked with pleasure, and one of her first words, I remember, was "roses."

By this time, however, my stomach had begun to bulge again and I was feeling poorly. Another baby was on its way. The midwife assured me that my nearly constant sickness was a sign my child would be a boy—that and the fact that I was growing very heavy behind and in my legs. I told Walter about these hopeful signs, and he smiled and patted my belly from time to time and called it "young Walter." I was so ill and uncomfortable during the last several months of my pregnancy that I simply had to give up all effort at activity and stay in bed. My mother and father were both concerned about me, and came to visit me. Father brought a physician from court who did little, other than to advise me to obey the midwife.

"Will I have a son, do you think?" I asked him.

"Only God knows that," was all he would say, even after I mentioned the signs the midwife had detected. "You must pray for one," he added, "just as we all pray for our queen to give England a son and heir." The queen continued in her unmarried state, and it was still hoped that she would marry Lord Robert and have a child to succeed her. But month after month went by, and it did not happen.

At last I felt my pains begin, and they were much worse than with Penelope. At first I was able to bear them fairly well, but after many hours I felt my strength ebbing and I could tell from the look on the midwife's face that she had doubts about my ability to bring my child into the world uninjured. I am not someone who yields to morbid thoughts, but I confess that in the second day of that long and anguished labor, I began to fear death.

I called for Walter, and for the priest from our parish, and also asked that little Penelope be brought in to cheer me. But

Penelope only cried, and had to be taken out of the room by her nurse. And Walter, his boots muddy from tramping through the thickets following a stag, did not know what to do or how to comfort me. Childbearing was after all women's work, and my failure to bear my child (not my weakness and neediness) clearly distressed him. In the end he threw up his hands and went out, leaving the priest to bless me and ask, in a tone that made me even more worried about my survival, that the Lord's will would be done.

I felt a raging thirst. "Wine! Give me wine!" I cried with as much vigor as I could muster, and continued to insist even though the midwife refused me, saying that if I drank wine my child might be born dead.

I was by this time half-delirious, and I remember hearing myself swear loudly at the servants, one of whom at length brought me some wine and obeyed me when I told her not to water it but to let me drink as much of it as I could hold, at a draught. Fortified by the wine, I decided to make a final effort to give birth to my child, even if it cost me my life. I strained as hard as I could, grunting and groaning, twisting the bedlinens and writhing while the midwife pushed down hard on my belly. I have never, before or since, felt such pain. It seemed to go on forever. But in the end I suddenly felt as though my body was being torn open, and then I heard, or thought I heard, a shrill cry.

I must have fainted, for when I woke it was dark and there was no one with me in the room. I saw by the light of the single bedside candle that the cradle was empty, and for a long terrible moment I thought, my baby has been born dead.

I wept then, from exhaustion and sorrow, and the sound of my weeping brought the wetnurse and two servants into the room. The wetnurse, I was overjoyed to see, was carrying my baby.

But she did not look at all content; she appeared vexed.

"You have another daughter, madam," she said curtly.

I held out my arms and took the tiny, red-faced baby. She was sleeping. I hugged her to me and murmured to her.

"Has the master been informed?" I asked.

"Yes, madam. He was not at all pleased."

"Never mind, little girl," I whispered to the child in my arms. "I thank the Lord for you, given to me in such pain and travail. I am thankful we are both alive."

I decided to name her Dorothy, a name I knew means Gift of God. She was, and is, my gift and I can never put into words how much I love her.

As a married woman I ceased to be a maid of honor and became a lady of the bedchamber to the queen, as did Cecelia. We were expected to serve at court for at least several months a year. I looked forward to my time at court for although it meant serving a capricious mistress it also meant diversion and amusement, sharing in the light flirtations, celebrations and chivalrous pastimes that made up the queen's days and nights when she was not attending to important matters or meeting with her councilors.

Walter too was at court a great deal, or doing the queen's business. He assisted my father, and was often sent on important errands and missions, entrusted with increasingly more important tasks as he proved himself loyal and dependable. Soon after Dorothy was born Queen Elizabeth sent Walter to Ireland to oversee the handing over of some royal lands from the Irish rebels. He accomplished this assignment swiftly and without difficulties, which impressed her. She soon sent him back on similar business. In all he was gone nearly half a year—our first long separation—and in his absence I was in charge of Chartley and our other estates, a considerable responsibility.

I learned a great deal in that time, asking the stewards to instruct me and enjoying much of what they had to teach about the management of our farms and orchards, the names and occupations of the peasants and villagers who worked them, the needs of our animals and crops and the challenges of blight and rot, drought and unseasonable weather.

Chartley itself, the old castle behind its thick grey stone surrounding wall, was a cold, drafty home even in summer. Walter's father refused to live there, preferring his smaller but much warmer lodge in the south. At Chartley the children needed fires in their nursery all year round, and the great hall felt as though icicles should be dropping from the ceiling. As if to compensate for this major drawback the beauty of the gardens delighted me. I loved to walk with the children down the long pebbled path between the tall flowering bushes wet with dew, through the kitchen garden, out to the greenhouses where fruit was cultivated even in winter and roses and rare plants from faraway places bloomed and shed their leaves and bloomed again.

I loved to take the girls into the orchards in the fall when the earliest pinkish-green apples, sweet-smelling and juicy, could be knocked down out of the trees with long sticks. One of the old farmers kept a fire going in the open air and we baked bruised apples in the embers, sprinkling them with sugar and cinnamon. Of such lovely simple pleasures was our country life made, and I relished it greatly—sitting in the swing between the great yew trees on the lawn, watching the shadow creep across the sundial, sucking the honey out of the blue salvia flowers, visiting the great black sow with her new pigs.

I relished it all, especially sharing it with my children—but I did not relish Walter. In fact I felt a growing aversion to him.

I grew to hate the hairy knuckles on his right hand, the way the hair stood out on his thick fingers when he counted out the coins from his strongbox in front of the fire. I hated the folds of pink skin at the back of his neck, the way he had of lifting his head like an alert predator scenting prey, the scrape of his voice, and the dull, thudding things that he said. His lack of humor. The way he looked at me with his small shrewd eyes, with a disgruntled, sulky look that said, you are an inadequate wife.

For I had no doubt that he found me so. I had failed at a wife's principal task—providing her husband with healthy sons.

I had failed, and so had Cecelia, but for a quite different reason. Her husband, Walter's second cousin Roger Wilbraham, never came near her. Unlike Walter, he had no need of more sons, his first two wives having provided him with four sons already. And, as Cecelia discovered, he also had a beautiful Spanish mistress, whom he kept tucked away in a village near his estate.

Oh, how she cried when she found out about that woman! She complained to our father, who threatened to have all Wilbraham's offices and incomes revoked if he did not rid himself of the other woman. But his threats were without force, because the queen refused to take the matter seriously. In her perverse way she shrugged off the entire problem, merely remarking that all men had mistresses and that Cecelia should learn not to complain about things she could not control.

"She's lucky to have a husband at all," was Elizabeth's callous rejoinder when our father approached her. "Let her bear with her lot, as the rest of us do, and not make demands."

Poor Cecelia was furious, and eaten up with envy. I don't believe she really wanted children—or Roger either, if it came to

that; he had a terrible temper and it was hard to see anything in
him that would appeal to a woman. Certainly Cecelia was neither
wifely nor motherly. She did not have an affectionate nature,
rather the reverse, and she lacked the forbearance to deal with a
difficult man, or the patience to nurture babies and raise boisterous
boys and girls into strong, courageous adults. Yet she craved the
status that being the wife of a well-to-do man and the mother of
a large family conferred. She did not like being called neglected
and barren. For although she was certainly neglected, it was by
no means certain that she was barren, merely untouched by her
callous husband, who hardly even spoke to her.

Though I never said it in so many words, I came to believe
that Cecelia was cursed with bad luck in life. I wished it were
not so.

My own share of luck came soon enough. My girls were still
very small when once more I found myself with a swelling belly
and became hopeful that this time I would give Walter the son
he wanted. Cecelia was envious of me and stayed away, even
though she lived only a few days' ride from Chartley. My dear
mother came to see me and stayed nearly a month, cheering
me and encouraging me in her softspoken way, and telling me
with a smile that she was sure my baby would be a boy.

My pains came on in the fall season and I felt that this was a
good omen. The fruit was ripe for harvest, the old farmer had
begun cooking the fallen apples in the embers of his orchard
fire and Walter, full of qualms and misgivings yet hoping for a
boy, forbore to hunt even though the season was well advanced
and many fine does and stags were abroad for the taking.

I heard Walter pacing in the antechamber while the midwife
stroked my belly and chanted the words of an old prayer.

I was delivered just before dawn, and as soon as Walter was
told I heard him bellow his joy. We were the parents of a son at

last. He was tiny and weak, his cry was faint and he did not nurse as lustily as Penelope and Dorothy had. But he was a boy, and that was all that mattered. "Young Walter" had come to Chartley Castle, the heir to the family lands and fortune, and I, his mother, was no longer a failure in my husband's eyes.

TWENTY

I T was a chilly evening, with a smell of rain in the wind, and the thick gilded curtains were being drawn in the queen's antechamber. There were only a few of us in the royal apartments, for Elizabeth was away from court for a few days, visiting her favorite Christopher Hatton at his estate of Greve-mere, and she had taken all the tirewomen and most of the maids and ladies of the bedchamber with her.

The chill in the dim rooms persisted, even after the curtains were drawn and the fires fed and we had drunk a warming posset brought to us from the kitchens. For before she left, the queen had quarreled with Lord Robert, a bitter quarrel, a lovers' spat; both had talked in tense, angry tones and the cold, unsettling aftermath of their anger could still be felt.

Lord Robert had been upset over Elizabeth's ongoing flirtation with Hatton, whose dark good looks and clever jests amused and excited her, and who was younger and in much better repute than Lord Robert himself and was not burdened with a shadowed past. Elizabeth enjoyed making Lord Robert jealous, it was as if she dangled other eligible men in front of him as if to say, see here, I can marry any man I choose, I don't have to pick you!

To be sure, she had shown the depth of her love (for I had no doubt she loved him, in her way) for Lord Robert by creating him Earl of Leicester and giving him the magnificent castle of Kenilworth in Warwickshire along with other rich estates and lands. She had even proposed him as a husband for her close relative and rival Mary Stuart, Queen of Scots, which would have made him "King Robert" in fact, just as in the title of the song the grooms like to whistle. But he still hoped to gain the chief prize, that of becoming Elizabeth's husband. No lesser reward would do. And as she continued to frustrate him and taunt him and deny him that chief prize, they quarreled.

They quarreled more often, it seemed to me, as the queen's reign went on. On that chilly evening, an evening I will always remember, their voices had been harsh and assaultive and after Elizabeth left for Hatton's estate I could hear Lord Robert stomping through her outer chambers, sputtering with fury.

When he came into the room where I sat by myself, reading, and saw me there he paused, momentarily confused. I looked up at him, expecting to see wrath. Instead his features were distorted in anguish. He tried to disguise it, but failed.

"Botheration!"

He sank down onto a pile of pillows beside the fire and drew his hand across his face. It was a large, strong hand, a man's strong hand, but it was not like Walter's, with thick fingers and hairy knuckles. Lord Robert's fingers were beautifully shaped, the knuckles smooth, the nails trimmed. I had always thought him a beautiful man, with a face and body worthy of a fine painter's brush. The portraits of him that I had seen, including the miniature the queen wore around her neck, failed to capture the rarity of his looks.

Even at his worst, as he was now, he was sublimely good-looking.

"Botheration, Lettie!" he said again. "What gets into that accursed woman anyway?"

I closed my book. He did not really want an answer to his question. He wanted sympathy—and relief. I felt an urge to go to him, to sink down beside him into the thick pillows, which I knew would be warm from the fire. His arms, too, would be warm. . . . But I stayed where I was.

"You know her! Tell me! Help me understand."

I shook my head with a smile. "You men are always saying how impossible it is to understand a woman—any woman. You dismiss us as mad creatures, ruled by whim—or by the devil. But for what little my opinion is worth, I would simply say that she is spoiled, and she enjoys taunting you, and she would probably be frightened if you ever turned away from her, or became cold and distant. As long as you pursue her, she can do as she likes with you."

I could tell that my words intrigued yet puzzled him. He let his hands fall.

"She would send me to the Tower if I abandoned my pursuit," he said, but his voice was less sure than his words. He paused, then continued in lower tones. "Or if I pursued another."

A silence hung between us. Then he held out his arms, and without hesitation, without thought, I was in them.

"Lettie, Lettie," he said again and again as I snuggled against him, lost in the breathless sweetness of being pressed so close, his warm breath on my cheek, the feel of his hands on my body, the rich scent of him, a scent of sage and rosemary and wine, with a faint whiff of the stables and of leather.

It was exhilarating, intoxicating, the feeling that ran through me as we embraced. It was as if he were taking me into his warmth as into the warmth of a burning fire, shutting out all the chill of the world outside. In the dim firelit room we were alone, inviolate, wrapped in our desire, fallen into a deep unfathomable place apart. A unique place where no one else could ever intrude.

He caressed me with such fervor that one of the pillows fell into the flames. Smoke rose in a black pall. I began coughing.

"The groom will come in!" I managed to say, struggling to free myself from his embrace and get up.

"Then we shall throw him out again!"

"But what if he should tell the queen . . ."

Lord Robert, laughing, had jumped up and was dousing the fire with water from a pitcher. Servants did arrive, alarmed by the smoke, and Lord Robert took my hand and led me into another room. Hearing the voices of Cecelia and several of the other bedchamber ladies, and knowing they would soon be with us, I tried to adjust my disarranged clothing and bedraggled hair, knowing it was hopeless. Lord Robert stood at the window, drawing the curtains aside and looking out into the windy night.

"Lettie! Something is burning! Don't you smell the smoke?" Cecelia said as she burst in, taking in at a glance my disarranged clothing and disordered curls. She looked quickly around the room, seeing Lord Robert's back as he stood at the window. She looked once again at me, with a look of mistrust.

"Your clothing! Your hair! Were you abed? Did the smoke awaken you?"

"A pillow seems to have fallen into the fire," Lord Robert replied coolly, without turning around. "It is of no account." And without glancing at any of us he walked with studied nonchalance from the room.

I admired his ability to disguise what must have been a tumult of feeling behind a mask of unconcern. For surely he had been as lost in fervor as I was only moments earlier. Surely he had sensed, as I did—a flush rising to my cheeks at the thought— that we had crossed together into another realm entirely, a higher realm of ardor so splendid, so rich in emotion, that we would never be the same again.

TWENTY-ONE

SOMEHOW the queen sensed a change in my relationship to Lord Robert, and she lost no time in punishing me for it.

I never discovered how she found out; perhaps there was something in his behavior that betrayed us, or possibly Cecelia did or said something to give us away. We were discreet. And in truth we met rarely as lovers, our moments of secret happiness were very few, though the exquisite thrill of our meetings, the anticipation of them, the glowing aftermath of each one, brought a sparkle to my eyes and a bloom to my cheeks that no one could fail to notice.

I told the queen that the cause of my happiness was that I had given my husband a son at last—but that excuse was soon blighted because my little Walter, never very strong, failed to gain weight and grow and before he was three months old, was in his tiny grave.

I cannot say I mourned him. I had not really known him, as

I had been summoned back to court shortly after his birth and his wetnurse and rockers had taken charge of him.

My sorrow at his death was in any case eclipsed by my loss of my dear beautiful mother, who died at about the same time. She had been ill, her weakness for wine and ale had drained her strength and left her faint and fragile. My father, putting faith in his prayers and not in the court physicians, had not told the rest of us in the family just how ill she had become and so her death came as a shock. I did not weather it well.

Meanwhile I was having difficulty coping with Walter, who when told of our son's passing was very low—and then very angry. He blamed me, overlooking the sad fact that many babies did not long survive their births and many mothers as well. I was at fault, he insisted, for having created in my womb healthy daughters but only a weak son. Walter openly and wrathfully lamented having married me, and knowing my attachment to Penelope and Dorothy, turned aside from them and ignored them—or worse, derided them, calling Dorothy "young Walter" and Penelope "my disappointment."

His anger did nothing to impede his lust. He seemed determined to have another son as quickly as possible, and to this end he energetically took his pleasure with me callously and often. When I did not become pregnant right away he had another cause to blame me. I was unyielding, he said. I thwarted his passion. I did not love him as a dutiful wife should. He grumped on endlessly about my shortcomings, actually making things worse because I became self-conscious and tense, bracing myself against his expected assaults, both physical and verbal.

I was sorry that our son had died, but unlike Walter, I did not yearn for another, or to be the mother of many children. Or, at least, to be the mother of many of Walter's children. For all my thoughts, now, were of Robert. What would it be like, I wondered, to bear his sons? His daughters? The idea was delightful, but of course I told myself it could never happen. Robert would never marry any woman but the queen. And I would be Walter's wife until the day he died—or I did.

Much to my relief, Walter was often away, sent to Ireland or elsewhere on the queen's business, or off in the country overseeing the planning and buying of supplies for her royal progresses. He took much pride in these tasks, and smug satisfaction in performing them in a way that pleased her. I, on the other hand, often found myself the object of Elizabeth's displeasure, and I felt certain it was because she knew, or very strongly suspected, that Lord Robert and I were lovers.

She slapped me when I handled her gowns clumsily. She shouted at me when I failed to keep up with her athletic dancing— she liked to dance galliards every morning, kicking and jumping vigorously in time to the quick, lively music and, when each dance ended, calling for the musicians to play another, sometimes six or seven tunes at a time. She shouted at me for having a whiny voice. She struck me and accused me of dalliance with her favorite Christopher Hatton and with Thomas Heneage, whom she had just created a gentleman of the privy chamber and who was at that time high in her praise because he pleased her by bringing green boughs and flowers into the council chamber and ordering the maids and grooms to fasten them to the walls. Elizabeth loved greenery, just as she loved the sound of birdsong and was soothed by the chirping and soft twittering of the caged birds in her bedchamber and audience chamber.

She loved the birds—yet once, when in a fit of angry vexation, she threw open one of the aviaries and let them all fly free, flapping her skirts at them and shouting.

How capricious she was! I thought it often, and told myself that rulers behaved in ways that baffled less exalted beings—or so my father was always saying. I knew from talking to others in the royal service that Queen Mary and King Henry had both been savagely capricious, and even young King Edward was prone to doing and saying crotchety, sour, unpredictable things at odd times and to doing cruel things to his falcons.

I began to worry about how extreme the queen's arbitrary, odd behavior might become, especially if she indulged, as she sometimes did, in too many cordials and became recklessly angry. If I allowed myself to dwell on this disturbing train of thought, especially at night when I was tired and could not sleep for worrying, I imagined that Elizabeth might blame me for seducing Robert and have me thrown into the Tower, or even executed.

I told myself that my fears were exaggerated, that I was in danger of becoming like Amy Dudley's elderly maid Pirto, fearing dire things that would never happen. But Pirto was dead. Mistress Clinkerte had brought me the news. She had died of old age, it appeared, and a broken heart, her body found slumped over Amy Dudley's memorial by the verger in the church in Oxford where Amy's remains had been placed.

Pirto! I was nothing like her, was I? Except that we both had secrets—and I worried that my greatest secret, my love affair with Robert, was already known to the queen.

There was one way I could find out. I could look in the book she kept by her bedside. The book whose margins served as her diary. Had she written there about Robert and me? Or how she intended to punish me?

I vowed to find out, just as soon as I could muster my courage.

TWENTY-TWO

IT took me awhile, I dithered and held back, but eventually I went into the queen's bedchamber—choosing a time when I was certain no one would disturb me there—and I cautiously opened the large old book she kept beside her bed.

There was no inkwell nearby, no writing implements on the table, and the book was closed—though the clasp, when I tried it, opened easily under my fingers. For a moment I wondered whether possibly she had stopped writing in it. But as I opened the book and began to turn the thin pages I saw the familiar spidery handwriting in the wide margins. She was still recording her thoughts, the events that made up her days.

Eagerly I read what was written there.

"Robert threatened my Little Black Hen (one of her pet names for Heneage) with a stick. So tiresome! His constant jealousy, his fits. He is getting old. I found three gray hairs in his beard. I laughed at him and told him to go dye it. And he did.

Fool! My Little Black Hen would never do so foolish a thing. Nor would my Christopher, though he would do anything for money. Christopher wants money, Robin wants power. Oh, for a man who wants neither."

Another entry read, "Quarreled with R. He is jealous again."

I saw that the queen had noted in her book what had happened recently with the Queen of Scots. How she had chosen to marry the handsome Lord Darnley, and was with child by him. ("This boy may be England's king," Elizabeth had written, though at that time Queen Mary's child had not yet been born. Elizabeth could not have known it would be a son.)

"We cannot dally together in my great bed," she had written. "We can never share Robin."

These words both repelled and puzzled me. Had Elizabeth really imagined that Robert would marry the Queen of Scots and bring her to live in England, and that he and his wife would share Elizabeth's favors? Did she mean that they would all curl up like kittens together, or cosy cousins, in the great cedarwood bed? Or could she possibly have meant the other, the sharing of bodies and lusts?

Elizabeth was a very strange woman, but that, I thought, would have been beyond strange. Beyond imagining. Only in my later years have I become more open to understanding how wide, how varied are the ways of human love. At that time I was shocked, uncomprehending.

I returned to my reading of the diary. One bit of writing, above all the others, caught and held my attention, and set my heart to pounding.

"R and L," the queen had written. "Are their hearts joined?" And then she added, "R and D. Mischief and woe."

I knew at once that by "R and L" she meant Robert and me.

And that what concerned her, more than our physical lovemaking, was whether or not there was a bond of romantic love between us. She suspected it, but she wasn't certain.

But what was I to make of "R and D"? Who was D? And what did she mean by "Mischief and woe"?

Try as I might, I could not dismiss the nagging question from my mind. Who was D? Was she Robert's lover? Was she young and beautiful? Was she unscrupulous? Would she take him from me?

Few women's names began with D. There was my daughter's name, Dorothy. And Diane, a French name that was occasionally given to the daughter of an English house. I had once heard of a nun called Deodata. None of the maids of honor or married women I knew had names beginning with D, other than Dorothy. And the Dorothys I was acquainted with at court would not appeal to Robert. They were plain, or aging, or petulant, or all three.

Perhaps D did not stand for a name at all, but a nickname. Elizabeth loved to assign nicknames to people. Often they were unflattering, especially the ones she gave to women. Dolt. Dunce. Donkey. I thought of others.

Then an image came into my mind. And a memory of a name, an odd name: Douglass. There was a young woman named Douglass who had come to court a few times. Girlish, pretty, flirtatious. Just the sort of girl who would appeal to Robert. A girl as I had once been, ten years before. She was one of the Howards, I remembered. Slender and graceful, with auburn hair a little like mine and a turned-up nose. I remembered seeing her dance and thinking, she dances almost as well as I do.

I asked Mistress Clinkerte if she knew of this girl named Douglass.

"You mean the wife of Lord Sheffield," she replied at once. "The one everyone has slept with."

"Everyone?" I said, trying to keep my voice light. "Surely not Lord Robert?"

Mistress Clinkerte guessed the seriousness of my question at once.

"Everyone," she said with finality. "From the grooms to the most exalted." And she began to whistle "King Robert's Jig" softly. "This Douglass Howard is worse even than Catherine Howard was, in her day," she added in a whisper. "Everyone knew about Catherine Howard and her lusts except the king."

"Does the queen know about Douglass's indiscretions?" I persisted.

"Of course. I don't know why she hasn't banished the girl from court. She would never be given a place in the royal household."

"No, of course not."

"Even Whaffer is astonished—and he has been at this court since the days of Lady Anne Boleyn and your own grandmother Lady Mary Boleyn, two of the most—"

"Hush, Mistress Clinkerte! I know well what is said of those two ladies."

"Mind your own reputation doesn't suffer," the tirewoman remarked. "With your husband away, and you with idle hours on your hands—"

She didn't need to finish her thought. I knew well enough what she meant.

She was right, I did have many idle hours on my hands, and I turned, joyfully, to Robert to fill them. Walter was often away, and when he was nearby we continued to find that we had less and less in common, less and less of that pleasant dailiness that binds couples who have been married for a number of years.

There was only a soured familiarity, a reluctance to converse. A withholding. And, on my part, a deepening physical loathing.

We were distant, yet we continued to share a bed, and on one of Walter's visits to Chartley I conceived another child. This time we both hoped it would be a boy, to take the place of the baby that had not survived.

For most of my pregnancy I stayed away from court, pampering myself and resting, getting fat from growing the baby—who was very large, making my belly swell much more than it had with any of my other children—and from eating quantities of ripe plums and peaches and the baked apples that the old farmer who tended the orchard roasted in the embers of his fire. Though I missed Robert, who came to visit me only rarely at Chartley, I was surprised to find myself quite happy. I sewed and embroidered caps and blankets for the new baby and made perfumes and cordials in the stillroom and fed the chickens and the songbirds that swooped in and out of the old trees that sheltered the dovecotes. When it was time to take my chamber to await the birth of my child I did so willingly, waiting patiently and prayerfully for my pains to come on.

Though the baby was very large, the birth was not an arduous or especially painful one. I had a skilled midwife and a woman from the village with swelling breasts who had been engaged to be wetnurse to my baby. During my labor she aided the midwife, who was her friend; she sat beside me and held my hand, saying comforting words and assuring me that all would be well. Before my pains began I had had my bed moved near the tall high windows of the bedchamber so that I could watch the golden leaves fall, and throughout my labor I watched them, concentrating on their floating, twirling descent onto the ground. I was in pain, yet all was stillness and order, thanks to the comforting words and the midwife's guiding instructions.

With her help I delivered my Robert at dusk on a November evening in the year 1567, just as the Evening Star was rising in the western sky. It was an omen, I thought. An omen of a grand destiny. I told myself that this boy, whose loud cries brought the entire household into the outer chamber to welcome the newest Devereux heir, might well become a great warrior, or a champion at the jousts, or a magnificent court figure like my beloved Robert, handsome and full of vigor and life.

I fell asleep dreaming of his great future to come, with his small fair head cradled in the crook of my arm, and a feeling of exceptional contentment suffusing me.

In all I was away from court for over a year, and in that time much had changed. When in response to the queen's summons I returned to my post as a lady of the bedchamber I discovered that Robert and Douglass Howard, Lady Sheffield, were not only bound together as a couple, as the queen had written in her book, but that they had become parents!

Elizabeth was annoyed and angry, Robert was in disgrace. Douglass was living far from court, on her husband's estate, with her bastard child. Her child by Robert. A child whose birth, I felt, could only lead to mischief and woe.

TWENTY-THREE

MY brother Frank surprised us all by arriving at Chartley with a Spanish pony as a gift for little Robert, beautiful pearl necklaces for Cecelia and me and a trunk full of gold.

I threw my arms around Frank's neck and kissed him on both cheeks, overjoyed as I was to see him after such a long absence. How handsome he looked, and how well-to-do, wearing a velvet doublet with embroidery of cloth of silver, silken hose and with jeweled buckles on his costly shoes.

"Frank! You should be at court! You would outshine all the queen's men, even the splendid Christopher Hatton, with his sparkling cloaks and ruffs and chains!" And you would compare with Lord Robert favorably as well, I thought, though I did not say it.

"Never mind my finery, Lettie. What about my gold!" And he had his trunk of treasure brought in—it took four strong men to carry it—and opened before our wondering eyes.

I could only gasp when the lock was opened and the lid

thrown back to reveal a horde of gleaming gold coins—Spanish ducats, Frank told us proudly.

"That's Peruvian gold," he said. "We were sailing north of Valparaiso when we came across two Spanish treasure ships. One was listing and the other we blew apart with our guns, but we saved most of the cargo. Oh, the silver! Tons and tons of it! And a great store of Spanish gold. What you see here is only part of my share."

Our father happened to be visiting Chartley when Frank arrived, and I hurriedly sent a messenger to Cecelia on the nearby Wilbraham estate, telling her that our brother was with us and urging her to come at once.

"Have you become a pirate then, son?" our father asked, taking in Frank in all his splendor and with his mound of coins. "Or are you still a good and honorable seafaring man?" Mother's death had aged father, we all noticed it. Yet aging had only sharpened his stringent moral standards. No one escaped his scrutiny—or his judgment.

In the years since I had last seen him, Frank had sent letters telling me how he had progressed from a mere apprentice, learning from an elderly captain how to sail a small ship up and down the Cornish coast to becoming a master himself, setting out for deeper waters and deeper profits.

"I serve the queen, father," Frank said. "I go where she sends my captain, Francis Drake. We have chased the Spaniards across many stretches of water."

"So that is the queen's gold you have there," father went on. "Not your own."

"It is part of my own share. Allotted to me by my captain."

"Yet those are stolen coins."

"Seized as a prize of war, father. Won on the battlefield of the seas."

Father shook his head. "Blood money," he said disapprovingly. "Give it back!"

A spark of anger ignited in Frank's dark eyes. "And to whom would you have me return it, father? To the Peruvian slaves who mined it, under the Spanish lash? Or to the murdering Spaniards, who sank three of our ships, with the good men who went down on them, including my closest friend?" He shut the lid of the chest with a resounding bang.

"No, I think not," he said. "I risked my life and fortune to win that gold, and the rest of my booty. I was nearly three years at sea with Captain Drake. Our barque almost foundered on a reef in a distant ocean, an ocean so far it has no name."

"It is known to God," was father's quiet reply. "The earth is the Lord's, and the fullness thereof. And we will speak no more of this at present." He turned his face away.

I took Frank by the arm and led him away from the others and into the nursery, where he met Penelope and Dorothy and my precious Robert, a big, smiling, energetic baby who roared in his high voice and waved his toy horse in the air. Frank swept him up in his arms and took him outside to see his pony, the girls coming with us, Penelope wrapping her arms around Frank's leg and Dorothy with one gentle hand grasping her uncle's doublet.

"And what about you, Frank?" I asked later, as we all watched the groom lead the pony around the courtyard with Rob crowing and laughing as he swayed from side to side, tied into the saddle by bands of strong cord. "When will you have girls and boys of your own?"

Frank smiled, a rueful smile. For a moment he petted the heads of the girls, then sent them off to play and led me over to a bench and sat next to me.

"I am married, Lettie," he said. "I married a wealthy woman, a widow who lives in Plymouth. She is there still, I believe. We are still husband and wife."

"But you did not marry for love."

"No. For money." He shook his head, as if in an effort to shake off the past. His eyes held sorrow.

"You remember how young I was when I left for the coast, to take up the apprenticeship I was offered. I was full of excitement. I was escaping father and his religion, all that dour talk of the devil and hell and damnation. I was getting free!"

"And I envied you that freedom. I have envied it ever since."

"But I had no money. Father told me that if I left, I would have to make my own way in the world. He said he would not give me anything, even if I was in desperate need. I knew that. I welcomed it. I wanted to prove myself, to prove to father that I could find my way without him and his dark view of life.

"For several years I worked hard and did well. I gained a knowledge of winds and tides, of the treacherous shores of the western coast with their rocks and shallows. I found myself at home among the men, real men, men who cursed and quarreled and got into drunken brawls in dark alleys behind low taverns. Oh, I had my share of those fights! I have a few scars I could show you."

I could not help smiling. Frank was so proud of his battle scars.

"I would be willing to bet that our father was never in a fight in his life."

We both laughed. "Not a scrap in a back alley," I added, "though I know he is locked in combat in the queen's privy chamber, with the other councilors, nearly every day. A more subtle sort of combat, but equally vicious. But please, go on with what you were saying."

"Well, after a while my master died, and left me his ship. He had no son of his own to leave her to. I was proud. I continued to do what he had done, taking the little vessel from one coastal port to another, and often to places along the coast where there was no port, in the dead of night, delivering wine or oil or soap or salt from France and taking on cloth or grain or sometimes lead from the local producers. Our father would turn pale if he knew how much trade goes on behind the backs of the royal officials!"

"He knows. All the court knows. Half the fine ruffs from France and Holland worn at our court come ashore in the dark and are never taxed. And much of the wine and spirits too."

"Well, I prospered—but I wanted to do more. See more. I kept hearing stories about Captain Francis Drake and his venturing. How he explored not only the coastal waters but the seas, how the queen favored his adventures and commissioned him to take Spanish prizes with the right to keep a share of the treasure he recovered. Sailing with him, becoming a part of his ventures, required money. Quite a bit of money. The widow told me that if I married her, her money would be mine. So I did. Heaven help me, Lettie, I did. Though I have regretted the marriage ever since."

"But not the venturing."

He smiled. "No, never that. Nor the pirating I did for England. But I paid too high a price for it."

"What price?"

He knit his brow. It was some time before he spoke again.

"There was a girl," he began softly. "A lovely trusting young girl, with soft brown eyes and gentle hands. Marianna. She was just sixteen. She lived with her family in the stinking hulk of an abandoned ship. Her poor father made what little he could as a renegade preacher, with a small congregation of sailors. He was filled with the spirit. I admired him. But there was never enough to feed all eight of them in the family.

"I loved her, I swear I did! But I saw that if I married her, I would have to support them all. They barely had enough to eat. Marianna took in the sailors' laundry, and her brothers gleaned in the fields after the harvest was over, scavenging like the rooks and the mice.

"Oh, Lettie, I saw that if I married her, I would never get to see the world. And every time I looked out to sea I wanted to break away from the coast, from my little vessel. From the life of being tied to others.

"So God help me, I took the widow and her money, and sold my small ship and signed on with Drake. I have been paid back a thousandfold—but I always regretted losing Marianna. When I went back to try to find her, the hulk was gone. Broken up in a storm, the entire family tossed to the winds. I was told that she died.

"If I ever have another ship, I will name it the *Marianna*. I will dedicate my entire life to her memory."

He put his head in his hands.

I put my arm around his broad shoulder, but I could tell that there was no comfort I could offer that would redeem what he had lost. Over the following days I was to hear much more about his remarkable travels, and his stories of the New World. But behind his words there was always a veil of sorrow. He had gone searching for adventure, and found much that was strange and wondrous. He had found gold. But he had lost something more precious, the source of his worldly happiness. He had lost his love.

TWENTY-FOUR

AS soon as I heard the clopping of the carriage horses at the entrance to the castle I became tense. It was Cecelia's carriage, coming from the Wilbraham estate nearby, and although I loved my sister I did not relish having to cope with her moods. In those days she was very moody indeed.

Her marriage, everyone acknowledged, was no more than two names joined on legal documents. Roger Wilbraham lived a separate life from Cecelia, and had since their wedding day. With the many official posts and perquisites that had come to him as a result of his marriage, especially his lucrative position as Master of the Queen's Ships (he was no longer Deputy, but full Master), he had prospered, and the one thing Cecelia could not complain about was the comfort in which she lived—alone. One of her husband's stewards came every month to bring her a bag of coins to keep under her bed to further her own whims and pleasures, and saw to it that her dressmakers and wigmakers, her physicians and apothecaries, and all the servants of her household were paid—and paid generously—from Wilbraham's own funds, as were all the costs of keeping up the estate.

Cecelia wanted for nothing, except contentment, and an overflowing heart.

The carriage came to a stop and I went out into the courtyard to welcome my sister. As she stepped down the vehicle listed heavily to one side, her weight pulling it sharply downward. She had become fat; "fat as butter," Walter said unkindly whenever he spoke of her. Her small eyes were all but lost in her round, fleshy face and her portly, corpulent body, encased that day in a tightly fitting, elegant gown of embroidered silk, was that of a middle-aged woman though she had not yet reached the age of thirty.

She wore, as usual, an elaborate wig, the hair twisted and tortured into an elaborate pattern. Ever since the day years earlier when the queen had ordered Cecelia's hair shorn she had worn a wig, often a bright red one like those the queen increasingly favored, and she had a collection of wigs in many styles and shades. (All of them made, as I now and then reminded her, from the hair of other unfortunate, shorn girls.) Her own mousy brown curls, which had always been sparse, had never grown back properly; without a wig she looked strange, one side of her head sprinkled with spiky hairs like a half-plucked chicken, the other side sprouting a mousy mane, ringletted but bare in patches.

Her teeth were still good—her best feature—and as far as I could tell, she had retained them all. (She bragged that she had.) But her complexion, which even in her youth had never been a rosy, healthy pink, was a sorry mess, sand-colored and blemished as it was with scars of the pox, scars that she tried without success to hide under layers of stark, unflattering ceruse.

Poor Cecelia! I knew that every time she looked at me she cringed, for the contrast between us, always strong, had become far more marked with the years. I retained my youthful loveliness (everyone said so), while her looks were growing less and less pleasing.

"So!" she announced when I drew her into the salon and she glimpsed Frank, "here is the prodigal pirate, returned at last!"

"A seaman, Cecelia, not a pirate. And a highly successful one, though I could wish he would dress with greater soberness," was my father's remark. He said nothing about Cecelia's own finery. Perhaps, I thought, he regards it as her reward for enduring a disappointing marriage.

But Cecelia only snorted.

"No man who serves Captain Drake can be anything but a pirate. Our queen favors it! But what is this I hear about a quarrel between you and my dear husband?"

There was not, I could not help but notice, any sign of an affectionate or even a civil greeting between Cecelia and Frank, though they had not seen one another for many years. They had never been fond of each other, as children they fought—I was the peacemaker between them. Were they about to fight again?

"Your dear husband, Cecilia, has done the unforgivable: he has come between me and my ship."

Frank's response was greeted by another, louder snort.

"And how has he done that?"

"By refusing me royal permission to leave Plymouth in my new ship, the *Gull*, to join Drake on his next voyage."

"What reason has he given?" It was our father speaking once again, frowning, his brows curved downward in disapproval.

"None. But I know the reason. Drake only wants one more ship to join his enterprise. And Wilbraham wants that valuable ship to be his son's. So he is denying me the official papers I need to take the *Gull* out of Plymouth harbor."

"Which son?" father asked. "He has several, doesn't he?"

"Four. But the one he favors is Sebastian. His son by his Spanish mistress."

Hearing her husband's hated Spanish mistress mentioned made Cecelia ball her plump fists and stamp her foot.

"I want that woman sent back to Seville! At once! Father, can't you help me? Can't you have her removed?"

"No, dear, but I may be able to do better than that—for both you and Frank. My spies tell me that Roger Wilbraham would like nothing better than to be free of his attachment to our family—without having to give up any of his offices, of course."

At father's words both Cecelia and Frank brightened.

"I had no idea," Frank began. "You never wrote me of this."

"I didn't realize it until recently. I am told that Roger went to the queen and requested that he be appointed master armorer for the port of Sluys, with an income of two hundred pounds a year and the right to purvey arms for the English ships berthed there."

Sluys in Zeeland was in the Spanish lowlands, the much disputed territories where the Dutch were in rebellion against the harsh rule of the Spanish King Philip and where, it was said, Protestants were being persecuted and killed by the hundreds. I remembered with horror the killings I had seen as a child, the burning of my tutor Jocelyn, the pitiless murders of the Anabaptists in Frankfurt. Sluys sounded like a terrible place. Yet Roger Wilbraham wanted to go there, no doubt because there was money to be made if he did.

"But even if he leaves England, he will still be married to Cecelia, and she will certainly not want to go with him," I said, looking over at her.

"I think father knows that!" she snapped back at me. "You have a solution in mind, don't you father," she went on, in the tone she used for no one but our father. "You will work things out. I know you will."

141

"If I can, child. I may be able to persuade the queen to grant your husband's request, though she will certainly never agree to pay him the two hundred pounds a year he is asking for, not when he already receives so much from the royal treasury for his other offices. And she cannot free you, Cecelia, from your marriage. For that, we will need the aid of the church."

"But the queen is head of the church," Frank put in. "Surely she can decree whatever she likes where faith is concerned."

Father glowered at him. "Do you imagine that the church is no more than a plaything of powerful men—and women? No! It is God's sacred institution. Only He decides what is and is not right, according to His dispensations!"

We all knew better than to confront father on matters of religion, and so went in to dinner, with nothing further said—for that day. But the possibility of removing the wrathful Roger Wilbraham from our lives acted like a tonic to our spirits, and we dined that afternoon, as a family, with more lightness of heart and laughter and good will than we had in many a year. And I thought, perhaps our fortunes are turning for the better, and I too will find my way out of my private, inner difficulties and struggles. My knowledge that the man I love is with another woman, and she has had his child, and the capricious queen, who knows all and governs all, holds everyone's future in her slender white hands.

TWENTY-FIVE

TRY though he did, father could not succeed in persuading the queen to grant Roger Wilbraham the office of master armorer for the port of Sluys, and when the annual payment of two hundred pounds was mentioned she threw a tankard against the tapestry-covered wall and called out, "God's teeth, Deacon (she had begun calling father by the nickname Deacon), who do you take me for, Croesus?"

Father bore with her, and ducked when she flung the tankard, but afterward, when he was no longer in her august presence, he very nearly swore himself.

"That woman should have married King Philip when she had the chance," I heard him say more than once. "What she needs is a husband to take her in hand and keep her in line!"

"But father," I reminded him, "if she had married King Philip, England would be a Catholic realm now. Surely you wouldn't want that."

But he only raised his eyes to heaven and muttered something indistinct. I knew she tried his patience immeasurably. And the older she got, the more insufferable she became.

It was growing clear to me that father was not going to be able to bargain with my brother-in-law Roger Wilbraham through obtaining the queen's favor. So I determined to do what I could to help. Or rather, to persuade Robert to help my sister and brother.

Robert was the most powerful man at court, even my father admitted that. Though the queen was angry with him at times, and was forever extending and then withdrawing her gifts and indulgence, there was never any doubt that the tall, commanding Earl of Leicester (as he had by then become) was the first among all the men at the royal court, and the most likely to achieve any goal he sought.

When I went to see Robert to ask for his help I was uncomfortable at first. Things had changed between us, because of his love—or was it mere lust?—for Douglass and because I had not seen him more than a few times over the previous year and more. Beyond that, I felt awkward because I was not in the habit of asking him for anything. I am independent, I rely on myself. I never looked on Robert as anything other than my beloved, I never tried to take advantage of him in any way.

I sought him out in the crowded Presence Chamber, where I knew he would most likely be found. I went up to him, feeling unsure of myself yet emboldened by my brother's and sister's needs.

"Lord Robert," I began, my heart beating fast, "I wonder if I might have a word with you."

His smile was both dazzling and disarming—yet I thought I detected a hint of my own uncertainty in him. When he led me into a window embrasure where we could talk without being overheard by the others in the room his first words to me were tentative—yet his dear voice, the voice I loved so well, was full of warmth. My doubts began to dissolve at the sound.

"Dear Lettie," was all he said. And then again, "Dear Lettie."

"Lord Robert," I went on, stumbling a little over my words, "my sister Cecelia—that is, Cecelia's husband—"

"Roger Wilbraham."

"Yes. My family hopes—" I sighed, then tried again. "My family hopes that a way may be found—"

"Your father has already told me of Wilbraham's demand—I'm afraid it is a demand, he thinks himself invaluable—to be made master armorer for Sluys. At an outrageous cost, I might add."

"Yes. And Cecelia will be glad to see the last of him. She hopes for an annulment of her marriage."

The lines on Robert's broad forehead deepened.

"The queen cares nothing for Roger Wilbraham, but she is not inclined to gratify your sister. She has an animus against her."

"Yes. She always has."

"The best way to deal with Elizabeth is to distract her. Set off fireworks, point to them, get her to pay attention to them, and while she is distracted, put a paper in front of her to sign. A very crude method of governance, to be sure, but one those of us on her council employ frequently."

"And what are the fireworks in this case?" I asked, enjoying the twinkle in Robert's eyes.

"I don't know. But for you, Lettie, I will find some."

And then he was gone, striding off into the throng of officials, clerks, men of law and petitioners that crowded the queen's chamber.

It was several days before I received a brief letter from Robert, asking me to meet him in a place I had never been before:

Southwark, the distant part of London across the broad, stinking river from the royal court. He said he would send an escort to take me there.

Why Southwark, I wondered. The place had a very bad reputation, as a gathering point of thieves and rogues and actors. Without telling anyone where I was going, I put on my cloak and covered my slippers with boots and waited for Robert's servant to arrive.

It took us forever just to cross London Bridge, the crowds were so thick, our carriage hemmed in on all sides by pushing, shouting peddlers and water-sellers and herdsmen trying to drive their sheep to Smithfield Market. Carts before and behind us broke down and had to be mended, packhorses lost their loads and laughing children climbed up to look in at our windows and shout at us demanding coins.

Robert had sent two of his servants to accompany me, young men in elegant liveries unaccustomed to the noise, stench and irritations of attempting to cross the bridge. One became ill, the other looked bilious but managed to retain his dinner. I did my best to turn my attention to the river traffic, the gilded barges of the nobles and officials, the small tradesmen's craft, bobbing up and down in the wind-whipped water, the oared wherries taking passengers from one side of the river to the other, the oarsmen singing or whistling as they rowed.

The water was turbulent under the bridge. I wondered how many drownings there had been, how many fugitives that had tried to swim their way to safety escaping from the queen's guardsmen, only to find themselves trapped in a swirling whirl-pool and dragged down to oblivion. There was death under the bridge, that was certain; equally certain was the sight of death on the bridge itself, in the form of grinning skulls—the beheaded remains of criminals hung there to rot as a warning to

others not to break the queen's peace or threaten her rule and
authority.

As we approached the far shore the stink of the river blended
with the putrid aromas of running sewers and drains and piles
of offal from the butchers' shops. I caught the faint scent of
flowers mixed with the rank, slightly sweet odor of decaying
flesh. Dead animals, the dead and dying poor lying along the
roadside, rotting fish and the pervasive stench of filth and decay
hung over Smithfield. It was no wonder they brought the bears
to fight the mastiffs here, I thought. Such bestial pastimes
belong in a place like this, where life is lived in squalor and
only the coarsest and most vile and cruel entertainments ought
to go on.

Much to my horror, my escorts led me to the place I found
most repellant: the bearyard.

"Lord Robert will meet us here," I was told. "He should be
along any time now."

But as it happened, it was not Lord Robert who joined us,
but my distasteful brother-in-law Roger Wilbraham.

Over the years the coarse, red-faced Wilbraham had grown
more stout and more choleric, disinclined to show even the
simplest courtesies to those around him. He sat heavily on a bench
overlooking the bearyard, scarcely glancing at me though he was
quite nearby, and said to no one in particular, "Lord Robert
comes anon." He then proceeded to take from his doublet pocket
a pouch of sweets, which he ate one after another, his eyes intent
on the dirt floor of the fighting arena, where servants were raking
the earth in preparation for the match to come.

It was as dismal a moment as I had known in some time, and
I had to fight a strong inclination to get up and leave. But it was
Robert who had sent me there, and I trusted him. I believed
that he had Cecelia's and Frank's interests at heart, and wanted

to help us. So I stayed, though I did not watch when the great lumbering brown bear was led out into the arena and I could hear the yelping and barking of the mastiffs becoming louder and more intense by the minute, though they were as yet out of sight of the growing crowd.

My two escorts in their fine liveries sat on either side of me, shielding me from the surrounding folk, a noisy array of Londoners and foreigners, mostly men though with a sprinkling of women of the streets—no women of quality that I could see—and peddlers who wandered among the rackety spectators singing and shouting their patter and waving knacks and foodstuffs, cheap fans and purses in hopes that someone would buy.

The great bear was chained to his iron post, the mastiffs led in. They were muzzled as yet, but still their keepers maintained as wide a distance as they could from the dogs' mouths with their treacherous teeth. Though I was far removed from the animals, high above them and separated from them by a sturdy tall fence, I could not prevent myself from drawing back. Roger Wilbraham, I noticed, did not draw back but rather sat forward as the dogs were led in, as if wanting to be more a part of the bloody contest to come.

At that moment there was a stir in the crowd and I saw Lord Robert arrive, with a dozen guardsmen, and accompanied by a man I did not recognize. A youngish man with a broad brow and a bright, open face and a curling reddish beard.

There were hisses from the crowd. Robert was feared, everyone knew who he was and knew that he was the queen's right-hand man, and therefore very powerful. But he was disliked. The hissing ceased when he looked around him, as if to single out his detractors. As soon as he came toward me and ceased to scan the crowd the hissing began again.

He came up to me and greeted me formally, though cheerily,

as he always did, and the guardsmen hurried to clear a bench for him and his companion to sit on. Roger rose and joined us.

"Milord Earl," Roger began, his dark eyebrows raised in surprise. "Had you not sent me a message asking me to greet you here, I would not have expected to see you in Southwark. And with such an esteemed companion."

"Master Drake lives here. Quite nearby in fact," was Robert's response. So this was the mariner and adventurer the queen favored so highly, Francis Drake.

"Near the bearyard?" I wanted to know. I was surprised to discover that such a valued man would make his home in such a disreputable place.

"Master Drake," Robert interrupted, before the captain could respond, "I have the honor to present to you a lady who is very curious by nature." He smiled indulgently, affectionately.

"Frank Knollys's sister, are you not?" Drake said to me, his broad Devon accent startling, his voice a bit hard to hear amid the noise of those around us. "Your brother is a fine seaman."

"I hope you find him so," I said, nearly shouting. "I know he values sailing with you greatly. In fact I have seen him recently, and he speaks of joining you again—if that is possible."

"Of course it will be possible," Robert put in. "My friend Francis knows that I, and my purse, stand ready to make it possible, at all times and in all ways. And in return he will reward me—and Frank too, of course—with a share of the gold and silver brought back in the ships' holds."

The contest between the burly chained bear and the dogs had begun. With one swat of his mighty paw the bear sent one of the dogs flying. He lay bleeding and though he struggled to get up, the struggle was futile. But the bear too began to bleed as the dogs tore viciously at his fur. He let out a mighty roaring growl, making the crowd cheer and clap energetically.

Roger too was roaring.

"My son Sebastian sails with Captain Drake on his next voyage. There is room for no other."

Robert took a ruby ring from his finger and held it out toward Drake.

"I think this will buy a few loaves of manchet, and a few yards of sail for the voyage."

Drake smiled and, taking the ring, slipped it onto his finger.

"Thank you milord."

Fumbling, Roger took a ring from his own finger and held it out to Drake, who looked at it with a slight smile, but did not take it.

"The earl's ring will buy many more provisions," was Drake's only remark.

"I have more rings. More treasure," Wilbraham insisted. "If you will allow me to present them, perhaps tomorrow—"

But Drake was holding up his hand to silence my pleading brother-in-law.

"It would take more treasure than you possess to buy a place in my expedition for your son—which is what I believe you are seeking."

The bear, shaking his head in fury and pain, drool and blood spattered all around him, and on the dogs' quivering flanks, had dispatched two more of his tormentors, but was tiring. Shouts rose from the crowd, fights were breaking out among the spectators.

"But do not despair," Robert put in. "There is something else you have to offer, besides gold."

"And what is that?"

"Your agreement to an annulment of your marriage."

His eyes widened. "But is that possible?"

"The queen can make it possible." Robert drew from his doublet a folded document with a pendant seal. "Once the queen signs this, you and Cecelia will no longer be husband and wife."

"Will she sign it?"

"Let us ask her. Come to Greenwich tomorrow, and with luck, all will be resolved—to everyone's satisfaction."

A roar went up from the crowd as the great bear tottered on its short legs, faltered, paws waving vainly in the air, and collapsed. The remaining dogs barked madly, circling the bleeding carcass and baring their teeth.

Nodding in agreement, Roger Wilbraham got to his feet, paid his curt respects to the others, and lumbered off through the crowd, shaking his head and muttering "He didn't put up much of a fight. Hardly worth the money."

And as we watched, the wounded and dying dogs were dragged off the killing floor, a new bear led in, and the dead bear, roped and chained, was dragged off while servants spread fresh earth and prepared the arena for fresh combat.

TWENTY-SIX

THE queen's tiring chamber was abuzz with the news that Douglass Sheffield's husband was dead.

"Poisoned," Cecelia said to the other ladies of the bedchamber gathered there, her voice toneless and hard with certainty. "And by your lover," she added, addressing me.

I had never admitted to Cecelia that Robert and I were lovers, but she was shrewd, she guessed. I did not deny it, to her or anyone else—but I did not admit it either.

"There is too much gossip at this court," I remarked. "Most of it is inaccurate."

"Your Lord Robert Dudley murdered his wife so that he could marry the queen. She won't have him—so now he has poisoned Douglass Sheffield's husband so that he can marry her! Everyone knows Douglass has had his child, though the poor little mite barely lived a few days—or was it a few hours?"

Douglass's baby by Robert, the one I thought of as representing "mischief and woe," had indeed been shortlived. No one knew just how long she had lived, as both Douglass and the newborn had been spirited away into the country and not until weeks later did word reach us that indeed the little girl had died.

Lord Sheffield had been furious with his wife, so the story went, whose many adulteries had been crowned by this illegitimate birth. He had been consulting lawyers and intended to divorce her, bringing scandal on both Douglass and the presumed father of the child, Robert—until gripped by a sudden terrible pain which soon led to his death.

"They say it was a gruesome end," put in the old equerry Whaffer. "I've heard he was in agony. He turned red and couldn't breathe. His insides felt as though a white-hot poker had been shoved up his—"

"That's enough!" one of the other bedchamber women snapped. "We don't want to hear any more. We will pray for the poor man's soul."

"And for the soul of him that did the deed," Whaffer continued. "Him that made poor Lord Sheffield suffer all the torments of hell and choke and fall over senseless."

"It's that poisoner of Lord Robert's," Mistress Clinkerte said. "That Dr. Julio. He must have put something into Lord Sheffield's food."

Robert's Italian physician was blamed for many a suspicious death at court, though no one had ever been able to prove that he was a sinister character. Italians always came under suspicion, to be sure; to be Italian was to be presumed a rogue, all too familiar with skullduggery and especially poisoning. But in truth it was Dr. Julio's association with Lord Robert that put him in a dark light. For it was said the queen had set her spies on him, as she had on Robert himself. And the death of Lord Sheffield was seen as confirmation that the royal spying was justified.

Try as he might, Robert had never been able to redeem his reputation after his wife Amy's death. Amy's brother John Appleyard had only made things worse for Robert by spreading the story that Robert had indeed been responsible for Amy's murder and then had paid Appleyard to conceal the truth.

I did not believe any of the rumors, and said so.

"Don't add to all the untrustworthy stories we are hearing spread about the queen's trusted councilor, Cecelia," I said. "The Earl of Leicester is very highly placed and greatly respected and men with such influence always attract envy and malicious gossip. If the queen were here she would shout at us all for telling lies.

"And what is more," I went on, "you are the last one who should be adding to all the gossip. You owe Lord Robert thanks for freeing you from your husband—and resolving Frank's difficulties with Wilbraham as well. He did it all, you know."

On the day following the bloody fighting in the bearyard, Robert had met with Roger Wilbraham in Greenwich as agreed, and after more bargaining and bribery, the annulment of Cecelia's marriage was made legal. Frank was allowed to leave Plymouth in the *Gull*, and a compromise was arrived at so that even Wilbraham's son Sebastian was accommodated. It was ungrateful of Cecelia not to feel glad for all that Robert had done, and I told her so.

I was stout and forthright in my defense of Robert, but in fact the news of Lord Sheffield's sudden death unnerved me. Was I wrong about Robert? Was it possible that he was indeed a murderer, using others, such as John Appleyard and Dr. Julio, to carry out his dark intent?

I thought I knew Robert as well as anyone could know him. When we were together—all too rarely at that time—and our bodies were pressed together, with such passionate abandon that I almost couldn't breathe, it was as if we were but one body. One heart. I could not possibly be closer to anyone than I was to Robert.

I felt as though we had bared to one another the deepest part of our selves. And yet—could that be only an illusion, created by the intensity of our lovemaking? For I knew that Robert was a man who could never be tamed, whose drives and desires would break any bonds put around him. There were wild places within him that he would never share. And I had learned, during my years at the royal court—that treacherous labyrinth of illusions and deceptions—that despite ourselves, we humans are beset by falsities. We deceive ourselves. All too often we are trapped in tangled webs of our own devising, webs of lies and delusions.

Robert loved me, and I him. And yet he had sought the love of other women, not only Douglass Sheffield but her sister, so it was rumored. And no doubt there were others. I did not delude myself into thinking him faithful to me—nor had he ever promised to be. He gave me as much of his love as he was capable of giving, and I knew that I had to be satisfied with that.

Could it not also be that he withheld from me the terrible truth that he was capable of murder?

"I am so frail, Lettie! So very frail!" Robert said as he collapsed after a banquet given by the queen in honor of the French ambassador.

He sank down onto a cushion-covered bench and, gritting his teeth, unfastened the jeweled buckle of his shoe on his left foot. He moaned and grimaced as he eased the shoe off his swollen foot, and with a practiced movement, swung his leg onto my lap.

"Rub me, Lettie," he said. "I hurt."

I barely touched his poor sore foot.

"Ow!" He yowled like a stray cat and pulled his foot back.

"It must have been all that dancing you did," I said, waiting for him to put his foot back down on my lap. "I have to say, you were not as spry as usual tonight."

"I hate dancing! I hate this court! I hate London! Damn it, Lettie! I want to sail away, with Frank, and never see this place or anyone in it again."

"Even me?"

"You can come and sail away with me."

Very gently, so as not to make him yowl again, I began to rub his foot, beginning with the heel and slowly working my way up toward what I knew was the sorest part, his red and bulging big toe. As I neared it I heard his sharp intake of breath and knew I could go no farther.

"The apothecary says that receiving bad news makes the swelling worse."

"Is that the same apothecary who gave me the foul tonic made with worm piss?"

"The very same. The queen swears by him. He helped to cure her pox."

"Botheration! She cured herself of the pox. She was too cross and stiff-necked to die. I never knew a meaner or more contrary woman in my life. Sour, hateful old thing!"

I knew that Robert, being so far out of temper, was not saying what he truly felt about the queen, to whom he was both loyal and devoted. He was in terrible pain, and the pain was making him livid and spiteful. He was paying a price for having entertained the banqueters; after the dining ended he and Ambrose had been the chief performers in a disguising, playing the principal roles in a pageant called "Gold of the Aztecs" in which they were costumed as brigands who stole a vast treasure and, after much dancing, threw off their costumes and were revealed as princes.

"She is not old," I remarked. I did not contradict his other words. "Not quite yet."

Robert was clearly exhausted as well as being in pain, but as he laid his head back and closed his red-rimmed eyes I realized that his fatigue came from more than carrying out elaborate, athletic dance steps. He looked anxious, as though he had not slept. His hair and beard needed trimming, and I was inclined to agree with the apothecary that the renewed swelling in his foot was probably caused by worry over bad news.

I massaged the distended foot, as gently and lovingly as I could, and I could tell from Robert's groans that I was giving him some relief. Presently he opened his eyes.

"Thank you, dearest Lettie."

We exchanged a loving smile, and the lines in his forehead grew a little less deep.

"I wish you could escape from court for awhile," I mused. "I wish you could go somewhere where you wouldn't have to listen to unkind gossip."

"You don't believe it, do you Lettie? What they are saying about Dr. Julio, and the death of Lord Sheffield?"

"I know nothing of how Lord Sheffield died, except that it was a painful death."

"I barely knew the man," Robert said, sitting up and starting to put on his shoe. I took over the task from him, carefully sliding on his silken stocking, then the shoe, finally buckling the jeweled buckle. I tried to ignore the grimace of pain that returned to his face. There was no help for it, I knew. He could not very well go barefoot through the rooms and corridors of the palace. And even if he did, he would limp.

I looked up at him.

"Will you marry Douglass?" I asked.

"She is not the one I would choose, if I could choose any woman." His voice was soft, loving. The look in his warm blue eyes told me that I was his favorite. Yet there was another . . .

"I always thought you would choose the queen."

"Ah! The queen! The man who marries her will have his hands full, that I know only too well. The French are after her, you know. They want her to marry the young Prince Francis, the one who is young enough to be her son! The ambassador has spoken to those of us on the royal council several times about this."

I hesitated, then asked, "Is she at all willing?"

Robert swore. "She likes him. They write to each other. In Latin, she says. Sometimes she adds a little Greek. She enjoys that. She has an odd streak, she likes learning. Comes from her father I suppose. She enjoys speaking and writing the old tongues, and she likes to write poetry too."

I was well aware that Robert had no such scholarly inclinations. He had spent his best learning years in the Tower, as he liked to say. Not much Latin or Greek taught there.

"Ah, Lettie," he sighed. "I wonder, what is the Latin word for big red toe that hurts? I must go and find the queen and ask her."

TWENTY-SEVEN

QUEEN Elizabeth's fortieth birthday was due to occur in September of 1573 and although lavish birthday celebrations were planned, as they were every year, no one dared to mention her age.

Women of forty were old—or rapidly becoming old. Or, if they were youthful, they were at least too old to have children, as a rule. So it was tacitly understood that once our queen reached the dreaded age of forty, she could not expect to have a child of her own, should she decide to marry.

Mistress Clinkerte, so far as I knew, continued to keep her silence about the queen's true physical state, the important secret that she had confided to me years earlier and that I had never told anyone, not even Robert. That the queen was not as other women, and could never have children.

Advancing years, childlessness, a querulous temper—and now about to reach the age of forty: I did not envy my mistress the queen.

But I had my own problems—and very serious ones, as they seemed to me then. Not family problems, thankfully. My girls were healthy and growing tall and lovely, Penelope full of fire (the Boleyn fire, some said) and Dorothy affectionate and more prudent in her manner of life. My little Rob was already sitting his pony well, flicking his small whip across the pony's flank as the groom led it around the paddock.

My children flourished—but my marriage withered. Walter was away in Ireland most of the time—indeed I had heard that he had a mistress there. Thanks to his years of service to the queen— and to Robert's influence—Walter had been raised to the honor of Earl of Essex, with the lands and wealth that accompanied that title. I was now Countess of Essex, though I had never sought high standing and was not in the least eager to be a great lady of the court. My father, suspicious of all worldly honors, was full of disapproval of this rise in my status, and my sister, as always, was consumed with envy. At least Cecelia was free of her unloving husband Roger Wilbraham, thanks to Robert's clever machinations. And my brother Frank was off at sea with Captain Drake—though still at odds with Wilbraham and his bastard son, vying for preeminence in Captain Drake's favor. I prayed that their rivalry would not lead to disaster.

It was not long before the queen's birthday celebrations that I noticed Douglass Sheffield (who at Robert's insistence had been appointed one of the bedchamber women) wearing Robert's ring.

I recognized the ring as soon as I saw it, a large, showy gold ring with an immense glowing sapphire, surrounded by diamonds. I had often seen it on his own hand. He told me it was a family heirloom that had belonged to his late grandfather.

That Douglass was wearing it could mean only one thing. The thing I had been dreading: that she and my Robert had become husband and wife.

"Has he married you then?" I demanded to know, surprising Douglass as she went about her tasks in the tiring chamber. The others in the room quickly withdrew, sensing a quarrel to come.

Douglass blushed, then hung her head.

"It has taken him two years, but yes, Robert Dudley and I have finally wed."

"What do you mean, it has taken him two years?"

"Two years ago he promised to marry me. And now he has."

I looked down at Douglass's waist, and saw the beginnings of a definite bulge.

"Is it because of the child you are carrying?"

She nodded.

"Surely you know that I am the one he loves."

I thought she would cringe, or run from the room. But she did neither.

"I believe he loves us both," she said. "But you are married, and I am a widow."

When I confronted Robert he denied that Douglass was his wife.

"She thinks that because we spoke a few words to one another we are married. But it isn't true. There was no priest present to hear the words we said. No witnesses—at least none who can be believed, since they were all Douglass's relations. And in any case, who can say what constitutes a marriage any more? You saw how easily the queen could dissolve the marriage between your sister and Roger Wilbraham, just by signing her name to a paper!"

"But if you are not Douglass's husband, what did happen between you? Why did you repeat whatever words you did say to one another?"

He shook his head. "Lettie! You know what that woman is like! She would not leave me alone! She gave me no peace!"

In fact I thought Douglass was anything but a harridan—more meek than irksome. But I did not argue with Robert. After all I was not present at whatever ceremony went on—assuming there was a ceremony of sorts.

"Did you do it because of her baby?"

Robert was silent for a time. At last he said, "I want a son, Lettie, even if he is baseborn."

"Her other baby died."

"This one, I hope, will live."

Thus it was that the boy Robert sired and Douglass bore, the boy given Robert's name, came into the world under a cloud of uncertainty. Douglass continued to assert that she was Robert's wife, while he continued to swear that he was not her husband.

As for me, I was certain of only one thing: that Robert loved me and I loved him, and that nothing—not words spoken before unreliable witnesses, not the queen's wrath, not my family's disfavor, not even Douglass's protestations or her bastard son, could separate our hearts.

TWENTY-EIGHT

IT was the hottest day of a very hot July, and we were on our way to Robert's immense castle of Kenilworth, our carriage bumping and jolting its way along a narrow lane so rutted it might have been a stinking alley in Southwark.

"God's teeth!" the queen cried out as we bounced our way over a stone, making the carriage sway precariously and causing her to swear and grab at her thigh through countless layers of silk and lace. "I'm all black and blue! Can't the man make a straight road! He boasts about all the money he's spent on repairing this damnable castle I gave him, why can't he fill in the holes we have to sink in to get there!"

Robert had indeed been boasting, to anyone who would listen, of all the money he had been spending on renovations to Kenilworth, by far the most magnificent of his many residences. In the few years since the queen's last visit, he said, he had put all the income from his lucrative import licenses into building an outer quadrangle for the servants' privies and new stables large enough to shelter at least five hundred horses. The profits he had from his licenses on the importation of velvets and oils, currants and sweet wines alone brought in just enough to pay the laborers, he told me; his income from the new tax on barrel staves helped to buy the quarried golden stone and heavy timbers for the gatehouse and the long yew walk. To redo the fireplaces in the old castle's hundreds of rooms large and small required new loans from the moneylenders, however, and a large loan from Francis Drake, who had brought back six tons of cloves worth an immense fortune from his recent voyage to the Spice Islands and who agreed to be Robert's bank.

All this was on my mind as we jounced over the rough road, the queen swearing and keeping up her angry tirade with every new shock and shudder.

No matter how his wealth increased, it seemed, Robert sank deeper and deeper into debt. He was not like Walter, who watched his money carefully and was reluctant to part with any of it, for any reason. Walter the listmaker, who kept careful records of his finances and put the records away in a special large coffer with a strong lock. While Robert was spending more and more on his great houses, Walter was profiting from his Irish ventures. Every time the queen sent him to put down rebel Irish lords he not only defeated them but seized their properties, and made them his own. Some of the lands and houses he sold, always profitably. Some he kept, the deeds rolled into tight bundles and stored in his coffer, under lock and key.

Robert had never been more in debt than he was in this summer of 1575, when he had borrowed the vast sum of sixty thousand pounds to provide weeks of feasting and entertainment for the queen and her large traveling party. The renovations to Kenilworth were not entirely complete; the chimneys were still being restored and new milking sheds and brewhouses built. But the many apartments for visitors, and especially those set apart for the queen, were complete, he told me, and no complaints were expected.

The day wore on, our hot and dusty journey continued. The queen often chose me as one of the attendants to ride in her carriage, as I am patient by nature and can be soothing when I try. But by the time we approached the great house, just at dusk, my patience was nearly exhausted and I longed for a good meal and a quiet room with clean rushes on the floor and newly washed linen on the bed.

Instead we were met with a deafening roar of cannon.

The queen, who was always terribly frightened by loud noises, put her hands over her ears and squeezed her eyes shut, failing to see the elaborate red and blue and white fireworks that burst over our heads in an explosion of color and light as the great house and vast adjoining lake came into view.

Trumpets blew, drums beat and as our carriage crossed the bridge that led from the road to the castle's wide stone entranceway giant figures loomed out of the gathering dusk, costumed as ancient mythic characters, bearing gifts to present to Her Majesty.

It was as if we were in the center of a vast pageant, with the god of the woods offering caged curlews and bitterns, the goddess of the earth reaching out with baskets overflowing with pears and cherries, an immense mermaid rising out of the lake to present slithering fishes and a dolphin spouting verses in Latin as each gift was presented.

Elizabeth had taken her hands from her ears and was rising to the occasion by accepting the gifts and thanking the givers. But it was plain to see that she was tired and travel-worn, and by the time we had taken off our dusty garments and arrayed ourselves afresh for supper, we could hardly hold up our heads, we were so weary.

Yet there was no respite to be had. Amid much clamor and joyous noise, Robert's entire household—hundreds of people— came out to greet the queen and the villagers from the neighboring settlements crowded in at the lake edge and applauded and screamed with delight as fireworks once more exploded in the sky.

Elizabeth called for a cordial and drank it down, then called for another as darkness closed in around us and the tempting odors of roasting meat and loaves fresh from the oven called us to the banqueting tables. Not until hours later did we find ourselves at last in the beautifully renovated rooms set aside for us, large rooms with high roofs and a great deal of glass, candlelit and welcoming.

We slept long and well in the soft beds, and even the weary queen was forced to admit that Kenilworth was among the finest houses in all her realms.

The following morning we hunted in the extensive park, stocked with red deer. Elizabeth prided herself on her abilities as a huntswoman, and rode out ahead of the rest of the party, reckless as she always was, never content until she had brought down her first deer.

A handsome buck had been spied, and she galloped swiftly after it, determined to bring it down. But before she could shoot at it, she screamed.

"They've shot me!" she called out, causing all those in the hunting party to gallop as fast as we could to surround her.

She was gasping, one hand over her heart. As we neared she raised her other hand, and managed to gasp out, "No hurt! No hurt! They missed!"

A hasty search produced only one possible would-be assassin, a small man in a green jerkin who was carrying a crossbow. The queen's soldiers, with Robert in the lead, quickly unhorsed him, seized his crossbow and began pummeling him and shouting at him. The vagrant arrow was found and brought to the queen.

She shuddered and turned aside.

"I thought for certain it was meant for me," she said, visibly shaken and pale. "I thought my enemies had gotten to me at last."

Robert broke the arrow over his knee and flung it to the ground.

"The fellow says he never meant to shoot at you, Your Highness. He was aiming at the buck, as you were."

"And you believe him?" Elizabeth looked at Robert, incredulous. "Surely you are not that naïve!"

But Robert only shrugged. "You know I would gladly give my life for you, Your Highness. And just as gladly kill any man who raised his hand against you. But this man, he is no assassin. I have seen him before, poaching in my park."

Elizabeth was contemptuous. "Such a one would make a perfect killer. No one would suspect him."

She turned to William Cecil. "Put him to the rack," she said. "Then see how innocent he seems."

And with those words she dug her heels into her horse's side and rode on.

TWENTY-NINE

THE lavish entertainments at Kenilworth went forward, with tilting matches and bearbaiting, pageantry and feasting and disguisings, each day bringing a new round of splendid diversions carried out in costly style. But the unnerving incident in the hunting park cast its shadow over every event. And what was worse, the queen and Robert fell to quarreling.

It happened in the richly appointed, extravagantly decorated apartments Robert had prepared for Elizabeth, while she sat before her looking-glass readying herself for a banquet and I and the other bedchamber ladies were in attendance. My father and William Cecil had just arrived from the court in London, bringing papers for Elizabeth to read and sign—for the work of government went on, even in the midst of the most elaborate entertainments—and she was irritated at having to attend to this unexpected business. She sat, pen in hand, restless on her cushioned stool, muttering to herself as she read and signed and flicking the papers here and there while tossing insults right and left.

I had often seen her act in just this way, and I knew from experience that in fact she was attending to the contents of the papers, as she would demonstrate later as the need arose. But at the same time she was registering her displeasure, making others suffer while she did what had to be done.

Presently Robert came in, elegantly garbed for the banquet he had planned and arranged with such care in a doublet and hose of silvered silk, amethyst buttons and buckles winking in the waning light.

"What, not ready yet?" he called out to the queen, his tone jocular and indulgent. "How much time does the wench need then? Has she no appetite, when my cooks have gone to such trouble to prepare three hundred dishes for her pleasure?"

"I am no wench," Elizabeth growled without looking at Robert. "I am your queen. And what I do here is more important than any feeding."

Robert sighed. "Please hurry, Your Highness, or the food will be spoiled."

She looked at him then, a baleful stare, freighted with displeasure.

"Then let it spoil. Surely I am more important than your woodcock pies and gilded calves' heads!"

"Your Highness is more important than anything," Robert said with a bow.

"As recent events have shown," William Cecil put in. "We were greatly distressed to hear of the accident in the hunting park. Should anything untoward happen, Your Majesty cannot be replaced."

Elizabeth put down her pen.

"Replaced?" she said, in quiet anger. "And why should I be replaced?"

"What Lord Cecil meant," my father put in, "was that in the event of your death—which heaven forefend—there is no one to carry out your responsibilities. It is a dread possibility we in your royal council have faced once before, when you had the pox many years ago."

"Yes," Robert spoke up, "and then, as you lay on your deathbed, you knew what to do. You ordered the council to name me Lord Protector."

"I know you better now," Elizabeth said wryly. "I would not make the same mistake twice."

Robert turned red.

"Must you insult me as well as ruin my costly banquet?"

Elizabeth shrugged. "I can do what I like," she said, looking at herself in the pier glass and adjusting her elaborate red wig. "And as it happens, I am not hungry."

"But others are," I heard William Cecil mutter. "Hungry for power."

Elizabeth chuckled at this, and Robert, infuriated, confronted her.

"Is this to be my reward then, for all my years of service? For the tens of thousands of pounds I have spent in the vain effort to give you pleasure? To be humiliated, cast aside, treated with less regard than a lowly servant? I who have loved and served you more loyally than anyone?"

"I believe Kenilworth is my reward to you, milord earl. You have it backwards."

Before more harsh, blunt words could be spoken William Cecil took a step toward the queen and cleared his throat.

"The fact is, Your Highness, this fearful accident—if it was indeed an accident, and not the work of an agent of the Spanish, as I fear it may have been—reminds us all of what is constantly in our thoughts. The urgent need for a successor to Your Highness's throne. You must marry. You must provide for the succession."

I felt a tremor pass through the women standing nearest to me, and a sharp increase in the tension in the room. Elizabeth stood, suddenly and clumsily, knocking over the stool she had been sitting on and nearly knocking over the table on which her papers were scattered.

"I did not come here to be harangued about the state of my virginity. Or the prohibited subject of my marrying or not marrying."

"We must discuss it eventually, whether the discussion pleases Your Majesty or not," my father said. "Why not now? When the fragility of your life is on all our minds?"

"You are fond of the French prince, are you not?" Cecil put forward. "Why don't we bring him here, so that you can meet one another. A French match would benefit our two countries. The prince would be a sound choice, young, intelligent—"

Robert's angry shout interrupted Cecil. "I am the queen's choice! I have always been her choice!"

"You are married already," the queen remarked languidly. "I believe you are married to Douglass Sheffield, who has had at least two of your children."

"That is vile gossip! I am not married to anyone!" He knelt before Elizabeth, head bowed, his voice constricted with strong emotion. "You must choose me, if you choose to marry anyone! You must!" He raised his face to hers. Hot tears flowed down his cheeks.

"You love me. You have always loved me."

There was a pause. Then the queen said, "Sir, you forget yourself." She adjusted her skirt, setting its folds into perfect alignment. I saw that her hand trembled, though her voice did not.

Robert stood, and began pacing the large room impatiently.

"Once and for all, I am no woman's husband! Yes, I have bastards. What lord in this realm has not?" I noticed that he pointedly avoided looking at my father as he spoke those words. My chaste, faithful father.

"Yes, I wanted a son," he went on. "Lady Sheffield provided me with one. He will carry on the Dudley name, as no one else in my family has sons, or is likely to have any. All but one of my brothers are dead. My sisters bear their husbands' names. Their sons are not Dudleys.

"And besides—" He hesitated. Clearly he was reluctant to go on, but forced himself. "And besides, the queen is not likely to give me a son of her body. No one speaks this truth, but everyone believes it."

Many in the room gasped at this daring avowal, which was clearly wrenched from Robert in great anguish. But Elizabeth did not allow herself to react. Though she continued to tremble, she contained herself. She did not allow herself to notice, as I did, how while pacing the room Robert had begun to limp on his gouty foot. I could tell that it was giving him pain.

"But if you cannot give me a son," he was saying, practically shouting and groaning at the same time, "at least make me Lord Protector!"

"And if I did," Elizabeth spat, suddenly finding her fire, "and you had to take my place, what would happen when you died? Would Douglass Sheffield's bastard succeed to the throne? *I think not!!* Now, leave me—and to hell with your banquet!"

Red-faced and shaken, his voice cracking, Robert shot back, "Then all is ended between us! You have been my playfellow, my bedfellow, my hunting partner and my mate—in all but law!

Married or not, we are and always have been together! I care
not who hears me say it! I speak the truth! But from this moment
forward, if you will not marry me, then I will marry any woman
I choose!"

Startled, embarrassed, the councilors and the royal attendants
shuffled nervously for the door, until stopped by the sound of the
queen's cheerful voice.

"Cecil!" she cried. "I am suddenly hungry! Escort me to the
feast!"

The councilor held out his arm, and, grasping it, Elizabeth
strode almost jauntily out of the room, all hauteur forgotten,
leaving Robert to glower in her wake.

The following year, Walter went to Ireland as he so often did.
But this time he became very ill.

"It is the bog fever, for sure," Cecelia murmured when the
news reached us. "He has caught it at last."

We learned, in a letter from one of his officers, how he was
brought to Dublin Castle where physicians sat by his bedside and
treated him with plasters and leeches. Penelope and Dorothy
both wept as I read the letter aloud, and little Rob nestled beside
me, trying to give me comfort. I read, with tears, how he wasted
and at last succumbed, grasping the hand of a priest as he took
his last breath.

I did what I could to help the children grieve. As for myself,
I could not help but mourn Walter a little. After all, I was a
widow now. And I was only thirty-five.

THIRTY

O U R wedding was private and the queen was not told about it. We were so discreet that even her spies did not find out. We exchanged vows in the traditional way, with a priest present, and Robert gave me the ring he had once given Douglass, the heirloom gold ring with a great glowing sapphire. I wore it proudly—though never at court, where the queen or her spies could see it.

Robert and I were man and wife—yet when I told my father after the ceremony he was not satisfied.

"It is bad enough that Lady Sheffield says she was married to the man you now call your husband," he remarked in his most moralistic tone, without making any attempt to hide his contempt for Robert. "Now you have made matters worse by exchanging a few brief words in secret, instead of being married according to the service of the communion book, and with relatives and friends in attendance as witnesses to your troth. It looks to others as though you have something to hide."

"But Douglass is lying, father! She and Robert were never married. She plagued poor Robert unbearably until he gave her his pledge, but that was all. He never repeated any vows, as he has with me."

"Nevertheless," father said in his gravest tones, "it is necessary to have a written understanding between Robert and Lady Sheffield, in case any question should ever arise as to whether they were married or not."

He continued to lecture me and harangue Robert until, in the end, a document was drawn up for Douglass to sign. We all met in a secluded bower in the gardens of Greenwich Palace, a place far from the noise and business of the court. Robert's steward brought the document in a pouch, and placed it on a table, inkwell and pen prepared and ready.

Douglass was in distress, her blond hair in disarray under her hastily-arranged cap, one of her sleeves hanging loose, having come untied, her eyes red-rimmed. I wondered whether she would bring her son with her, and was glad to see that she had not. She picked up the document and began to read it. She had not read far before she looked up from the paper, with tears in her eyes, and shook her head.

"No!" she said. "I cannot! I cannot!"

She looked at Robert, then at me and finally at my father. She shook her head again, more decisively this time.

"Look at me!" she cried, tearing the cap off her head to reveal a strange sight. Among the thick curling blond locks were bald patches. And the scalp revealed was not white but red, an angry red.

"See this!" she shouted. "Look at this! I am being poisoned! Everyone knows that a slow-working poison makes a person's hair fall out! I am being poisoned, and there is only one poisoner here! My husband, Robert Dudley!"

A growl escaped Robert's throat and he reached out to slap Douglass. My father quickly stepped between them.

"Hush, girl, and do as you are bid. I assure you, it is the queen's wish as well as the wish of those of us gathered here."

"My stomach hurts all the time," Douglass insisted, grasping her waist. "I retch. I am ill."

"You are probably pregnant," Robert snapped. "And certainly not by me! Half the men in the court have bedded you!"

"But since my first husband died, only you have married me! And now you are trying to kill me!"

My father took a step toward Douglass and, firmly grasping her by the arm, helped her to sit down at the table.

"Lady Sheffield," he began, deliberately choosing not to call Douglass "Lady Dudley," did you love your late father, and obey him in all things as was his due?"

"I did."

"If he were here now, he would guide you as I am doing. He would tell you to sign this document. All we need today, is for you to sign. What is happening to your hair, or any churning in your stomach, is of no account."

"But I am being poisoned!"

My father picked up the pen, dipped it in the inkwell, wiped it, and handed it to Douglass. She wept, her shoulders crumpled. But she signed.

I heard Robert heave a sigh of relief. And then I saw him draw a heavy pouch from his doublet and hand it to his steward, murmuring "Give this to her." It was, I felt sure, a pouch of coins. For Douglass, and for their son. And in return for signing a paper filled with words she believed to be false.

As for me, I was not certain what to believe. I wanted to trust my Robert, my dearest husband, who I knew to be a man of many failings as well as strengths. I hoped fervently that Douglass's falling hair and stomach pains were caused by something other than poison. I prayed that it was so. I prayed that we would have a long and happy marriage, blessed with children who would love us as much as we would love them. I prayed for our future, knowing that nothing is ever certain in this world, and that in marrying Robert I was taking a chance.

To satisfy my father, Robert and I were married a second time—this time at Wanstead, which became our favorite home, with my father and Robert's brother Ambrose and other relatives and witnesses present. Robert's chaplain married us, and was careful to follow the ceremony as written in the communion book.

When asked, no one in the small group of witnesses protested that he or she had anything to say against the marriage. But then, Douglass Sheffield was not present, nor was the queen. And the queen, in time, had a great deal to say, once she discovered that I, her rival, had at long last married the man she loved.

THIRTY-ONE

SHE did not find out right away. Indeed it was many months before word of our marriage reached her, and when it did, she was in a state of near panic because she had just survived another attempt to kill her.

Or so everyone believed.

I had never seen the queen so frightened as on the day of that attack, when she came into her bedchamber soon afterward, clutching her chest and short of breath. Her always pale face was ashen-white, her eyes were large and startled, with a stricken look—not unlike the look in Douglass Sheffield's eyes when she signed the document saying she had never truly been married to Robert.

I was to remember that look in the queen's eyes for a long time to come.

According to what Whaffer told us all, gathering the bedchamber staff and tirewomen around him in a small room where we would not be disturbed or overheard, the attack happened just as the queen had been about to board the royal barge for a trip upriver. It was to have been an important trip, for she had with her a French courtier named Simier, a Frenchman who had come to England to discuss her future marriage to the French prince Francis.

Suddenly, Whaffer said, as she was about to step down into the barge, there was a loud shot.

An arquebus had been fired. The bargeman, standing very near the queen, cried out and fell. Blood spurted from both his arms. The French courtier Simier ran for his life, deserting the queen. Others ducked or ran or shouted for help.

Amid the chaos, Elizabeth cried out for Robert and in an instant he was at her side, Whaffer told us, shielding her with his body, hurrying her back into the palace for safety. Once she was there, and surrounded by trusted guardsmen, Robert went down into the vessel and wrapped the bargeman's wounds with his shirt, shouting for Dr. Huick and demanding that the man who fired the shot be brought to him.

We were full of questions. Had the assassin been found? Was he taken to the Tower? Who was he?

For several hours these questions remained unanswered, while we bedchamber ladies took on the difficult task of trying to soothe the queen's nerves. We brought her cordials. We urged her to lie down and take some rest, though she was unable to sleep; her eyes remained wide open with that haunting startled look which made me so uneasy.

"Strike, or be stricken! Strike, or be stricken!" she murmured again and again. Unable to rest, she paced in her bedchamber, drawing aside the curtains and bedhangings again and again and even looking behind the tapestries for hidden assassins.

"You need not fear, Your Highness," my father told the queen. "The assassin was not firing at you, but at the Frenchman Simier.

Simier is a criminal. He killed his own brother! And do you know why? Because his brother was sleeping with Simier's wife! The assassin was sent by the wife's relatives, or so it is said."

"Can you be certain of this?" Elizabeth asked. "The assassin at Kenilworth was not shooting at any Frenchman, but at me. I believe it is the Spanish who send the assassins. They want me dead."

Father shrugged. "The French are all sunk in wickedness. They are capable of anything. The idea that Your Highness should consider choosing a husband from among them sours my stomach, if I may be so bold as to say so."

"You may not! Besides, you know as well as I that England needs an alliance with France, as a counterweight to the evil designs of King Philip."

Hearing this exchange, as I stood with the other bedchamber ladies in attendance, I was glad to see that talking with my father was bringing Elizabeth back to something of her old courage and confidence. But she was still pale, and somewhat short of breath, and her eyes were wide with fear.

"After what happened today, will you agree to send this Simier back where he came from, at least until you have had a chance to weigh the consequences of a French marriage?"

"Certainly not! I have already given the matter more than enough thought. Simier may be a coward and a criminal, and he certainly showed me no chivalry today, but I will allow him to stay. Now, leave me in peace."

With a respectful bow, father left the room. The Frenchman Simier was allowed to remain at court, and after a brief investigation it was determined that the arquebus shot was not the deliberate act of an assassin, but an accident. The man who fired the shot apologized and was not punished. Such was the official response—but I knew the queen persisted in her belief that the Spanish were seeking to kill her.

"Two near-fatal accidents within the space of a few years?" I remarked to Robert. "The queen nearly killed both times? That could hardly be coincidence."

"Fatal accidents do occur at royal courts," was Robert's response. "The queen's own father, King Henry, had a terrible accident on the tilting ground and nearly died. Queen Anne Boleyn was so frightened that she miscarried her child. And the father of the French Prince Francis died of wounds suffered in just such an accident, riding at the tilt."

I remained unconvinced.

"Do you think Elizabeth will marry this French prince?" I said after a time. "Even though he is said to be as small as a dwarf and weak and horribly pockmarked?"

"Marry she must—and soon. The stronger the Spanish grow, the more she needs an ally. Besides, she likes this boy. They write to each other in Greek and Latin, as I have told you. He is witty, and she likes a witty man. She can't wait to meet him—even though I am sure that the thought of marriage frightens her. She can't stand the idea of anyone having rule over her, and the husband is the head of the wife, even if he is much younger, and even if she is a queen."

"Then you have doubts."

"Some, yes. But she may surprise us all, and fall in love with the prince once he arrives."

I did not think so, but I said nothing further to Robert just then.

Prince Francis did arrive very soon after the frightening episode with the arquebus, though he came without pomp and was received without ceremony. I glimpsed him once or twice during his brief visit, as he sat talking to Elizabeth, both of them laughing, clearly enjoying each other's company. He was even uglier than I had been led to believe. Truly the runt of Queen Catherine de Medici's royal litter. Her eldest, also named Francis, had been the childhood friend and frail young husband of Mary Queen of Scots and had died before he was seventeen. Her second boy, Charles, had not lived to be much older. The next to inherit the throne, Henry III, was then king, and had survived to the age of twenty-eight, but was said to be in fragile health, with weak lungs and an infirm heart. So this prince, Elizabeth's pet, was not likely to be long-lived or strong—which, I supposed, could well have been a part of his appeal for the vigorous, hardy Elizabeth. If she married him he would soon make her a widow, but a widow who in time of need could call upon the armies of France.

The very private visit was over within days, and the prince went back to France, leaving it to his royal brother's ministers to discuss the possible terms of a marriage treaty. But he left his creature Simier behind, to accomplish a final task. A fateful task.

To persuade the queen to marry the French prince Simier told her, first, that she was right in thinking the Spanish were hoping to kill her, and that he had been told that assassins were on their way to England to accomplish this gruesome mission. And when she responded with fear, he told her that she could no longer count on Robert to protect her, for Robert now had a wife to protect—a wife named Lettice Knollys, to whom he was bound by ties not only of loyalty, but of love.

CHIRCY-CWO

ELIZABETH was frightened. But not too frightened to banish Robert from court and to summon me into her presence, in such a cold fury that I feared I might be locked in the Tower and sentenced to death.

"I have never trusted you, you She-Wolf," she began. "I knew when you entered my household that you were a wayward girl, not to be trusted. I was told what happened in Frankfurt. The shame you brought on your family! But your father promised me he would keep you on a tight rein. I thought that he had. Now I find that you have stolen from me the man I hold dearest in all the world."

How I found the strength to answer her as I did I will never know. All I know, all that I can remember of that long-ago morning, is that when she looked at me with such chill fierceness in her light eyes I suddenly realized what it was that she was seeing.

For it came to me all of a sudden (having caught a glimpse of myself in one of her many pier glasses) that she was seeing, standing before her, not a She-Wolf but a beautiful woman, much younger than herself and still very lovely—enviably lovely, so that men still wrote her poetry, and sought to paint her portrait. (Yes, it happened. And not infrequently.) A woman of whom she had been jealous ever since I first came to her court.

I realized that the sight of me must be extremely vexing to her, and not only because I possessed the beauty that she lacked, but because I had triumphed over her! I, Letitia Knollys, now Countess of Leicester, was reveling in the love of the most handsome, the most desirable and splendid man at her court.

I possessed the love of her life.

And this gave me strength. I straightened up. I felt my power. And then I spoke.

"Where is my Robert?" I demanded, ignoring her rebuke. "Have you put him in prison? I insist on seeing him. I am his wife."

She continued to regard me with a flinty stare. She refused to be roused to passion.

"And it is only because you are his wife that your life has been spared. If I ordered your execution, he would never forgive me!"

"You would execute a woman of royal blood then? A woman whose right to the throne may well be higher than yours! My mother was King Henry's bastard and if the gossip about Anne Boleyn's infidelity is to be believed, you are not royal at all! You are the daughter of the musician Mark Smeaton, or some other lowborn man!"

She raised her hand as if to slap me, and I stepped back. She did not pursue me. Instead she motioned to her guards to leave the room. We were alone.

She paced for a moment, frowning, thinking. Then she came to rest.

"You will leave court as soon as I dismiss you from this room," she said. "And you will not return. But before you leave, we will have an understanding."

"You will not harm me or my children or anyone in my family," I began. "You will not deprive Robert of his lands or offices. If you do, I will reveal all that I have read in your daybook and all that I know of the death of Robert's first wife."

I could tell that this last threat startled her. I knew the truth about Amy Dudley's death, and it seemed evident to me that the queen did not—and that she would very much like to.

"You will allow us to live together quietly, and will not trouble us."

I could think of nothing else. I grew quiet.

"Clearly you are a child when it comes to striking a bargain, She-Wolf. Are these the strongest terms you have to offer?" She smiled. "As long as I am sovereign, Lord Robert will continue to serve me, in whatever fashion and whatever place I determine. Your life and his will remain mine to command, as befits loyal subjects. I may, if I choose, snuff them out at any time. Never forget that.

"Robert may love you, certainly he lusts after you. But those bonds, however firm, will fray in time. While his bond to me is enduring, more enduring than you can know. And while it endures, you will always take second place in his heart, and in his life. Never forget that. Now go!"

I would have liked to speak, to deny all that she had said, even though deep down I knew it to be the truth. But I had no words. I had run out of defiance. As the queen spoke, I began to feel a tremor of fear, faint at first, and then stronger and stronger. In the end I was glad to leave her presence, which I did promptly and with the curtest of bows.

Where was Robert? What had she done with him?

Once out of the queen's apartments I ran, picking up my skirts and hoping I would not trip, racing down the narrow dark corridors of the palace, slipping on the uncarpeted stairs, praying with every step that Elizabeth would not change her mind and send her soldiers to seize me and imprison me, shutting me in the deepest of her dungeons and telling my jailer to throw away the key.

THIRTY-THREE

OUR son Robert was born in June of my fortieth year. He was large and long, with blue eyes and reddish hair, and unlike my fifteen-year-old son Rob, who had been a lusty baby, crying a lot and wriggling and never at peace, this boy was calm. I nursed him myself and he ate well. He slept beside us in his carved wooden cradle trimmed in crimson velvet. He was barely two months old when Robert ordered a very small suit of armor made for him, and when he was home he liked me to dress the baby in it and take him out in my carriage.

"There now, Baron Denbigh," Robert said to him, using the title that came to the boy as heir to the earldom of Leicester, "you are fit to guard the queen. When you are a little older I will teach you to use a sword."

Robert's delight in our son was beyond measure. His face shone with pleasure whenever he saw him, taking him in his arms and talking softly to him, lifting him onto his shoulders and doing his best to gallop around the kitchen garden—limping on his sore foot—neighing like a horse and laughing. All his life, ever since the time, decades earlier, when he had lost most of his family in the bloody aftermath of his father's plot to seize the throne, Robert had longed for an heir. A son to carry on the Dudley name and restore honor to the Dudley line and ancestry. Little Denbigh was all he could have wished for, he said, ignoring the baby's slight physical imperfection—one of his legs was a good deal shorter than the other—and his somewhat glassy-eyed stare.

Robert's other son, the boy he called his "base son" by Douglass Sheffield, was rarely mentioned, though I knew that he too gave my husband pleasure. His son by Douglass was raised by nurses and tutors, in a country house not far from his mother's. When little Denbigh was born Robert's base son was seven years old, growing like a weed and showing a fine intelligence. Robert took pride in his quickness, and though he did not see him often, he made his love and regard felt.

Thankfully, Douglass made no further trouble for us. She married a second time—proving, by her marriage, that she had never really considered herself to be Robert's wife—and did not go to court often, or so I heard from Cecelia and my father. She was a foolish woman, I thought, selfish and shallow. She cared little for anyone besides herself. To be sure, I was prejudiced against her and secretly envied her her share of Robert's affection. And it had been affection, not love. Of this I felt sure—and would have, even if he had not sworn to me that he had never loved Douglass, only lusted after her youthful body.

My own body had grown fuller, more voluptuous, after little Denbigh's birth. I ate my fill, I napped, I took less exercise, and inevitably my gowns had to be let out. I never grew fat like Cecelia, of course, merely fuller and more rounded. I was pleasing to Robert, and that was all that mattered.

When brother Frank came to see our boy I could not help but notice that he looked wistful, gazing down into the cradle. He had not brought a pony for our new son, as he had for Rob when he was born, but he did bring a chest made of beautifully carved silver. Inside were coins and gems.

"Souvenirs from our latest voyage," he said with a smile, referring to his remarkable journey with Captain Drake, a journey that had taken the small convoy of ships all around the globe. Something no Englishmen had ever done before—and I suppose no others either. "Put this away in a safe place for your son, for when he grows to manhood."

Robert and I both thanked Frank heartily, congratulating him on surviving his perilous voyage and telling him he was being entirely too generous—though I knew that Robert, who was always short of money and too much in debt, would undoubtedly take a loan from the baby's chest as soon as he decently could. He would mean to pay it back of course—he was no thief, and did not covet what did not belong to him—but he was improvident. His good intentions would probably not be fulfilled.

"Never mind," Frank said, brushing aside our thanks. "It is only money and money only buys things. Not love. What you two have together is worth more than all the treasure in the world. And now you have your son, to make your love complete."

Robert put his arm around me as Frank spoke, and I felt anew the glow of love, and a motherly pride. I thought, no woman was ever happier than I am right now, this moment.

But at the same time I felt sorry for Frank. I knew that he was thinking of his own lost beloved. His Marianna. After he had been with us a day or two he spoke to me about her, of how he wished he had married her when he had the chance.

"And your wealthy wife, what of her?" I asked.

Frank shook his head. "She died several years ago, while I was at sea. And yes, since I know you must be wondering—she left me her fortune. Not that I need it. I have a fortune of my own. We brought back a great many chests of Spanish coins when we finally sailed into Plymouth harbor at the end of our long voyage."

Robert ordered little Denbigh dressed in his tiny suit of armor for Frank to see. The baby crowed, and Frank laughed with pleasure.

"He is a proper lordling!" Frank declared. Then he looked more closely at the child, an expression of concern replacing his pleasure. "What of his leg?" he asked. "Has your physician examined it? What does he say?"

Robert and I both began to speak at once, but I stopped, letting Robert answer. Our little boy's short leg troubled us very much, as did his seeming inability to focus on us. He seemed to stare off into nothing, and did not reach for us, or for bright objects the way other babies did. The way all my other children had.

"We are concerned about his leg," Robert said. "We have had Dr. Julio and several physicians from London come to examine him. They say the shorter leg will grow to match the longer one—in time. They can find no reason why it hasn't."

"We want to take him to court, to let the queen's physicians look at him," I added. "But she is angry with Robert and won't allow it. And as for me, she refuses to let me come anywhere near any of her palaces. She hates me and calls me the She-Wolf."

"Everyone says she is a strange woman," Frank murmured. "They say she treats her most loyal servants worst of all."

I reached down into little Denbigh's cradle and put my finger into his small white palm. He grasped it firmly.

"Remember how our father used to say that kings and queens

do not act like other people?" I said, looking over at Frank. We exchanged a smile.

"I hope your boy will soon be running and playing as lustily as any other," Frank said. "No doubt his leg will lengthen. He will outgrow his armor before you know it. Then he can join this Bond of Association I have been hearing so much about since our return."

At Frank's mention of the Bond of Association a tremor passed through me. Recently Robert had, with other noblemen, formed an organization which he insisted was necessary to protect the queen. Members of the bond were sworn to kill anyone who succeeded in assassinating Elizabeth—or anyone on whose behalf the attempt to assassinate her was made. Intended to prevent violence, in fact it seemed to me that this association might well promote it, by inciting blood feuds and an enduring chain of bloody reprisals. I hoped I was wrong. When I confessed my fears to Robert he merely looked somber and told me that the times called for extreme measures.

"Let there be no doubt in anyone's mind," he said at his most earnest, "there is already a war across Christendom. The Spanish King Philip views all Protestants as enemies of God. He is sworn to destroy them—to destroy us—one by one. He has already begun this horrible extermination in Holland and Zeeland and the other Protestant provinces of the Low Countries. Thousands of innocent people are being rounded up and tortured, shut up in dungeons and starved, put on the rack and stretched until their bones break."

"Just like the wretched Anabaptists in Frankfurt," I said. "When I was a girl. They were bound hand and foot and thrown into the river to drown—and not by the Spanish, but by other Protestants. Calvinists like my father."

I couldn't help remembering the horrors I had witnessed in

Frankfurt, or the hideous burning of my tutor Jocelyn, a victim of the Catholic Queen Mary. Undoubtedly the most ghastly thing I had ever witnessed. I had seen at first hand what savagery was unleashed when rulers and churchmen decided that other men—and not only men, but women and innocent children too—were following Satan instead of the true God. All sense of our common humanity, I knew, was laid aside when such brutality was loosed. And now Robert was telling me that King Philip was expanding his cruel crusade to destroy all Protestants.

"Our Bond of Association is only the beginning," Robert was saying. "There will have to be much larger and stronger bonds, and armies, indeed we must mount a crusade of our own, to defend and protect what is ours."

Strong words, and fearsome ones. I thought of them often in the coming days, as I sat by our little son's cradle, my finger gripped by his tiny hand.

THIRTY-FOUR

"IT is the end of the world," Mistress Clinkerte announced as she busied herself with my little son's newly washed laundry, folding his small blankets and stockings and caps and putting them in the great wardrobe that stood in his nursery. His nurse and rocker Margaret looked on, evidently feeling put out that her usual duties were being carried out by someone else.

"The end is coming. It will be here soon." She was chewing her herbs as usual as she spoke, and the scent of them filled the room. Little Denbigh, who had been fussing unhappily in his cradle, had fallen silent and was dropping off to sleep. I sat beside his cradle, watching him, alert to his small movements, his occasional rapid intake of breath.

"Everyone believes it," Mistress Clinkerte went on, looking askance at me when I failed to respond to her announcement. "Surely you have heard of it here in Wanstead."

"I have," I said, keeping my tone noncommittal. I had never been one to put much faith in prophecies. I had noticed, in the course of my lifetime, that they rarely came to pass.

"They say a great empire will fall. That thrones will topple. One throne in particular." She sniffed.

"Thank you, Margaret," I said, addressing the rocker. "Will you leave us please?"

It seemed to me that the implication of Mistress Clinkerte's words was clear, and I did not want the servant to hear disloyal things said about the queen.

Elizabeth had thawed slightly in her attitude toward Robert and even, as I thought, toward me. Robert was just then away, as he so often was, on court business. But before he left court, bound on his diplomatic mission, he got permission from the queen to send Mistress Clinkerte to me, knowing that she would be a comfort and a help as I struggled with my sorrow and frustration over our little Denbigh and his physical troubles. I took this to be a gesture of sympathy on her part, for Robert had told the queen candidly of our son's stunted growth and his inability to walk or talk. He was just then entering his second year of life and it was clear he was suffering from some mysterious affliction, some curse whose precise nature no physician could seem to discover.

Cecelia said flatly that I had been too old when I bore him, others that Robert had been too old and ill to sire a healthy son. My father muttered darkly about sin and the wages of sin—but then, he said this about nearly every event he heard of; his view of life was becoming more and more negative as he aged. I wondered what he thought of all this talk of fate and disaster about to fall upon the world.

"Great harms are sure to arrive in the Year of Doom," Mistress Clinkerte was saying. "The year fifteen hundred and eighty-eight after the birth of Our Lord."

"Hasn't a great empire already fallen?" I said, more to make idle talk than to argue with Mistress Clinkerte. "That of the Indians in the New World?"

"Pish! That was nothing . . . a few painted savages dancing around a campfire. No! It will be England that falls—or perhaps the entire world."

She went on with what she was doing for a time. I gazed down at my son, who had fallen fast asleep. I pulled his small blanket higher and tucked it in around him. How much he looked like Robert! The same reddish hair (though Robert's was growing grey), the same bow-shaped mouth, long lashes . . .

"The queen certainly believes it," Mistress Clinkerte resumed after a time. "She claims she doesn't, but I see how nervous she is, how worried. She has a great book of prognostications and reads it nearly every day. Sometimes she even reads it aloud, softly, under her breath.

"Famine and drought will come," I have heard her read. "But all the gold will be burned. Plagues will come. All mankind will come to an end."

"Dark sayings indeed. But I imagine every generation has heard such things—and we are still here."

"This time the stars align against us. I have heard Whaffer say it, and he's no fool. He told me that when he was a boy he heard about the Year of Doom. He hopes he'll be dead before it comes."

"Good old Whaffer! I hope he lives forever!" I could not help but say.

Mistress Clinkerte threw up her hands. "The day will come, when you will have to believe that all I say is true. Mark my words, it is the end of the world!"

I did not put any faith in the alarmist warnings of Mistress Clinkerte, who was growing old and—surely!—even more credulous. I did not want to allow myself to be swept up in the rising fear of doom that I heard so many people give voice to. After all, I had more than enough to worry about with my dear little son failing to thrive, and my daughter Penelope more than old enough to be married, and proving to be far more willful and dangerously independent than I was at her age, and my daughter Dorothy, a good and mild-natured girl, showing far too great a partiality for a common seaman. I needed to find them good highborn husbands, or to find a remedy for my boy's ills. I did not want far darker worries about the end of the world to invade my thoughts.

Yet when Robert, weary from the tasks the queen continued to heap upon him, echoed the doom-laden message I had been hearing from Mistress Clinkerte, I had to take it more seriously.

"It's true, Lettie," he said in his tired voice as he gulped some cold roast pheasant and venison pasties and drank deeply from a tankard of beer. He had ridden all night in order to have an entire day to spend with me; the queen could barely spare him even for an hour, he said, but he had stolen a day and a night to be with me at Wanstead. Arriving at dawn, exhausted and ravenous, he had been glad for the food I had waiting for him.

"I wish I could say otherwise, but the prophecies are too numerous and too believable to be ignored," he went on. "Remember the predictions about the coming of the Mouldwarp, the monster-king who would kill and maim and cast down the church? No—you wouldn't remember, you are too young. But it came to pass, that was King Henry. That demon Mouldwarp."

He paused to eat and drink, then went on. "And the prophecy about how the earth would shake and a tall monument would be brought low? Sure enough, the steeple of St. Paul's burned to the ground, and there was a great quaking of the earth—and all in the year it was supposed to happen."

"I remember that." It had been shortly after we returned from Frankfurt I think. Or near that time. London had been full of rumors. And sure enough, we had our earthquake and then the church tower burned—and a lot of the houses nearby burned with it.

Robert finished his meal and a servant took his plate away.

"I'm afraid we must prepare to face disaster, in whatever form it may come, in the year fifteen-eighty-eight. The Year of Doom, they call it. Wars, famine, drought, 'a tumult in the earth,' one prediction says. 'An empire will fall.'"

Suddenly his face brightened. The weariness that had been so apparent in his tired eyes and slack mouth disappeared, and a hint of the playfulness I so enjoyed in him came to the surface.

"Well then!" he said, "if an empire must fall, then it must! But let it be the greatest empire of all! The empire of Spain!"

CHIRTY-FIVE

To say that Robert and I were happy would be to understate the truth by a long English mile. What mattered to us both was that we were together. That we took great joy in one another, year after year. Our love did not fade, our devotion grew. Only those who have known such happiness can understand my words. And can understand how inadequate words are in trying to convey the great and enduring force of love.

But the queen, ever the enemy of our love, did her best to separate us, calling Robert to court for months at a time to play his vital role on her council, and at other times also for the most trivial of issues. She summoned him to sit for the portrait painter, saying she wanted a portrait of herself with him in the background. She required his presence at the weddings of minor officials and the christenings of their children. She sent him with his soldiers from town to town across much of southern England, raising trained bands and securing fortifications and reporting back to the council on the state of the realm's defenses. Anything to take him from me, to weaken his strong ties to me and to our son.

"She needs me," Robert would say curtly when a messenger arrived at Wanstead from the court, bringing a hastily scrawled note from Elizabeth. "She is fearful. She requires my presence."

And he would go, every time. I knew it would be folly to complain, or to point out the queen's true motive in demanding so much of his time. He served her. He was loyal to her. And, in a way that caused me a certain amount of jealousy, he loved her.

They had been lovers, this I knew. But they were lovers no longer. I trusted that Robert was faithful to me, and I did not question that trust. He served her, but his heart was mine. His heart was mine, during the long separations, the nights of missing him and often dreaming of him. The days when I needed him and he was not there to help me.

I needed him more and more as little Denbigh grew weaker, and I grew more and more certain that he would never walk or talk or grow to be like other boys. For his third birthday Robert ordered another small suit of armor made for him, and had his portrait painted wearing it. Frank sent him a small chair to sit in, beautifully carved and upholstered in red velvet. But I knew by then that he would never sit in it, for he could not sit at all and simply lay in his small bed, all but unmoving, from early morning to late at night.

I sat beside him, keeping watch, saying my prayers, reading a little from my book of psalms and nibbling at the food Mistress Clinkerte brought me.

It was Mistress Clinkerte who finally came to me one morning and, after looking down at the still body of my son, his small chest barely rising and falling with each breath, said gently that she thought Robert might be sent for.

She was right, of course. And the tone of her voice was gentle—which was unusual, as she was normally brusque and firm. Her very gentleness told me just how gravely ill little Denbigh was. Yet my anger flared at her words, and I resisted at first. I resisted admitting the worst, and I resisted telling my dear Robert what I feared.

In the end I knew what I had to do. I had to tell him myself that he was needed. I called for my maidservant to bring my riding cloak and boots and, with two grooms as escort, mounted my fastest horse and rode, with all speed, to Nonsuch Palace, where Robert was in attendance on the queen.

Tired and thirsty, but filled with a sense of great urgency, I rode up to the palace gates and, without so much as stopping to be acknowledged by the guards, went on to the inner courtyard and hurried inside. My grooms were right behind me.

I knew Nonsuch well, having often stayed there during my years as maid of honor and bedchamber lady to the queen. I made my way to the royal apartments and on into the chamber where the council usually met.

"I am the Countess of Leicester," I announced to the guards at the door. "I bring vital information for my husband."

One of the guards knew me. With a nod he opened the chamber door.

I burst in, and looked anxiously around the council table for my husband.

He was not there.

Instead I found myself looking into the shocked, alarmed faces of William Cecil (who had become Lord Burghley), Francis Walsingham, and my father.

"No, Lady Leicester! You ought not to be here!" cried one of the other councilors. "You are not allowed at court! The queen—"

"Where is my husband? Why is he not among you?" I demanded, my voice tight.

"Father! Where is Robert?"

But my father merely threw up his hands and turned his head away.

"What is it? Has something happened? Is he with his soldiers?"

None of the men would look at me. Several were muttering to one another.

Then an awful thought struck me. Before anyone could stop me I ran out of the council chamber and into the queen's private apartments, which were immediately adjacent to it.

The first room was empty, in the second was only a startled boy, sweeping up the ashes in the hearth.

But in the third room, the queen's small, private dressing room, I found them together.

I stopped at the threshold. I caught my breath. I could not believe what I was seeing.

Robert was kneeling before the queen, who was standing, his hand on one of her wrinkled, scrawny bare legs, reaching up toward that part of her that Cecelia always scornfully called "her royal maidenhead."

She wore only the scantiest of lacy undergarments. Her aging, scraggy body, withered and puckered and white as a mushroom, was ugly. The room was filled with the scent of musk. The musk with which Robert scented his codpieces.

I stood, dumbstruck. The queen's face turned bright red. She shouted for her guard. Robert, pale and frightened, lowered his wayward hand and got to his feet, standing in front of Elizabeth, shielding her from my unwelcome stare.

Then, in an instant, before the guards could arrive and seize me, I was out of the room, my grooms at my heels, hurrying not along the swept, torchlit corridors of the public part of the palace but along the narrow, dark, urine-stained warren of corridors where the servants ran, carrying loads of food, pails and buckets, firewood and bedding. I ran among the throng, my eyes blinded with tears, stumbling on the uneven stones beneath my feet and wanting to cry out no, no, no, with every painful step.

CHIRTY-SIX

*Y*OU *must understand. You must."*

I heard Robert's throaty, pleading voice through the thick oaken door of our bedchamber at Wanstead. I had gone back there, wounded and heartsick, feeling betrayed, angry, cheated—and filled with an overwhelming desire to lash out. At my husband, at the queen, at the world.

Yet once I was back in my own home my arms felt as though they were made of iron. I could not move. I managed to go in to see little Denbigh, and found him in the same state as he had been when I left. Still clinging to life, but painfully thin and feeble.

Exhausted, I went to our bedchamber, needing to lie down and rest, when I heard Robert's voice outside the door. Evidently he had ridden after me from the palace. My heart sank, hearing him speak.

"Please, Lettie. Let me in. Let me explain."

I had locked the door, and meant to keep it locked. I remained silent.

"Lettie!" He banged on the door with his fist. "Lettie!"

I put my hands over my ears.

"You don't understand. You can't think that I—that we—"

"Go away! Go away and leave me in peace!" Now Robert was silent—but his silence was brief.

"I am going to stay here until you listen to all that I have to say! When you saw Elizabeth, she was terrified. I have never seen her so frightened. She was having one of her nervous fits. She had just been attacked! Again! A Welshman this time. A sniveling little Welshman with a knife. He nearly slit her throat! He was disguised as a guard. No one knew what was happening at first. But we stopped him in time. She fainted away. When she recovered, she couldn't stop screaming."

Though I kept my hands over my ears, Robert's voice was loud, and I could hear every word he said. He spoke in explosive fragments, panting with the urgency of his message. He was telling me that Elizabeth had come very near death.

He pounded on the door, this time with the flat of his hand, then with something made of metal. The hilt of his sword, I imagined.

"Listen to me, Lettie. You found us together because she had sent all her tirewomen away. She tore off her clothes. She was beside herself with fear. I was trying to make her decent again. I didn't want—I couldn't bear it if—" He broke off, overcome by emotion. "Half those old men around her—they already think she's losing her wits. I couldn't let her go out among them naked . . ."

I took my hands from my ears. Was it true? Had I misinterpreted what I saw at the palace? Was he merely being protective of Elizabeth, and not lecherous or erotic?

It was just possible. But it was also possible that he was telling me what he hoped I would accept, rather than the truth. I hesitated.

"Let me in, Lettie."

"No."

"Let me in!"

Exhaustion. Confusion. Anger. And with it all, a nagging sense that my feeling of being cheated and betrayed was giving way before the onslaught of Robert's convincing words. The queen *had* come under attack, several times that I knew of. She was subject to alarming nervous fits. I had witnessed them often enough. She did send her tirewomen away with screams and threats. And she did trust Robert, and only Robert, and want him near her for reassurance and help.

Robert had fallen silent. Had he given up, and gone away? Would he come back? I went to lie down, but could not close my eyes for long.

Then I heard a scraping sound, and men's voices outside my door. Several men. Shouts. A metallic clang.

And then, all of a sudden, there was a tremendous bang and the solid, heavy oak door was shattered. Robert rushed in. I screamed.

In an instant he was in the room, crossing to the bed, his strides long and powerful. I cowered beneath the quilted silk but he grabbed my shoulders and held me down where I was, looming over me, half-frowning, beside himself with—what? Concern? Anxiety? Or something darker? I could not be sure.

In that moment, he was not my husband. He was a man in the grip of a violent passion. A man who had just broken down the door with a battering ram. And who now held me immobile, subject to his will.

I could not breathe. I struggled under his weight, knowing

even as I did so that it was useless to resist. He was too strong for me. He had always been too strong for me, his vigor, the force of his desire, his raw animal potency. It was this very power that had drawn forth my love. And that even now, amid my fear, drew forth my lust.

"Lettie," he was saying, "I will not let you suffer by thinking the worst of me. I love you. I am your true and loving husband, today and always. You must believe me."

And he bent his face to mine and kissed me, a kiss that did not taste of betrayal. A kiss that lasted half the night, and brought with it the full restoration of love.

Love was restored, but hope, alas! was not.

Our dearest little Denbigh died the following night, in the still dark hour just before dawn, with the candles guttering and the birds just beginning to chirp sleepily in the trees outside the windows. I had been holding his hand. I felt his grip relax, his small fingers grow limp.

"So dies the house of Dudley," Robert said solemnly. We looked at one another, but said nothing.

I had my children, Robert his base son. But our boy, the longed-for child who would carry the Dudley lineage into the next generation, who would, Robert had once hoped, one day marry into royalty, was gone.

He was buried in his small suit of armor, and laid in a costly tomb. His gravestone was simple, and praised him as a boy born of a noble lineage, a boy of great promise. A promise blighted, to our great sorrow, before he was out of childhood.

I could not give Robert another son. I was past my bearing

years, and in any case I did not have the strength for another arduous labor. The travails of childbirth were past, but the travails of mourning had come upon me, and I would not soon put them aside.

CHIRTY-SEVEN

IT was high summer, young Chris Blount, our handsome new Master of the Horse, was overseeing the redesign of our stables and also having a sundial made for my pleasure. I sat in the garden amid the roses, inert, lost in my thoughts, feeling very alone.

When young Chris brought me violets I smiled and thanked him, but absentmindedly. I was no longer present to the world, something was pulling me deep within myself, so deep I was all but unaware of my surroundings. The heat clung to the stones, the lizards slithered along the old walls and baked there, eyes half-lidded, until driven to dart away to shelter under the roof. The fish in the pond took refuge from the glare of the sun under broad wet leaves. But I, motionless and silent, sought no shade. I sat where I was until the sky clouded over and rain began plashing in the birdbath. Mistress Clinkerte appeared then, clucking her tongue and chiding me for being so careless, for letting the rain ruin my gown and the sun my complexion, and led me indoors.

In truth I no longer cared how I looked. My once vibrant auburn hair was fading and my skin, which had been rosy and surprisingly free of lines for so long, had begun to show faint wrinkles and had lost its glow. Dr. Julio brought me a tincture of St. John's wort, which he assured me was sovereign against melancholy and sleeplessness (I slept very badly just then), but I could not detect any change, and soon stopped taking it. Besides, I was uneasy taking any medicine from Dr. Julio's hand; there had been too many sinister rumors about him and the dark purposes to which his skills had been applied.

I sat by the hour listening to the steady soft hush of the rain, listless and idle. Eventually I went to bed, and fell into a troubled sleep, haunted by the notion that I had lost a vital part of myself and that I was, in memorable words I had once read, "a body without a soul."

Small, daily, necessary tasks brought me back temporarily from my listless state: attending to the wandering beggars who came to the door, thin and pale and anxious, asking for bread (I fed them all, always, at our table and sent them away with full baskets of bread and fruit), the old ostringer from Hampton Court who came to live in one of our cottages, his skin paper-thin, his voice cracked and broken, who was ill and needed medicine, the match proposed for Penelope, with all the legal questions it raised concerning portions and jointures and inheritances.

And then there was young Rob, my strapping, good-looking dark-eyed son, my dear child of the Evening Star, so concerned about me and so attentive in the time following little Denbigh's death. Rob was eighteen, an outstanding student at Cambridge, as yet unmarried and full of ambition like his stepfather. It was hard to believe this gifted boy was the son of dull Walter, he shone with such charm and easy grace. Not for him his father's tedious listmaking! He hovered near me, bringing me my cloak or my book (though I could not manage to read anything), making sure I had my posset or my tincture, trying to lure me into conversation, to shake off my brooding.

Rob was set on going to court, serving the queen, and making his name in the world, and was eager to talk to me about this, but because of her animus against me Elizabeth would not allow him near her. He showed admirable patience, I thought, confident that, with the threat from the Spanish growing greater, she would summon him to her service before long.

Meanwhile my dear husband was laboring under his own season of grief. He went for long solitary walks, accompanied only by his dog Boy, his favorite hound, his long face as sad as the hound's, limping on his sore swollen foot, his temper short and when he spoke, which was rarely, his tone querulous. I barely saw him for days on end, and when he did seek me out, it was to tell me that he was thinking seriously of retiring altogether from the queen's service.

"It is just too much, Lettie, far too much, at my age and with my infirmities," he remarked one morning while being treated by a costly bonesetter he had heard of, one Ezard, from Paris. He sat with his leg elevated, his large red foot exposed, as the bonesetter applied a stinking paste to his engorged toes.

"All the piles of letters and reports to read—more than ever now that the number of spies and informants has grown so great—and all the endless wrangles with Burghley and his crookbacked son on the council, and with your father, who crosses me on everything! And forever keeping the queen soothed, amused, making her feel as if all the best ideas are hers. Oh, I tell you, it is not a task fit for a slave, much less an aging lord like me! And I have been at it these twenty-five years and more!"

I sat by quietly, letting him go on uninterrupted, knowing he needed to talk.

"Pardon, milord," the bonesetter was saying, "but I must ask you, when did this most recent attack of the swelling begin?"

"I fell off Roan Gallant, my Irish galloper. After that I could not even pull my boot on. Ten or fifteen days ago, is that right Lettie?"

I nodded. "The pain comes on worst at night. He cries out in his sleep. His head is hot too, and he cannot make water."

"He cannot make water?"

"He tries, but there is only a dribble."

"Botheration, Lettie, I can speak for myself!"

"Pardon, milord, but if you cannot—relieve yourself—then you may need a surgeon—"

"None of that, thank you! All I need is for you to make the swelling in my foot go down, so I can get my boot on, and ride to Buxton, where the baths always do me good."

The bonesetter, frowning, said no more, but I could tell he thought Robert was dismissing his ailment too lightly. I knew better than to speak up, however; like the Frenchman, I frowned and held my tongue. Trying to sway Robert would only lead to frustration and would not do him any good.

The bonesetter began smearing goat's grease on the red foot, making Robert squirm and then swear loudly.

"If you prefer, milord, I can cut a vein. Or there are the leeches—"

"No! Get on with it! Ah! Ow!"

Finally, after half an hour of pain and loud protests, Monsieur Ezard completed his ministrations and drew forth from his bag a sealed vessel.

"A cupful, every day," he told Robert. "It will greatly help the swelling and the pain."

"What is it?"

"Worms, pig marrow, herbs and a secret ingredient known only to myself."

"I won't eat worms," Robert said flatly. "I have had worm piss prescribed to me before."

"This is not to eat. It is a balm. You will use it. And you will feel better." Even as I said this I thought, making sure you take your medicine will help me. Will give me something more to do, and cause me to brood less too.

With a bow, the bonesetter presented Robert with his bill.

"Lettie! Where are my eyeglasses?"

I found them and brought them to him.

"What's this? Thirty pounds, for some goat's grease and worms?"

"For my expert knowledge and advice, milord."

Robert looked dubious, but agreed to the sum, telling the Frenchman to present his bill to the steward.

Monsieur Ezard bowed again. "As soon as I receive payment, I shall send the secret ingredient," he remarked as he left the room.

"Damn the French!" was Robert's response. "And the Germans and the Burgundians and the Walloons, and the Flemish, and the damnable Spanish above all!"

Robert was far from at his best, as a husband or lover or companion. Our marriage required much compromise and understanding from me, and though I did my best to provide it, I could not help feeling, in those dark days after the loss of our son, that too much was being asked of me.

Though I hesitate to write it, the truth was that I sometimes thought Robert and I had waited too long to marry. That by the time we married, even though we knew much happiness together, Robert's best years were behind him. The queen and Douglass Sheffield had his best love, and I was being given the dregs.

Naturally I thought this most often when Robert was at his worst, feeling his age and in pain. I always loved him, I was devoted to him. But I was more and more aware that I was married to a man long past his prime, and I wished, selfishly, that I had had more years of the stronger, healthier, more playful Robert at my side. I was only forty-three when little Denbigh died, and Robert was much older.

It was not only the swelling in his foot and other ailments that brought my selfish, ungenerous thoughts to the fore. His body was changing in other ways. His handsome face was much more lined, his cheeks pouchy. His mouth often turned down at the corners, like the queen's did when she was at her most disapproving. He was losing his hair. And his skin, that skin that had once been so extraordinarily soft, smooth, inviting to the touch, had become dry and puckered. His stomach, while not fat, had a growing bulge, and his limbs were not the supple, shapely limbs of—of, for instance, our new young Master of the Horse Chris, who had the body of an Adonis.

I know that my disloyal thoughts (if so they might be called) were brought on in part by my own low spirits, yet they plagued me then. I prayed to be lifted out of my despond, and in time, thanks in part to events around me, I was restored to my former self. Gradually Robert too found his way back to a sort of contentment, though the scar of our joint loss with the death of little Denbigh went deep, and never fully healed.

What began to bring Robert out of his grief was a project he had long been working at, a project close to his heart.

For many years, ever since Robert had fought alongside his two brothers Henry and Ambrose at the Battle of St. Quentin and had seen Henry fatally struck with a cannonball, he had been concerned with the plight of elderly soldiers, especially those left injured and unable to serve. There were many in want of care, and since the closing of the monasteries by Elizabeth's father there were no longer hospitals run by the monks to provide for them. Robert was slowly building a hospital in Warwick, though he had never been able to spare much time to oversee the works. He now roused himself to complete the building, and by the time winter came he had achieved his task.

Eighty old men, all survivors of the wars, some who had gone with King Henry to fight the French in the long ago 1540s, took up residence in Robert's hospital, to receive care and treatment at the hands of skilled physicians and apothecaries. Robert dedicated the hospital to his late brother, and put a commemorative stone by the gate.

"To my beloved brother Henry Dudley," it read, "whose valor was proven in battle and whose memory shall never die. May all who serve be forever honored and cared for."

I thought it a worthy endeavor, and told Robert so. I did not mention the cost. My husband was extravagant, and always had been. He borrowed against our lands to build his hospital, and endow it for the future. Would the debts ever be repaid? I had my doubts. We always had moneylenders at our gates. Somehow Robert and his bankers managed to keep them satisfied—temporarily. He never spoke to me of money matters, and I had learned not to ask.

It was when Robert told me that he was going to London to witness the execution of the queen's would-be assassin that I knew he had fully thrown off his grieving and sour bad temper.

"They are going to kill the sniveling Welshman," he announced. "And I intend to be there to see it. Do you know, Lettie, the pope himself promised to pay the man handsomely if he murdered the queen! And promised him forgiveness too—in the eyes of the Catholics, of course."

I urged him to go, to see justice done. All the members of his

Bond of Association would be there, he said. In strength. As a warning to the many Catholics in England who still hoped that Protestantism would be overturned and put their faith in Queen Elizabeth's cousin Mary Stuart, who carried the blood royal of the house of Tudor in her veins.

Robert rode off, with a strong band of soldiers as escort, and I watched him go, rain pelting down and the road a bog under his horse's hooves. I knew it was what he needed to do, despite his talk of retirement from the queen's service. Just as I knew, soon afterward, how he would respond to the summons that arrived at Wanstead in his absence—a summons from Elizabeth, appointing him Captain General of her forces being sent to the Dutch provinces, to lead the fight against the menacing armies of Spain.

THIRTY-EIGHT

ROBERT'S spirits could not have been higher when he went aboard his flagship for the journey to Sluys. The queen had forbidden me to see him off but I went anyway, and we shared a final hug and kiss before he stepped into the longboat that rowed him to his vessel, the *Albion Triumphant*.

I was sending him off with a trunk full of new linen shirts and the black silk nightcaps that kept his ears warm in cold weather. Beyond that he had his bathing tub, dozens of soft towels and a looking-glass. There was even a new coach in which he planned to ride among his troops when he celebrated their victories.

I sent him off in all his finery, his cloak, doublet and breeches of blue and purple velvet lined with scarlet, his tall black hat with blue and purple plumes, his perfumed gloves trimmed in black silk and gold.

He was a splendid sight as he waved to me from the deck of

his ship, colorful banners fluttering from the halyards, flags flying from the masthead, the ship's great culverins thundering a salute that shattered the still morning air.

A loud shout went up from the onlookers as the queen's barge rowed out, delivering her to the *Albion Triumphant* to join Robert for the first part of his journey, the voyage downriver to Canterbury. As I watched, he received her on board, presenting her with a gift of blue and purple garters trimmed in gold. He had shown them to me before we left Wanstead, saying "She'll like these. She loves garters," and trying one on for size, making me laugh.

I went on watching and waving until the ship rounded a bend and hove out of sight, her fleet of companion vessels following. I hoped all would go well for Robert and his men—five thousand footsoldiers and a thousand mounted men—and in particular, for two of his men, my dear Rob and Chris, our Master of the Horse who had become Rob's friend and fellow soldier.

The two boys—I still thought of them as boys—looked strong and stalwart as they embarked, along with the aging Whaffer, who had offered himself as their servant and horse groom. They were high-hearted and optimistic about the outcome of the invasion, joking about how they were going to make short work of the Spaniards and be back in a few brief months, before their armor could rust or their horses' manes needed trimming.

Despite the jests and bravado, I knew that the threat to England's security was very real. My father had been saying so for years, and the majority of those in the royal council agreed. The Spanish King Philip had come to dominate much of the globe, with his vast territories in the New World, his rule over Naples and Sicily and Milan, and his dominance in the Low

Countries. With the recent conquest of Portugal, he acquired that country's farflung empire—plus a large navy and a great many skilled mariners.

So I had heard—and until recently I had also heard that our queen was very reluctant to go to war. But now she had changed her mind. She had decided to challenge Philip in the area where he was most vulnerable, the rebellious Dutch provinces that owed him allegiance but fought him at every turn. If English arms could shore up the Dutch rebels, then perhaps the Spanish menace could be reversed.

For a month I waited impatiently for a letter from Robert, and when one came I devoured it at once. He wrote at length (how did he have time, I wondered) of the joyous reception given the English troops by the Protestant Dutch. Of how he might have been the Messiah Himself, so great was the shouting, the adoration, the noisy celebrating that greeted him in every town and village.

"Save us, good Lord Leicester, save us!" the people called out, making him burst into tears.

The tears, I knew, were more from exhaustion than emotion. My Robert was surely driving himself too hard, forcing every last ounce of strength from his aging body. It was his way, he could not stop himself.

I went on reading the letter. Its tone turned from elation to apprehension. He wrote of the sorry state of the Dutch provinces, once thriving and prosperous, with green fields and bustling harbors full of ships, now a weedy wasteland, the harbors silted up, the ships empty and rotting at their moorings.

"I fear I cannot save them, the good Dutch Protestants," he wrote. "I fast and pray, I sing psalms with them, to show I am sincerely on their side. But they quarrel among themselves. And we are constantly short of supplies."

He wrote that my young Rob was acquitting himself very well, and had been given a command of his own, and that Chris too was proving to be a strong and courageous fighter (and brawler, he added) and that old Whaffer, robust and spry despite his age, was the only one in the company who never got sick and never complained.

Robert's letter made me want to join him, there in Flanders, to shore him up in his discouragement. But of course I did not dare. Even if I tried to make the crossing alone, in secret— perhaps taking Mistress Clinkerte with me as my attendant—my presence would soon be discovered by the queen's spies. Robert would be blamed. He would be made to suffer. So I stayed at Wanstead, waiting for more news.

While waiting I was distracted by events in my family. My lovely Penelope married the brash, self-important Lord Rich, a tall, burly man of large appetites who tended to muscle others aside and whose shouts of command to his servants seemed to sing out through every room in our thirty-five-room manor. He was as rich as his name, though poor, I could not help thinking, in kindness and generosity of spirit. Robert didn't care for him but thought him an excellent match for the strong-willed Penelope, as he could both bring her a title and keep her in check. After a few rebellious outbursts she agreed to marry him, and the wedding went forward. Before two years had passed they had two children, two boys, and Penelope was pregnant again—and repenting her choice of husband.

Meanwhile there was another wedding in the family, this one unexpected. My dear Dorothy, whose sweet, compliant nature had only grown more affectionate over the years, surprised us all by marrying her longtime love Ned Mudge, a common mariner without lands or a title or any prospect of acquiring even modest wealth.

We had known for some time that they were sweethearts. But Robert had forbidden Ned to see Dorothy and sent him away. As Dorothy never mentioned him after that, we assumed their infatuation had ended. Yet Ned had not gone very far away, only to the next village and Dorothy continued to meet him in secret. Finally, amid the bustle of preparations for Penelope's rather grand wedding, Dorothy had slipped away to join Ned and they had gone together to the village church where a sympathetic priest married them, braving Robert's wrath.

Dorothy's courageous, impetuous act took me entirely by surprise. My fiery, self-willed Penelope had always been the one to follow her own daring path, yet in the end she agreed to make a conventional choice in marrying Lord Rich, while Dorothy thrust convention aside and married for love. Her bravery humbled me; I had after all married Walter, the partner my father chose for me, and a man I never loved. Only late in life did I find the daring to marry the man my heart led me to—and then only because it was what he wanted, what he made possible. Ned Mudge was no Robert Dudley, to be sure. He was just a strong, quiet, affectionate man who I knew instinctively would always stand by my daughter and take care of her, however humbly they lived.

Did Dorothy, in the end, make the wiser choice? I came to think so, though at the time she suffered much criticism and I was blamed for not preventing the perceived tragedy of their wedding.

I was dismayed as well as surprised by what happened, but not angry. I knew what it was to follow my heart. I only prayed that Dorothy would not, in time, regret being plain Mistress Mudge while her passionate, beautiful sister was Lady Rich living in a grand manor house. But Dorothy was not inclined to be envious, and when she and Ned came to me to admit what they had done and ask my blessing, and she held out her hand with the modest gold ring to show me, I could see how proud she was and how much love she felt for Ned, who clearly treasured her.

They were full of hope for their future life together. Not for them the dour predictions of death and destruction and the fall of empires. They seemed wrapped in a protective mantle of love—or so I saw them, through a thick veil of sentiment. Love would keep them safe, no matter what darkness fell upon the world.

And darkness there surely was. The news from Flanders was growing more ominous. Robert wrote of desertions among his men, brought on by hunger and lack of warm clothing, of the quarrelsomeness of the stubborn Dutch and the rising costs of warmaking and the sadly high numbers of English dead. Valiant dead, he wrote. So many fine men lost, their lives sacrificed in what seemed to be a losing cause.

The land, the canals and rivers that snaked through it, the very skies seemed to be turning against the English, Robert wrote. He cursed the incessant rain and cold, the quagmire underfoot, with horses sinking up to their gaskins in mud and the weeping clouds drenching men, animals and equipment alike.

"The damnable guns won't fire, Lettie," he wrote. "We can't keep them dry. Our armor rusts on our backs, no one does what they promise to do, all is lies and blame and rot!" he went on, his bitterness fairly burning off the page.

He asked me to send him more shirts and six pairs of thigh-high boots, and confessed with chagrin that his splendid new coach had sunk beneath the mire of the Sluys marshes, never to be seen again. His poor swollen foot was giving him great pain, and he had run out of goat's grease to assuage it. (He did not mention Monsieur Ezard's worm tonic, but he did not need to.)

Robert saved his most caustic words for Roger Wilbraham who, he insisted, was undermining the entire English venture by his corruption and outright theft. Instead of using his posts as master armorer for the port of Sluys and Master of the Queen's Ships to buy arquebuses and pikes, powder and ball, salt fish and rice and oil, "the rogue Wilbraham," as Robert called him, was keeping the money from the queen's treasury for himself. Meanwhile more men and horses were falling sick and dying and the Dutch cause, like the ill-fated coach, was sinking into the mire. Which meant that the hated Spaniards were coming closer to achieving their goal of conquering England.

It was the valuable commodity called the white eagle, the saltpeter necessary to fire the gunpowder, that aroused Robert's worst fury. The rogue Wilbraham, he wrote, was rumored to be taking all the stores of white eagle and selling it to the enemy. "To the enemy!" He underlined the hated words. "They say his son Sebastian smuggles it to England and hides it in a cave somewhere near Fowey. From there the Spanish ships come ashore to buy it, protected by local Catholics who want to see Elizabeth overthrown and Mary Queen of Scots reign in her place.

"Oh Lettie, I am surrounded by treachery here. Nothing but treachery."

I hardly had time to react to Robert's doleful letter when I heard a furious galloping and then shouts in the courtyard beneath my windows. I looked out and saw a man being carried into the house. My first thought was, is it Robert? Has he been badly hurt? Have they brought him home to die?

I rushed down the stairs and into the entryway and saw, at once, that the man being carried, moaning, in through the wide doorway was not Robert.

I felt enormous relief—and then concern. For as I came closer I saw that I was looking into the ashen face of young Chris Blount, whose torn shirt was covered in blood and who was being laid on a table, dying, before my eyes.

THIRTY-NINE

HIS brow was wide and high, his lips bow-shaped and soft, like the lips of a child. He had the face of a noble Roman. A noble nose, with a high prominent bridge, and his eyes, when he opened them on the third day after he was brought to Wanstead, were a deep unfocused blue. He was still very pale, but a little color had come into his cheeks, and his voice, when he struggled to speak, was unmistakably Chris's voice, the voice I had so often heard saying solicitous things. May I bring out your cloak, milady? Shall I move the bench closer into the shade for you, milady?

I had thought for certain that he would die, but his underlying strength, the strength and vigor of youth, saved him. Or perhaps, as I thought later, it was at least in part my care of him during those critical days that saved him.

For just as I had with little Denbigh, I sat by his bedside, making certain that his wound—a terrible wound, a deep gash in his chest and side from a musket ball, red and swollen and oozing a stinking liquid—was tended properly and often by the French bonesetter Monsieur Ezard, who had joined our household and was available to attend to any and all illnesses. Someone was always ill, as our household was large—well over a hundred servants—and Robert and I believed in offering care not only to our servants but to their families when needed.

I sat beside Chris, looking down into his handsome face, keeping a cool wet cloth on his hot forehead—he had a dreadful fever—and saying my prayers. My prayers were answered on that memorable third day, when for the first time Chris opened his eyes and spoke a few words.

"Don't mother him too much," Mistress Clinkerte said tartly when she passed in and out of the chamber where Chris had been laid in an ornately carved, wide oaken bed. "And don't forget that you are a married woman, even if your husband is far away!"

I rebuked her sharply for her suggestive words, implying that my care for Chris arose from a deeper emotion than concern for a sick member of our household. Yet her remark worried me a little, for she knew me well, and I wondered, in my sleepless state, whether she might be right. Was I more attached to the patient than I ought to be? But no, if Robert were home, he would kiss me and tell me he admired my dedication and care. He would not reprimand me, or hint that I was giving the handsome patient undue attention.

Over the following days, as Chris began to recover, he talked more and more. I was eager for him to tell me all the news of my husband and son. But sensing that thinking of the warfare and the hardships he had endured might upset him and slow his recovery, I encouraged him to tell me about his family instead, which he seemed eager enough to do.

His father, he said, was a landless knight, a poor relation of the Blount family whose most notorious member had been Bessie Blount, mistress of Henry VIII. Bessie had been honored with the title Mother of the King's Son because her boy Henry had been considered the king's likely heir. But young Henry had died before he reached the age of twenty, and Bessie had retired into obscurity in the countryside.

"We are poor relations of the Blounts," Chris said with a smile, adding that his father was long dead and his mother, without resources of her own, lived in Exeter with a distant relative who housed her out of charity.

"So you see there is nothing distinguished in me or my lineage," he said.

"But you are an honored soldier," was my response, "and a veteran of the wars."

"And your husband Lord Leicester has given me the post of Master of the Horse to all his forces. He rewarded me after the Battle of Hondschoote. The post comes with a salary, or at least it will, when payment is finally made. None of us have been paid for months."

These last words were uttered in an undertone. I was aware, from Robert's letters, that his men were in want of pay, and had been for at least a year, while they fought the seemingly endless battles in Flanders.

"Not that I am complaining, milady. It's just that we need our pay. We have not eaten well in a long time."

"Is Robert—Lord Leicester—very thin?"

"I'm sorry to tell you, milady, but yes. He has shared our hardships. He is like a skeleton—but such a lively, energetic skeleton! You should have seen how he labored when we were trying to help the Dutch hold Sluys against the Spaniards. He was everywhere at once. You should have seen him! He never slept, he just worked, making sure each of the guns was placed just where he wanted it, and checking each of the supply depots, sailing around every inch of the harbor, checking the tides and currents and plotting where the shoals were and how they could be avoided. He supervised the sounding and marking of the entire main channel, and some of the side channels too. Nothing escaped him. He even checked the fit of our blue and purple uniforms, and—"

I stopped the flow of Chris's excited words by putting my hand over his, lightly. I did not want him to exert himself too much. But as my hand brushed his, I could not help but gasp. For at the touch I felt a burst of heat, as if a tiny tongue of flame had leapt up. I quickly drew my hand away, and forced a bland smile of reassurance.

"I know I would have been proud of him," I murmured. "He always did have the most remarkable energy."

Chris was looking at me as if stunned. I was suddenly certain that he too had felt that spurt of heat that passed between us. He was wide-eyed. Perhaps, I thought, he doesn't know what this means. What to make of it.

I let the moment pass and, getting up from my bedside perch, pretended to busy myself looking through the papers on a nearby table.

"Robert writes to me often," I remarked. "In his letters he says that the paymasters are dishonest."

I turned to look at Chris, who nodded.

"Very well then. I will gather what funds I can and find someone to take them to Sluys. To try to make up some of the arrears in wages."

"Not to Sluys, milady. Sluys is lost. As is Antwerp, and Zutphen, and a dozen other towns we tried to defend."

I felt the color drain from my face. Sluys is lost, I thought. Then surely all is lost. Sluys was the most important town in

Flanders, the town that had to be held at all costs, if the Spanish threat was to be averted.

Robert had told me before he left that it was at Sluys that the great fleet of Spanish barges was going to congregate, barges to be filled with thousands of soldiers and equipment. From there, guarded by a massive fleet of Spanish and Portuguese galleons and merchantmen and smaller vessels, the invading army would cross the Channel and land, their landing made safe by an immense barrage of culverin fire from the guardian fleet.

It was a terrifying vision, a vision of disaster. And now, it seemed, there was no way to prevent it.

FORTY

CHRIS saw my distress at once.

"It was all about the white eagle, milady," he said, his voice low and confiding. "And there is still hope that even though the great towns have been lost, the battle to come may be won."

"I don't understand."

"No, of course you don't. Let me tell you how we came to lose the town, and then you will see."

"Are you sure it won't tax your strength too much, to revive terrible memories of strain and conflict and loss?"

But he only smiled. "Old soldiers love to tell how they got their wounds. Even if they are only thirty-two."

So that's how old he is, I thought. I assumed he was much younger. I was forty-five myself, and feeling my years. Though when I was with Chris I felt at my youngest.

"Well then, as I said, it was all about the white eagle, the precious stuff that mixes with the gunpowder to make it explode."

"The saltpeter, you mean." I knew about saltpeter from hearing Robert talk to his officers about it when discussing military supplies.

"We call it white eagle, because when it heats up, it becomes a puff of white smoke and flies off, as if it had wings. There's never enough of it, we always run short, and it costs the earth— 'the stuff's like diamonds,' Lord Leicester always says—and what happened was, he found out that the rogue Wilbraham had gotten hold of most of our reserve supply of white eagle from our camp and was going to sell it to the Spaniards."

"What?"

I sat back down beside Chris and listened intently to what he was saying.

"We had been guarding the waters and marshes around Sluys for months, and had nearly managed to keep the town from falling to the Spaniards, but then, well, we lost too many men, and a lot of them had deserted anyway, not being paid nor fed, and we could see the end coming. The town was in shambles, with no one to protect it but the local burghers and some Walloon volunteers. We couldn't protect the entire harbor, we had too few ships, and besides, all manner of treachery was going on there. People running through the streets and along the quays. Everybody trying to save or steal what they could and hiding everything in cellars and holes in the ground. We could hardly tell the soldiers from the townspeople. All the shouting and rioting! I tell you, milady, it was terrible.

"Then we heard somebody yelling 'Fire! Fire!' and sure enough we saw fire shooting up from part of the town wall. It seemed like half the citizens came running out all at once, trying to escape the fire, with their arms full of treasure and their children tagging at their heels and crying. Oh, I tell you, that town of Sluys was ripe for the plucking.

"Come nightfall, Lord Leicester and his chief officers were on the *Albion Triumphant*. Rob and I were there with the others. Just then one of the watchmen set up a signal that Sebastian Wilbraham's galliot was coming out along a side channel. She was heavy in the water.

"Now, the rogue Wilbraham's son Sebastian was well known to us as he was smuggling goods back and forth between Sluys and the English coast. At first we thought he was helping us, being paid by the queen's agents. But then, later, Lord Leicester found out from his spies that Sebastian was a traitor, like his father. He was being paid by the Spanish to steal our stores and sail them to hidden coves on the English shore where English traitors—Catholics—were waiting to unload them—"

"To prepare for the invasion," I interrupted. "The invasion Robert told me the Spanish are planning."

Chris nodded.

"So the white eagle, as you call it, was sold to the Spanish to be stored on the coast, so it would be ready for the invading army to use."

"Lord Leicester was sure that the galliot was riding low in the water because her hold was full of the stolen white eagle. He was determined to pursue her and recapture it.

"We did our best, but it was dark, and the tides were running high and the whole mass of marsh and tidelands was like a huge pot on the boil. Big waves, higher than our masts, some of them, were coming at us from all directions, it seemed. And to make everything worse, it was raining. It rained and rained and rained. Such rain as only happens in Flanders, I'm guessing. As if all the sluice gates in the world had opened at once and the waters came gushing out."

"What did you do?"

Chris raised his eyebrows and shook his head, as if in disbelief at the memory of the chaos of that night.

"All of a sudden it seemed that the Spanish were everywhere. All around us. As if they had been waiting for us. We could hear the thunder of their guns, though how they could fire in the midst of such a downpour I could not imagine.

"We did our best to fire back. Rob, your brave son, helped the gunners load the culverins and aim them, even though the Spanish batteries were trained right on him. It was a wonder Rob survived that night. Shot was flying all around him. All around us. The noise, the rain, the smoke—we were all coughing and spitting. As for me, the last thing I remember was lifting shot to a gunner when a white-hot torch passed through my chest. I must have fainted. Next thing I knew, I was here at Wanstead."

The look he gave me was full of gratitude, and warmth, and unmistakable admiration. "With you, milady."

"I'm so glad you survived it all," was all I said, and I was quick to add, "and Robert will be very glad to see you when he comes home. He is on his way. The queen has summoned him. She has rewarded him with the post of Lord Steward Her Majesty's Lieutenant Against Foreign Invasion."

"An impressive title indeed."

"And a great responsibility. The defense of all England will soon be in Robert's hands."

FORTY-ONE

HE Year of Doom broke over us like a storm, harsh squalls of alarums spreading throughout the kingdom.

The cry went up from Milford that the Spanish had landed, thousands strong, and that their deadly cannon were being hauled up into the Welsh hills and their murderous soldiers were marching south toward London.

Voices from the north shouted that the whole countryside around York was in revolt, and that the Catholics were going to take over the kingdom, even though their champion, Mary Stuart, had at last been executed and the realm freed of her menacing presence. Reports came from the capital that the queen was dead and the entire city engulfed in flames.

No one knew what to believe. Had the Spaniards killed the queen? Or had she fled? Were the last days of the world come upon humankind, as had been predicted these many years? Would there soon be, as predicted, a sign in the heavens—a rare second eclipse of the moon—that would mark the beginning of the end?

At Wanstead, the servants were abuzz with rumors and tales they heard in the village, and with each fresh rumor I did my best to stay calm and counsel patience and common sense. Despite my efforts, our household was being depleted; dozens of our grooms and valets and maids deserted the manor to take refuge where they could, some in isolated villages far to the north of us, others in caves in the distant hills, all frightened into believing that the farther away they were from others—and especially from the court and capital—the safer they would be when the moment of doom arrived.

When there was a monstrous birth in the nearby village a fresh wave of fear caused havoc among our servants. A baby was born with two heads and four arms and legs, and the midwife, in terror, took it into the parish church where the parishioners ran screaming into the cemetery and fell on their knees in dread.

"It is a sign!" Mistress Clinkerte announced to all who would listen, her eyes wide with fear. "The end is coming closer!"

Certainly the enemy was coming closer. The Dutch coast was after all only a few hours' sail from the beaches of England and the Spanish were there in force, set to embark their tens of thousands of men by barge and prepared, it was said, to cross the Channel in a single night. The trained bands, local militias, were arming and marching every morning, people were buying guns and swords, armor and gunpowder (all of which went way up in price) and it was said that anyone who possessed gold was hoarding it, in anticipation of the terrible slaughter and chaos to come.

I found it very hard to sleep in those tense days. The very air seemed thick with dread. People's behavior changed. They avoided one another's glance, hardly spoke, acted as if under threat. Uneasiness prevailed.

Even the elements seemed to be giving us the message that nothing was as it had been. Unseasonable weather broke down upon us, thunderstorms, downpours, ferocious winds that tore at the budding plants, preventing them from coming into their spring bloom. The trees in our orchards were bare of new fruit. Come harvest, I thought, there will be no fruit, no crops. Nothing to gather into our barns. But then, perhaps there will be no harvest season this year, because time will have ceased altogether and our lives will be over.

I tried to stay close to the manor, as I was still looking after Chris in his recovery and taking more than my usual share of responsibility for the running of the household and lands. But when I did go out, I could not help but notice that the roads were full of carts and mounted riders, some grim-faced and galloping in furious haste, others merely looking forlorn and uncertain as they loped along. Whole families were on the move, their possessions piled on the backs of beasts, their children riding precariously on plodding nags. Some of these wanderers came to our door, and I gave them what I could, doing my best to ease their fears, all the while knowing I was not heeded.

Robert had returned from Flanders some months earlier, limping badly and, I thought, much aged. He was filled with rancor, mollified only slightly by the queen's granting of his grandiose title as Lord Steward Her Majesty's Lieutenant Against Foreign Invasion. He complained that though the title sounded very important, it was in fact no more meaningful than the title she had given her Frog, her French wooer, a few years earlier—Defender of the Liberties of the Low Countries Against Spanish Tyranny. She gave words, he complained, but did not give adequate treasure to go with them.

Most of all, Robert felt aggrieved—deeply wounded, in fact—by what he called Elizabeth's betrayal. He had discovered, to his horror, that all the while he had been leading his men against the Spanish in Flanders she had been negotiating in secret with the enemy behind his back. Negotiating to end the fighting and bargaining with the lives of the English soldiers in a vain attempt to arrive at a truce. She was undermining everything he did—and every sacrifice his gallant soldiers and mariners were making. The belief that she had broken his efforts was like a rapier to the belly, he said. It was plain to me that Elizabeth had exploited Robert's vanity—was still exploiting his vanity—while robbing him of the glory he sought, the glory of victory. And leaving him hollowed out inside, bereft of trust and eaten up with resentment.

There was no use my reminding him that the queen's mind and strategies were unfathomable, built up of layer upon layer of subtleties. That negotiation—devious, treacherous negotiation— had always been her prime skill. Robert knew this as well as I did, yet when he found out that he, the commander of her forces, had been no more than a pawn on her chessboard of deceit, the realization shattered him.

He blamed Elizabeth, and not his own military shortcomings, for the failure of the campaign. Even as he prepared for the onslaught yet to come, the arrival of the major Spanish invasion force, his grievance continued to rankle, causing him to pay far less attention to me and to the wellbeing of our lands and dependents. He had been given the responsibility to prepare the headquarters of the royal defensive forces at Tilbury, on the Thames south of London, and as the spring came on he spent nearly all his time there, overseeing the convergence of the trained bands in the burgeoning military camp, and laying in stocks of arms, including a treasure trove of two hundred and eighty old bows that had belonged to his father, discovered by chance as he was rummaging among long-forgotten stores.

"If only we had had these in Zutphen," I heard him mutter. "We might have won there, the tide might have turned."

I knew better than to pester him or disturb his errant thoughts. I left him to his musings, and was not entirely sorry when he left for Tilbury, as his dour presence had darkened the atmosphere in our home and made all the other difficulties we faced harder to deal with.

My brother Frank had been with Robert during his Flanders campaign, as captain of his own galleon, the *Marianna*, bought with purloined Spanish gold. In the present crisis Robert had given Frank the responsibility of supervising the coastal defenses, and before setting off to begin this task, he came to Wanstead to see me.

Tall, lean, and commanding in appearance, his dark hair beginning to be flecked with grey, my dear brother looked every inch the admiral as he strode through Wanstead's wide entrance. Francis Drake had in fact created him Rear Admiral, an honor reserved for few men. I was very proud of him, and told him so as we embraced. Chris, who seemed never to be far from me in those days, greeted Frank whom he had known in Flanders. I saw Frank look quickly from Chris to me and back again, a look full of speculation. Had he guessed that Chris was more to me than a guest, and a close friend of my son's?

"Come and have something to eat," I said, taking Frank's hand and leading him to the long oak table. "I expect you are hungry."

He sat down somewhat wearily and sighed. "I had a very tiring ride," he admitted, "and a plate of food and a tankard of your best ale would not come amiss."

Chris excused himself to let us talk.

"Lettie, I've come at father's request. He is at Tilbury with Robert, and is gathering the family there. He thinks you will all be safest if you stay under the protection of the soldiers. If you will gather your things, we can go as soon as I fill my belly."

I thought a moment, then agreed. I went to call for Mistress Clinkerte and told her to pack a small trunk. Meanwhile I put on my riding clothes and boots.

"What about the servants?" I asked when I returned to the dining room. "Those that are left, I mean—we have lost so many, some to serve in the militias, of course, but most because they have simply run off."

"Chris will stay here, will he not? That is, if you can spare him." Frank winked.

"He would be at Tilbury himself, if not for his injury," I said stiffly. "He nearly died, aboard the *Albion Triumphant* when Robert was pursuing the traitor Wilbraham. As you probably know."

"I know what I know," was Frank's enigmatic reply. To my relief, he said nothing further about Chris but ate enthusiastically and rapidly, clearly eager to be back on the road. We were soon mounted and riding off amid Frank's escort of mariners and soldiers. As we went along Frank told me what had transpired in recent days with the Spanish fleet—all of which came as a revelation to me, as we had had no reliable news since Robert's departure for Tilbury Camp.

"We were waiting in the Plymouth roads, the most part of Drake's squadron, when word came that the Most Fortunate Fleet—that's what the Spanish call it—had been seen by watchers off Penzance. Right away we saw the beacon fires, blazing away all up the coast as far as we could see. We waited for the ships to come our way, and met them there in the roads, and took them on.

"How they fought! Especially the Portuguese, in their immense carracks, standing high and rocking mightily with each wave. The Portuguese ships were the best of the lot, they would not give up, no matter how many holes we blew in their sides! The wreckage from those ships . . . the sea was filled with spars and masts and shredded sails. And bodies too, though the mariners of that fleet gathered their own, and saved many.

"The greatships of the fleet were heavier than ours, but ours were faster, and we kept them always to windward, so they were never able to run in toward our coast, not even the pinnaces. We chased them up the Channel, and fought them again off Portland Bill, and then again off the Isle of Wight. Drake in the *Revenge* was fierce and daring, but the *Marianna* was often in the van, I had her fitted with culverins that could throw a nineteen-pounder right onto their decks at a thousand yards.

"They hove off toward the French coast and we followed, until we had them trapped before Gravelines. I tell you, Lettie, that was a grand day! We brought so many of them down, and would have taken many prizes but a storm blew up and the wind changed and they got away before we could run them up onto the banks. They were lucky! I brought the *Marianna* back south as I was ordered to do, but most of the others in our squadron stayed on beating northward in pursuit. The Channel is full of ships, but the Most Fortunate Fleet has suffered much, that I can say for certain."

I looked over at Frank, wanting to tell him once again how proud I was of him, but knowing that he would only wave my praise aside. Unlike Robert, he did not seek the glory of victory or success, but to carry out the task, and to carry it out well and thoroughly. I thought, not for the first time, what a fine man my brother was. Yet even as he recounted his adventures I noticed that he still carried the mark of sorrow on his features. The old sadness from his youth, that had never left him. He was a widower, but had never loved his late wife, theirs had been a partnership based solely on commerce, the commerce of the sea. His heart had always belonged to the girl for whom his ship was named, his long lost Marianna.

"It sounds as though you have them on the run, like frightened hares," I said. "And what of the hundreds of barges full of Spanish footsoldiers that Robert told me of, have they been sighted as well?"

Frank shook his head. "We have had no sign of them as yet. But when they come, they will find a strong army waiting at Tilbury.

"Before I deliver you to father," he added, "I must go to Rundle Head. I promised to talk with the men of the land watch there and take word of any sightings they may have made to Robert."

We rode to the coast and climbed a hill, leaving our mounts with the escort waiting below. Frank climbed nimbly, I more slowly and with some care.

"Forgive me but I must go on ahead, with all speed," Frank said, adding "I was due hours ago."

I nodded assent.

The August day was fair, the sun hot on my back as I continued the ascent up Rundle Head. When I finally neared the top I paused, looking out across the expanse of dark blue water, a brisk wind lifting my skirt and threatening to pluck off my hat, which was tied securely under my chin. The water frothed with whitecaps—wild horses, we used to call them as children—and at the base of the outcropping, wave after wave rolled in to smash against the rocks, sending spray high into the air. The smell of the sea was strong and pungent. I breathed deeply, filling my lungs with the welcome coolness, glad to catch my breath.

As I looked down I caught sight of a small stretch of beach, and what looked like a tiny cottage built in against the rocks, away from the foreshore. A lone figure stood before the cottage, a woman dressed in black, one arm up to shade her eyes. Like me, she was looking out to sea.

Turning my glance back toward the wide blue emptiness that stretched to the horizon, I was aware of the outline of a ship coming into view, rising and falling on the shifting rollers, her wide sails bellied out by the wind. One of the sails was tattered, and the wind blew through it, sending the shreds out like streamers.

I heard shouting and looked over to where Frank stood with half a dozen other men, all watching the ship as I was. Then a second ship, smaller than the first and faster, hove into view, overtaking the other. There came the shattering boom of a gun. Was it from one of the two ships? I could not tell.

As I watched, the figure on the beach below me caught my attention once again. She had begun to walk out toward the rocky shore. It crossed my mind that she intended to signal to the ships. Why? Was she a Spanish spy? Or was she luring them to their doom on the rocks?

Squinting, I thought I could barely make out a man, leaning on the taffrail of the ship nearest the promontory. But then a wisp of spume arose to obscure my view.

Clouds were scudding in across the Channel. I scanned the horizon for more ships but did not see another sail. Frank was waving to me, then clambering over the cliff edge toward where I stood.

Out of breath when he reached me, he managed to gasp out, "See, there, it is the great Biscayan! I sank her twin off the Isle of Wight! And the other is her storeship. See how light in the water she rides! She is nearly empty. That means the Biscayan is out of arms and food. Without powder and shot and food, the fleet will have to refit or retire. I must get word to Robert—to father—to the queen."

He grabbed for my hand. But just then, as I turned to accompany him, I glanced down at the shore below, and saw the black-clad woman leap into the water.

I gasped. "Frank! That woman! She's going to drown!"

"What woman?" His voice was gruff.

"I've been watching her. She walked out along the sand. I thought she might be signaling to the ships. Now she's jumped into the sea."

"A madwoman. Some madwoman."

"No, Frank, no." I began to scramble down the hillside, in the direction of the beach below, dislodging rocks as I went. If Frank would not help the woman, I would.

"Lettie! There is no time for this! We must get to Tilbury, to tell the good news!"

But I went on, nearly falling as I half-slid, half-ran down the cliffside, my impatient brother following me, unable to catch up with me as we both plunged, nearly losing our balance, toward the wet yellow sands.

FORTY-TWO

I arrived first, my boots sinking down as I tried to run toward
the water's edge. Frank was calling out, but by this time he
too could see the woman's flailing arms as she fought the
oncoming waves and tried to stay afloat. She was not far from
us—the beach was narrow—but the sucking sand held me back,
and I felt myself moving with frustrating slowness. Frank went
past me. He was still shouting, but now his shouts were for the
woman.

"Hold on! You there! Hold on!"

As I watched, still moving forward as quickly as I could, I saw
Frank reach the shore and press on, running out along the slippery
rocks to where the woman was fighting the waves, clutching at
the flinty shingle, trying in vain to gain a handhold.

Frank flung off his doublet and dove into the water. For a
moment there was no sign of either the woman or my brother.
Then, suddenly, both burst up into view, gasping, just as a wave

crashed over them and I thought, they are both going to drown for certain.

There was nothing I could do. I watched, I prayed. I waited for what seemed an age, willing the surge to recede.

Eventually it did, leaving two supine bodies in its wake.

Frank managed to get to his feet and, taking the woman in black by the wrists, dragged her up onto the sand until she was out of danger of another breaking wave. I went toward them.

"Is she dead?" I called out.

Instead of answering Frank turned the woman over onto her back, and looked down into her face, gently lifting away the long strands of black hair that obscured her features.

He looked down, puzzled, then leaned down farther to look more closely.

"It can't be," I heard him mutter. "It can't be." Then, more loudly, "I don't believe it."

"Is she alive? Is she breathing?" I asked. But even as I said it I could see the rise and fall of her chest. And in a moment she opened her eyes.

Frank was kneeling over her, and I knelt too.

She saw us, she looked at Frank—and then she smiled. Such a smile as I had never before seen on a human face. And Frank smiled back, and took her in his arms, and wept.

For there, on the rocky foreshore of that windswept beach, he had at last found his love.

FORTY-THREE

WHEN the queen rode into Tilbury Camp on her proud, high-stepping white gelding, her head held nobly aloft, her lined, aging countenance full of cheer and exuberance, the silver corslet that encased her bony chest gleaming in the sunlight, such a cheer went up from the men that might have been heard twenty miles away in London.

They roared, they clapped, they whistled into the rising wind off the river.

"Gloriana! Gloriana!" came the sound again and again. "Long live Gloriana!"

She rode in among them, her red wig glittering with diamonds and waving purple plumes, and halted to salute them as they stood in their ranks, with only the yeomen of her guard in close attendance.

"You are all my guardsmen!" she shouted back to the cheering men. "I need no others! I know I am safe among you."

She raised her silver truncheon and shouted "Strike or be

stricken" and once again an outcry rose from ten thousand throats, and echoed out over the camp and out to the palisaded walls and beyond to the river and the crowds gathered on its far shore.

"See how she laughs in the face of danger," I heard a man near me say. "See how brave she is, our dear old queen! She's not a whit frightened of a few Spaniards!"

From where I was standing inside Robert's blue and purple pavilion I could peer out through a small opening and watch the soldiers standing in their ranks, the queen riding amid them, with Robert on his powerful grey stallion on her right hand and my Rob, her Master of the Horse, on her left.

"The Great Lord, the Earl of Leicester," I heard some voices call out as Robert passed. Hated he might be, and despised for his failure in Flanders, yet he was nonetheless the queen's chosen champion in this tense time, and all the men in camp knew it. Despite his years, his scraggly white hair and beard and puffy scarlet cheeks, he carried the weight of command, he was the queen's man. On this day he disguised his inward dismay well, and waved to the soldiers with the hearty enthusiasm of a much younger man. Only I could detect the lines of worry on his sagging features. And when the queen's horse stumbled, nearly throwing her, and alarm spread through the massed ranks, it was Robert who was at her side in an instant, grasping her by her corslet and arm and saving her from a fall.

"No hurt! No hurt!" she cried, grinning. "Milord Lieutenant is at hand!"

I saw that Rob joined in the applause and shouting that greeted these words, graciously yielding the pride of place to Robert though he himself was by far the nimbler rider and his mount, I happened to know, the faster steed.

The contrast between Robert's cumbersome, stout figure and

my son's graceful svelte form could not have been more pronounced. My husband, once the most handsome man at court, had long since yielded that honor to young Rob, whose beauty was of a different order entirely. Robert had the dark, empassioned countenance of an irresistibly seductive gypsy, while Rob's face, with its wide brow, deeply thoughtful dark eyes and sensitive, curving mouth was the face of an alluring poet, manly yet tender, even visionary. Not for him, on that afternoon, the concerns that plagued Robert: worries over the army's small size (Robert had been expecting forty to fifty thousand men to come to Tilbury Camp), over the dearth of arms and provisions, over the as-yet-uncompleted bridge of boats to connect Tilbury Fort with Gravesend, where, according to the reports of spies, the Spaniards were expected to land.

I knew what weighed on my husband's mind: how could the queen be kept safe? And when would the great fleet arrive, what day and what hour, with its accompanying horde of barges loaded with Spanish fighting men?

When I arrived in the camp with Frank and Marianna I was told that my father had arranged for all of us in the family to be sheltered in the largest of Robert's three pavilions, where we would be guarded by a troop of eighty elderly veterans, volunteers from the old soldiers' home Robert had built. Frank went at once to convey his information about the Spanish ships to the queen's officers, taking Marianna with him, but I went right to the largest of the blue and purple pavilions, and once inside I found Penelope and her two oldest boys, Dorothy and her little girl, and my sister Cecelia, who to my amazement came up to me and kissed me on the cheek. Whaffer, standing guard at the tent flap, nodded to me while my father, nearly bald and stooped and looking even older than his seventy-four years, came up to me and wrapped his thin arms around my shoulders.

"I should be out there, among the men, following your husband's orders," he confided, his cracking voice forlorn. "I can still shoulder a musket, after all, and every man is needed. But his officers sent me back here. They said I would only be in the way when the fighting started. I can still carry water, though. They are going to let me carry water to the wounded."

I quickly learned that Penelope's husband Lord Rich had raised a band of two hundred men from his estates and was training with them, there in the camp. As a pikeman. Dorothy's husband Ned was helping to build the bridge of boats. And Cecelia, fat as she was (Walter's old phrase for her, "fat as butter," came to mind unbidden), was a good horsewoman despite her girth and had volunteered to carry messages.

"What can you do, Lettie?" she asked me.

"Isn't it enough that she is here to support her brave husband and son?" was my father's tart reply. I had to smile, as I had never before heard my father defend me against his favorite Cecelia. Apparently I had earned his favor at last.

The tumult in the camp went on for days, and each day the queen, who was staying at a nearby manor house, came to visit the men and hearten them with her cries of "Strike, or be stricken!" and her impetuous bolts into their midst on her white horse.

On the third day a shaggy-looking, dirty man was brought in chains to stand before Robert and the queen. As he passed, dragging the heavy, clanking metal attached to his wrists and ankles, the soldiers spat on him and worse, shouting "Traitor! Judas! Scoundrel!" and throwing him to the ground again and again. As he struggled to rise I caught a glimpse of his bleeding face and stony, glaring eyes.

It was Roger Wilbraham!

"We found him trying to sell his white eagle to some

fishermen off Gravesend," said Frank at my elbow. "The Spanish buyers never arrived, so he tried to find others. We took him. He'll be hanged at first light."

Cecelia came out of the pavilion and, marching up to her former husband, began beating him with her riding crop.

"See here," Elizabeth shouted to Cecelia. "Let the rogue pass. He'll find himself without a head soon enough."

Reluctantly Cecelia obeyed, but not before she had flung a curse at Wilbraham, and added a swift kick. Then she retreated behind the tent flap.

"My good people," Elizabeth's voice rang out, only slightly hoarse from having addressed the men of Tilbury loudly and often in recent days, "you may well wonder why it is that I stay here among you, rather than seek the safety of a strong castle far from the coast." She tossed her head. "Well, this is why! Englishmen do not run, nor English women neither. And I am safest here, where traitors are brought to die for their treasons and good men are gathered to defend our land."

When the shouting and clapping had died down she went on. "Besides, I am told this very hour by our brave mariners that the mighty Spanish fleet is going down to destruction. Their ships are leaking, they lack powder and shot, they have lost their rigging and many men have perished. Their decks are full of wreckage and the sea is a grave for many a great ship. They have gone north in hopes of finding safe harbor and threaten us no more."

Rising as high as she could in her saddle, Elizabeth cried out in her loudest voice, "THE LORD GOD HAS DESTROYED OUR ENEMIES!!"

Now the cheer that broke was like a mighty thunderclap, a great crash of sound, a blow upon the ear, a noise so shattering that I had to cover my ears with my hands and squeeze my eyes shut to endure it.

"And while we must remain vigilant," Elizabeth said, her small light eyes shining as she spoke, "and pray for His continuing miraculous favor, I am resolved, whatever comes, to live or die amongst you all, and lay down for my God and my kingdom and for my people, my honor and my blood, even in the dust."

In that moment I could not deny that, for all her petty malice and deceit, all her jealousy and selfishness, her vanity, her infuriating need to control and torment those around her, she was marvelous. I joined the cheering, and clapped until my hands were nearly raw, and embraced all those around me, Penelope and Dorothy and my weeping old father, and Frank and Marianna too, and sent up a prayer of thanks for what we had been spared. For even though I had seen with my own eyes the menacing galleons that threatened us, I was no longer afraid.

"Let them do their worst," I heard Frank say. "Let them come again if they dare. We will stand firm with our queen, and die as one, before we let them take our England."

FORTY-FOUR

M Y Robert!

It was all too much for him, the constant effort, the strain, the fear. The ceaseless work of superintending the military camp. He collapsed into Rob's arms, just as Rob was helping him try to mount his horse despite the pain of his swollen foot. Rob, Chris and Whaffer carried him to his pavilion and from there he was brought home to Wanstead.

Three physicians were in attendance when he arrived, along with the bonesetter Monsieur Ezard. Robert was put to bed in our large airy bedchamber, dressed in his soft nightgown of patterned velvet, the windows closed to keep out the first chill draughts of autumn.

He was very ill indeed. I could see it in the physicians' faces, and in the way the bonesetter, who I had come to trust as a friend, gently took my hand and simply said, "Say your prayers, Lady Leicester. And I will add mine."

I scented Robert's bedclothes with cloves and citron, and

scattered lavender on his pillow to help him rest. His long face was pinched and sad, the eyes sunk deeply in their sockets. He licked his lips and I helped him to drink, but his lips remained dry and cracked and he was having trouble swallowing.

His first words to me were, "Why hasn't she come?" He had been at Wanstead for nearly three days by then, three days of pain and a slow wasting away.

"I'm sure she will, if you should need her."

Robert's dry lips turned upward slightly. I bent closer to hear his soft words. "What do you mean, if?"

He was quiet for a while. I sat beside him, holding his thin cool hand. He watched me, with the same ghostly smile playing at the corners of his lips. At length he spoke again. His words were more like croaks than words, but I understood him.

"Death came to the king, and the king said, 'cut off his head!' Death came to the maiden, and the maiden said, 'come into my chamber, and dally here awhile.' Death came to the poet, and the poet said, 'I have long been expecting you, old friend.' Then death came to the philosopher, who nodded in greeting, but said nothing. Death said, 'I have come, O master, to learn from you.'"

He reached out to touch my arm. "Help me to be a philosopher, Lettie. I only ask that you be with me when the portal opens, and I lay this wretched flesh aside, and step through."

I agreed, weeping.

He slept for hours, then woke suddenly.

"Did you know he has gout, just like me?"

"Who?"

"King Philip of course. I hope his is worse." He laughed and dropped off to sleep again.

By the fourth day he was tossing uneasily in his sleep, crying out, delirious at times. He murmured the words "white eagle" again and again, and talked about the second eclipse of the moon, and waved away the physicians who tried to bleed him, knocking the cups from their hands as they tried to cut his arm and open a vein.

Chris stood by me through the long hours, and my children were sent for and also Robert's base son, though he sent no message in response and never arrived.

One by one our servants came in, many of them in tears; each knelt by his bedside, and he stretched out his hand in a sort of benediction. The gentleman ushers, the almoner, the steward of our household, the chaplain, the grooms and maids, the stable boys, even the scullery maids came to speak a few words to the Great Lord, whom they regarded with a mixture of veneration and fear. It was all he could do, at the end, to muster the strength to reach out his hand to each of them. I sent them out of the room so that he could rest. Many reached out to me as they passed, and murmured a word or two. I thanked each one, though like Robert I was weary and longed to sleep.

The vigil seemed long. Every few hours Robert would wake and murmur "Where is she? Why won't she come?" It was no good my telling him that I was right beside him, for it wasn't me he wanted. It was her.

Once in his delirium he called out, "The horses, Lettie! The horses! Oh, the beautiful horses! They threw them all overboard! The Spanish! They drowned the fine horses!" Deep sobs rose from his thin body. Then, "My dear ones, my Bay Gentle, my Persimmon, my Roan Gallant, my Great Savoy—good gallopers from Ireland—yes—such a good pace—"

I had Robert's elderly dog Boy brought in, and laid gently down on the bed beside him. He reached out to stroke the old dog's head, and smiled. A little later he reached out to me.

"It will be well, Lettie," he said, his mind suddenly clear. Then, "I thought I heard her coach."

Lord forgive me, I lied then, knowing he could have no peace otherwise.

"But you did hear it, beloved," I said. "She was here. We tried to wake you but you were sleeping too soundly. She couldn't stay. She said to tell you how much she loves you. How much she has always loved you."

Hearing this, he nodded, and laid his head back against the soft pillow, and sighed. "The portal—" he whispered. For a brief moment a light came into his tired eyes. He stroked the old dog's head, he looked over at me, but then the light was gone, and he took his last breath, and quietly left us.

I bent my head. My dearest, my love, my heart of hearts—

My Robert!

FORTY-FIVE

IT was nearly a year after Robert died that I married Chris. Frank and Marianna were married in the same ceremony, and family and servants gathered to hear us recite our vows and afterward, to join in the exuberant dancing and eat wedding cake and wish us well with shouts and toasts.

We had a simple wedding, in the chapel at Wanstead. We did not care for pomp or show; I could not afford it, Robert having left me nothing but debts and Frank, who had once prided himself on his treasure in stolen Spanish gold, having spent nearly everything he had buying ships and arms and paying soldiers at the time of the dreaded invasion by the Spanish fleet the year before.

A quiet wedding was best, for the last thing I wanted was to draw attention to my marrying Chris. There had been malicious gossip—some said it was gossip started by the queen—about me and my much younger husband. Chris was many years my junior, and looked even younger than his true age, with his splendid strong muscular body and unlined handsome face and athletic agility. It was said that he and I had been lovers while Robert was in Flanders, and that on Robert's return, I had poisoned him so that I could become Chris's wife. One of Robert's chamber gentlemen swore that he had seen me giving Robert a cup of wine poisoned with ratsbane, and when I heard this (it was utterly absurd, of course) I could not help but be reminded of the ugly stories that circulated after Amy Dudley's death.

There was another rumor as well, and this one, I confess, was partly true. It was said that I married Chris for his inheritance.

Perhaps I would have married him anyway, I will never know. But in fact, as I have said, Robert left me heavily in debt, indeed hopelessly in debt, and by a great stroke of good luck Chris's uncle Timothy died not long after Robert did and left Chris his fortune.

No one had expected this, least of all Chris, whose lineage was honorable but his means small. Uncle Timothy had quarreled bitterly with his only son, and shortly before he died, he altered his will to disinherit his son and make Chris his heir.

To me it seemed providential, as Chris had been saying for a long time that he loved me but was reluctant to even suggest that we might marry. He often said that he had nothing to offer me but his heart—a beautiful sentiment which was, alas! quite true. But when I found myself in difficulties and he became a man of some wealth, a marriage seemed appropriate—indeed, for me, it could hardly have been more timely, for I was in dire need, and mounting distress.

Robert had been in his tomb only a matter of days when Robert Cecil, the queen's young private secretary and the son of her venerable councilor Lord Burghley, came riding into the courtyard of Wanstead with several dozen brawny laborers and a score of large carts. Once admitted to the house—he could hardly be refused entrance, being an officer high in the queen's service—he began directing the men to remove the furnishings.

"And what do you imagine you are doing?" I demanded.

Cecil went on with his self-appointed task. "Lord Leicester owes Her Majesty twenty-five thousand pounds. The furnishings of this house will be sold to recover a portion of that debt."

"But my husband left this house to me."

"That may be, but the queen—or rather the royal treasury—is confiscating the contents. If they are found to be of too small worth to satisfy the debt, the house and lands may be seized as well."

It was no good my railing at Cecil, as I watched piece after piece of my beloved hangings and screens and tables and plate being carried out by the workmen and taken to be strapped into the waiting carts in the courtyard. In vain I complained indignantly that the queen was heartless. That she had caused my husband pain on his deathbed by refusing to send him any word of consolation or coming to see him.

"She has been much occupied by affairs of state," was Cecil's curt reply as he lifted a small table beautifully adorned with inlaid woods, a particular favorite of mine, and tossed it to one of the laborers. He lifted it with difficulty, for he had little strength, being dwarfishly short and cursed with a hunchback.

"Robert served her all his life. He deserved better."

Cecil raised his small head and gave me a calculating look.

"He was well compensated for his—services." A low chuckle escaped his narrow lips, though his eyes held no mirth.

This slur made me furious.

"My father will hear of what you are doing this day," I said at length. "He will not tolerate such treatment of me."

"Your father," said Cecil, huffing with effort as he helped to roll a magnificent Turkish carpet into a long pale cylinder, "was among those on the council voting to recover the funds Lord Leicester owes to the treasury—or rather, the funds his estate owes." The carpet having been taken away, Cecil spat on his hands and wiped them on his hose. "Apparently you are unaware of how depleted the treasury is."

"Or how rapacious the queen's councilors are."

It took a full two days for the contents of Wanstead to be unceremoniously swept out from under me, though I was not left in want or without a place to lay my head. Cecelia provided me with temporary furnishings and linens from her well equipped house, and our servants, who treated me with particular kindness in those sad days after I lost Robert, offered their own possessions, some very modest, to make me comfortable until the empty, echoing mansion could be restored to something like its former condition.

But the queen's demands did not stop at Wanstead. She also insisted that the contents of Robert's magnificent London house be seized as well, along with the wondrous interior glories of Kenilworth (which Robert had left in his will to his ailing brother Ambrose), and all the fine horses from our stables and other stock on our grazing lands. It was as if, instead of grieving Robert's loss and honoring his memory, she was determined to snatch away everything he had ever owned.

To take it all from me, and leave me nothing of him except his tomb, and the memory of his love.

In the end I could do little but acquiesce, and the queen's depredations were not all I had to face as Robert's widow. His vast debts led to lawsuits, demands from creditors, angry quarrels with people who claimed he had wronged them or injured them in some way. Chris came to my defense, as did Frank and Rob, I had attorneys to plead my cause and when all else failed, there was Chris's bountiful inheritance to pay at least some of the debts and appease those who harassed me.

And there was Marianna, my gentle, affectionate new sister-in-law who was tough as granite beneath the surface of her kindness and good nature, and who stood by me almost like a true sister at every turn.

Frank's chance rediscovery of Marianna had reaffirmed my faith in the mercies of a loving Providence. How, decades after losing her and believing her to be dead, had he come across her at the very time she was in despair and in need of rescue? I thought about that strange coincidence often—though in truth it was no stranger than the timely arrival of Chris's inheritance, and his offer of marriage to me. There was much talk, in those days, of the hand of God having delivered England from the Spanish menace. Certainly, I thought, the hand of God has been prodigal; certainly that all-merciful hand has been stretched out to Frank and to me—and certainly to Marianna.

She was no longer the slim, lithe, beautiful girl Frank had known and loved in his youth. But in her forties she was still slim, could walk briskly and for miles, and her features were pleasing. Her black hair, like Frank's, was streaked with grey and her eyes were no longer the trusting, innocent eyes of a virginal preacher's daughter but the knowing, somewhat world-weary eyes of a woman who had endured and survived years of poverty and pain, largely on her own.

When she and Frank had been in love, she had been living with her family in the abandoned hulk of an old ship. Then, Frank was told, the ship had been washed away in a storm and the entire family—so it was thought—had perished.

"But we had moved out of the ship before the storm came," she confided to me one afternoon as we sat in my bedchamber at Wanstead with the warm autumn sun pouring through the tall windows. "We found shelter in an old farmhouse with a leaking roof. Oh, I was glad for that farmhouse! It was abandoned. No one ever came to turn us out, so we stayed. My father was ill and could no longer preach. My mother and I and my sister planted a garden for food and raised chickens. We had just enough. We didn't starve."

She looked down, and a shadow passed across her pleasant features. "It was a very hard time. One of my little brothers caught a fever and died. My oldest brother left to go to sea and never came back to us. I prayed for Frank to return but he never did. I married—though it was always Frank I loved, deep down—but after a few years I discovered that my husband already had a wife. And a cruel temper as well."

"And you never had children?"

She did not reply right away, but took her time.

"I had a little boy," she said, her voice very low. "He only lived for a few days. My husband—"

I raised my hand. "No, Marianna. I don't want to hear it."

She nodded. "No. You don't."

"My dear," was all I could say. "I'm sorry, my dear Marianna."

Clearly she had suffered much, but her manner and bearing were calm and graceful, her voice steady as she continued.

"There is more," she said. "When you saw me on the beach below Rundle Head, and came down the hill toward me, I was living alone, hidden away, in fear that my vengeful husband might find me. I had no family left. I did not know where to go or what to do. Everyone said the world was about to end, and then I saw the Spanish ships, and I thought they would land and kill us all. I was in despair—"

"And so you jumped into the water."

She nodded.

I reached out my hand, and she took it, smiling.

"But the world hasn't ended, and the Spanish are gone—for now—and you and I are sisters. Isn't it amazing?"

FORTY-SIX

MOTHER! Where are you, mother? I want to talk to you!"

It was Rob's loud, importunate voice. The voice that made people jump in alarm, or run to do his bidding. Now that he was twenty-six, and married (he had married the insipid daughter of Francis Walsingham, shortly after I married Chris), and a father, his sturdy body was beginning to have the weight of maturity. His strong voice was low and commanding.

"What is it dear?"

My tall, broad-shouldered, overbearing son burst into the room, the look on his arrestingly handsome face somewhere between a grin and a teasing leer. He had gained a reputation for roistering and bluster; I knew that he and Chris went out at night in search of the disorderly pleasures all healthy young men were drawn to. Had I been younger I might have minded. As it was I tended to ignore what my husband and son did, never doubting their love for me—though I did doubt their judgment, and at times told them so.

"There you are mother!"

Rob, for all his loud and importunate ways, was irresistible. People were drawn to him. He brought excitement with him wherever he went. He stirred things up. His strength of will, his refusal to be restrained, were a tonic, a refreshing change from the old times and the old ways. For like it or not, the queen and her aged councilors—all but young Robert Cecil—were seen more and more as decrepit relics from a previous era. Visitors to Elizabeth's court, Rob told me, went there to admire the carefully preserved artifacts of her early reign: her old-fashioned gowns, cut in styles that made young woman laugh at their quaintness; her caps—such caps as no woman would dream of wearing in the up-to-date 1590s—her first throne, so starkly plain compared with her present throne upholstered in soft brown velvet and sparkling with diamonds and sapphires, enormous pearls and emeralds that shone in the firelight.

More and more, Elizabeth was seen as the past, Rob as the future. Though past and future had become staunch companions, and the queen had taken Rob into her inner circle as her favorite attendant, her preferred opponent at cards, her strong arm to lean on when she appeared before her subjects. Occasionally she even turned to him for advice, though he did not rise to prominence in her royal council, a fact that increasingly irked him.

Indeed the queen herself irked him more and more, the higher he rose in her favor. She was after all an old woman, with an old woman's impatience and demands, while Rob, whom she called her Wild Horse, was a young man in his prime, answering to no demands but those of his own views and needs, and chafing at any restraints or shackles Elizabeth placed upon him.

Theirs was clearly a close relationship, but one cankered by constant strain.

"There you are!" Rob kissed me on both cheeks. I could smell his strong odor of musk and perspiration. His face was red with exertion. I ordered one of the servants to bring him a tankard of small beer and asked him whether he wanted anything to eat.

"No, mother. I have not come about food, but about you! You and the queen, that is."

"You know she wants nothing to do with me."

He waved my comment away with impatience.

"I am determined to bring you back to court! It is where you belong."

"The queen would not agree."

"God's bones! She is cantankerous and old. She never agrees to anything! She must be cajoled—or forced."

My son's words made me uneasy. Why was it suddenly so important that I return to the royal court? I had never expressed any interest in returning, quite the contrary. I had no desire to be near Elizabeth, with her deepgoing resentment of me and her well-known capacity for seeking revenge and doing harm.

"No, Rob. As you know, I am perfectly content in the country, far from London and its stinks and noise. In fact, Chris and I are moving even farther away, to Drayton Bassett." Drayton Bassett in Staffordshire was another of my late husband's manors, one spared the queen's depredations. It was a small but comfortable house of some twenty-seven rooms with outbuildings, farms and a granary.

Rob drained his tankard and asked for another, wiping his mouth with the back of one large hand.

"The fact is, mother, your place is at court. With your royal blood, and the queen lacking a successor—"

"My royal blood! Well, yes, mother always hinted that she

believed herself to be royal, through her mother. But of course she had no way of proving such a claim. And in any case, even if she had been the king's daughter, she was his bastard daughter."

"But Elizabeth is only a bastard!" Rob put in. "The Catholics certainly think so. That makes her claim to the throne no stronger than yours—or mine."

I was surprised and dismayed to hear Rob say this. Until that time I had never heard him talk of the sucession—or indeed of any crown issues, other than military matters.

"I hope, Rob, that you do not entangle yourself in dangerous discussions about the queen's right to the throne."

"Why not? It is an important topic just now, since she has no child and must choose who will succeed her. I have heard it said that once, when she was very ill and likely to die, she appointed my stepfather as Protector. Is that true?"

"Yes, though the council opposed her. The decision caused much bitterness."

"Why shouldn't she name me Protector? Or better still, heir to the throne? I am far better suited for the role than my stepfather was. I am stronger, and braver. I can make myself obeyed. And he was hated, while I, as you may have noticed, am liked."

It was true. As I have said, Rob possessed a quality that drew others to him. The older he got, the more prominent he became as the queen's preferred attendant and escort, the more he was admired. Chris told me that in London, it was not uncommon for a small crowd to form at the gates of the royal palace when Rob was expected to pass by.

Though Rob pressed me to talk more of these matters I refused, merely saying that we would continue our conversation another time. But I was alarmed. Such rash assertions from my son left me in no doubt that he was inviting disaster. And apparently he wanted me to be at court, nearby, to support him in his foolhardy scheming.

I tried talking to Chris, pointing out how dangerous it would be for Rob to try to meddle in the sensitive question of the succession.

"Men have lost their heads for less," I remarked. "Most of Robert's family was imprisoned in the Tower when his brother Guildford married Lady Jane Grey and tried to take the throne by force. Executions followed. Elizabeth herself was put in prison when she was suspected of plotting to take the throne from Mary. Rob is walking on deadly turf."

"Then I am walking with him," Chris said staunchly.

I stared at him in disbelief.

"Surely you don't mean—"

"I intend to stand with Rob, whatever he decides to do." I had never seen my husband so resolute. Or so lacking in prudence. It was clear to me that, when it came to Rob or his plans, Chris would not listen to reason.

In the meantime, what was I to do? I felt helpless in my distress. Trying in vain to sleep at night, I was constantly awakened by bad dreams, dreams in which, amid a babel of voices, one voice stood out. Rob's voice, saying, "Come to court! You must come to court! I am determined to bring you back to court! It is where you belong! Come now!"

FORTY-SEVEN

I N the year my father died, the crops failed, and hard cold rains soaked the sodden earth, bringing starvation and sickness and a great many deaths. England suffered, and Scotland and wild Ireland too, so it was said. Our storehouses were quickly exhausted; our laborers gathered what they could from the dismal harvest into the barns at Drayton Bassett, hoping to have enough food to keep the estate workers alive and to share with the villagers, and praying that we would not lose too many of our animals though the cattle grew very lean in that year and even the chickens—those we spared from the stewpot for the sake of their eggs—were scrawny. I supposed that the worms they fed on were drowned by the heavy rains, though when spring came the robins, who fed on the same worms, seemed sleek and active, their numbers undiminished.

It was a year of great dearth, and want, that year of 1596 when I had my fifty-fifth birthday. My dear sister-in-law Marianna, having known want herself for much of her life, became the angel of mercy for our villagers, taking it upon herself to organize and oversee the giving out of grain and dried vegetables and even helping to collect mushrooms from the woods—for mushrooms, as every woodsman's child knows, are very nourishing, as long as the poisonous ones are avoided—and to harvest the thin inner bark of pines and birches to grind into flour for making ash cakes.

Then came the sad news from London. I was informed that father had died, suddenly, just after a stormy council meeting ended. I suppose I should not have been surprised, given father's age of eighty-two, but he had not been ill and it was hard not to imagine him at his perennial tasks of governing. He had, after all, been a fixture of the royal council for decades—for most of my life, in fact. The news of his death caught me unprepared and left me dazed, coming as it did amid the daily crises caused by the spreading famine and the mounting unrest and criticism of the queen.

Chris and I went at once to the capital to attend father's funeral service and to make arrangements for his burial. What we found there shocked us: a stark panorama of want and panic, with the death carts rattling through streets choked with refuse and pathetic scenes of begging and misery at every turn. I had seen plague, I had passed through deserted villages devastated by famine. But I had never seen such an alarming sight as the capital in the dearth year, with the Famine Bells (as I called them) tolling constantly for the dead and angry crowds collecting to curse the queen and troops of soldiers in the streets to prevent uprisings. The treasury, I noticed, was particularly well defended, with fresh supplies of guns and arms being brought in under heavy guard through the massive old iron gates.

I was glad, in a way, that my father had not lived to see the worst of the want and looming chaos. The clusters of disaffected citizens with signs that read FEED US, LEAD US. The murderous apprentices—ever the most volatile of the capital's fickle populace—with their improvised pikes made from sharpened stakes and the long knives and hatchets hanging from their belts. The riverside hovels where thin mothers in rags tried in vain to comfort crying children.

My father's splendid obsequies were held at St. Giles's, as was fitting for a nobleman and a valued officer of the royal household and adviser to the queen. As soon as the ceremony was over, the coffin was brought out to be taken to Rotherfield Greys for burial, in accordance with my father's will. Rob was among the pallbearers, and as soon as he came into view, the waiting crowd outside the church broke into riotous cheers. Their shouting drowned out the Famine Bells, and their noisy excitement quickly attracted more and more people, until it seemed to us that half the population of London was swarming in to see Rob and cheer for him.

Feed us, lead us! they chanted again and again, until at last father's shrouded coffin was laid in the coach and Chris and I began the slow journey into the countryside, relieved to leave the shouts and noisome stinks and pathetic sufferings of London behind.

I was summoned back to court, to serve the queen as Mother of the Maids—the post my own mother had once held when I was young—in the second year of the famine. It appeared that Rob had done what he said he was determined to do: he had managed to cajole or pester the queen into making a place for me in her household.

I was wary of her even so. When I went to join the court,

and was summoned into Elizabeth's presence by a tall young yeoman, I was trembling, and my heart was beating far too fast.

I had been told to present myself in the royal dining room at a certain hour and was careful to be on time. My instructions were to wear a white gown with black trim, and not to adorn my hair with gems. A bearded guard in a gold doublet, carrying a heavy wooden halberd, admitted me to the cavernous, elegantly appointed room, its walls hung with embroidered hangings woven of rich silks of purple and blue (Robert's colors, I noticed) and its floors covered with fresh, sweet-smelling rushes perfumed with rosemary.

At the head of the long bare dining table sat the queen, her high-piled red wig a harsh contrast to the lush colors of the silken hangings, her garishly painted old face a caricature. Her bright orange gown hung open across her sunken chest; she wore nothing beneath it. Was she being brazen, or was she unaware? I could not tell. The sight of her was disturbing, for she had aged a great deal since I had last seen her at Tilbury, and she had a distracted look. She pulled nervously at her long fingers, sitting there at the empty table, the jewels in her wig and at her wrinkled throat sparkling in the candlelight. I thought, for a brief moment, that I saw tears glittering in her flinty eyes.

While I stood watching, two gentlemen, one carrying a silver rod, the other an elaborately embroidered cloak, entered the room and, having knelt before her, spread a heavy cloth of ivory linen on the long table. Behind them came more gentlemen carrying a golden plate with bread and an immense ornate saltcellar, and then, in procession, there entered several dozen servants in scarlet livery, each with a heavy plate of gold on which sat a small serving of food.

So she still eats sparingly, I thought, remembering how little she had eaten when I had served her years before. It is not only because she is so old that she is so thin, it is because she starves herself. I remembered Robert telling me that poison had been found in her food many times.

Twelve trumpeters came in, playing a fanfare, and behind them were half a dozen kettledrummers. While the queen ate, the musicians played lively dance tunes. Only there was no one there to dance. Only the servants, and myself, and the queen, whose feet would not be still and who seemed to bounce and sway to the tunes as they echoed around the walls of the immense room.

As she ate, she drank, cordial after cordial, and hummed along with the music. She paid no attention whatsoever to me, and after what seemed like an hour or more I was weary of standing and longed to sit down. I had not eaten since early morning, and the delicious smells that rose from the gold plates—the food mostly untouched—were tantalizing.

She was humiliating me. She was demonstrating her power over me by keeping me standing there while she nibbled at the abundant food. I was wary, on guard. Yet at the same time I was angry. For was I not, like herself, of royal blood, as Rob had reminded me? Did I not carry the blood of the great Henry Tudor in my veins, just as she did? We both resembled him, after all. Surely we both had an equal right to dine in the great hall of his palace, heirs to his mythic legacy, cousins in the flesh if not in law. What did it matter that my grandmother had been the king's mistress and not his wife? Had not Elizabeth herself been declared a bastard?

I felt my stomach lurch. On impulse I did the unthinkable. I marched to the table and seized an untouched plate. No one stopped me. Trembling, the heavy plate shaking in my hand, I sat on a bench and began to eat, fearing with every bite that the queen would shout an order and I would be dragged from the room.

Instead she took a draught from her cordial and said, in a voice frosty with scorn, "Help yourself, She-Wolf. There is plenty for all."

FORTY-EIGHT

1S that a wen on your forehead?"

The queen's tone was sharp, her expression flinty. She had finished her meal, and waved the plates away. I remembered well the day, years earlier, when I had first come to court, and she had asked me the same question.

"Is that a wen on your forehead? A wen is the mark of a whore."

"I don't believe so, Your Majesty."

"It quite spoils your looks. And you are getting on."

The servants and musicians filed out. We were left alone in the beautifully appointed, echoing chamber with its vaulted ceiling and tall windows. Elizabeth clenched her fists and leaned forward toward me, elbows on the polished table, her loose gown flapping unbecomingly.

"You are here for one reason, She-Wolf: to keep a tight rein on your son. Take heed, lest he go too far."

There was no need for her to say more, or for me to respond.

I had seen for myself the excitement Rob was able to engender in the unruly crowds; in such an atmosphere, and given the darkening attitudes of Elizabeth's hungry subjects, violence was only too likely to erupt. And yet, I realized, if she were to restrain or imprison Rob, his supporters would be even more likely to rise against her.

She was clever, as always. In bringing me back to court she was using me to put a damper on my hotheaded boy and his ambitions, while at the same time making it clear to Rob, who was devoted to me, that she held me in her power and could, if she chose, do me harm.

We were both her pawns—but Rob, with his wide, soldierly appeal, was by far the more dangerous, more a wayward rook than a pawn. A rook indeed. A castle. A bulwark standing in her path, with the weight of the populace behind him.

Though the royal court of the queen's ripe (some said overripe) years was quite a different place from the youthful court I had known in my girlhood, I soon settled into its uneasy routines, and began to discover what was expected of me. My official title was Mother of the Maids, with responsibility for overseeing the conduct of the highborn unmarried girls sent by their parents to adorn the royal apartments and make advantageous marriages. But my true function, I quickly discovered, was to serve the queen's needs, wherever and whenever she voiced them. In an odd way—odd because of her long-held enmity toward me—she trusted me more than she did younger people or those less familiar to her. The bumptious rising generation that came of age in the closing years of the century alarmed her, though she tried to hide her fear; the truth was, she was feeling the weight of her years, and the nearness of old acquaintances, of family, gave her ease.

"Lettie! Lettie! Bring me my cane! My eyeglasses! My cordial!" she would call out, her voice hoarse from shouting and complaining. "Lettie! That fire is too hot! It hurts my eyes!" "Lettie! Take away that looking-glass! I look too ill! No one should see me in this state, not even these old eyes of mine!"

Sometimes, when the painful gout in her right thumb became too strong to bear, she called on me to write for her. She had secretaries, to be sure, learned men who could couch her letters and official messages in elegant Latin, but it was easier for her to dictate to me, and she admitted—in one of her rare bursts of praise—that she found my large, round handwriting easy to read.

She was often gruff and even more often rude, she could be cutting and cruel, and the women who served her had long since learned to duck when she flung her slippers with a cry of "*Point de guerre!*"—a swordsman's cry—and to suffer in silence when she boxed their ears playfully and pulled their hair. Though I must note that when she pulled Rob's hair, sometimes yanking forcefully enough to bring tears to his eyes, he grew angry. It was a tense, bitter game between them; she liked to rile him, to see how far she could go with her barbed playfulness before he would turn on her with a snarl or storm out of her presence with an oath.

For Rob's sake I bore up under the weight of her demands and criticisms as well as I could, indeed, I thought, as well as anyone could, given all that had passed between us, all that was unspoken but everpresent, but when her black moods came upon her even I was unable to cope.

At her worst she became capricious and savage, murmuring "Strike, or be stricken! Strike, or be stricken!" and hurling pots and tankards and even heavy silver candlesticks at those of us who triggered her sudden fury. Everyone learned to watch out for these squalls of anger, and to leave her presence. In the grip of her frenzy she paced angrily up and down in her privy chamber, stamping her feet, calling out shrill oaths and threats, lifting the rusty sword she kept near her and thrusting it into curtains, closets, anywhere she imagined her enemies lurked.

Rob seemed almost to thrive on the rough and tumble of Elizabeth's caprices, and to welcome the contest of wills. I watched as they played cards, raced their horses through the park, even in the rain (for the queen continued to ride and hunt, to the despair of her physicians), danced to the lusty tunes of the galliard and even the acrobatic volta, argued and tussled, sometimes coming to mock blows, sometimes ending the quarrel amid convulsions of laughter.

It was rough play, to be sure, and Rob was always careful to let the brittle old queen win whatever contest arose between them. But I never saw the battling carried to the point of injury. Perhaps my presence prevented it, I don't know.

I could see that Elizabeth had a fondness for Rob, but she was not at all in thrall to him, not even a bit, as she had been in thrall to Robert. What was more, it was very clear to me that she saw through him. She knew full well that what he sought was not her company or even the honors she could bestow, but her power itself.

I knew my son, and I knew the queen. I could see that Rob imagined that he had charmed her, that he could, when he chose, exert his will over her. He was not so deluded as to imagine that she loved him; he knew, as we all did, that her love had been for Robert and Robert alone. But he imagined that, with Robert dead, he had stepped into Robert's place in her life. And that one day, before long, her mask of embattled rulership would slip, and she would feel her mortality, and then—why, then he would be there, waiting for the summons to take over in her stead.

And Elizabeth, clever, treacherous Elizabeth, allowed him to keep his illusion.

To say that there were constant strains at court in those

tense days would be far too mild a statement: there was ceaseless combat. Rob was a member of the royal council, but mere membership in that inner circle counted for little. What mattered was the ability to dominate the council, to sway others, and this Rob seemed incapable of doing. The subtleties of politics eluded him; he was no match for the master, the crafty, brilliant, dwarfish Robert Cecil. My father was no longer there at the council table with his dour viewpoint but steadying presence. Walsingham too had died, as had Hatton. The aged William Cecil, Robert's father and the mainstay of the council in Elizabeth's youth and middle years, was tottering toward the grave.

The issue endlessly discussed, endlessly debated, was the very issue that Rob cared about most. Who would assume the throne when the queen died? What if she were to die suddenly, leaving the realm unprepared? Could she be persuaded to make a will, to name her successor? Could she be made to see that until she did settle this question, there would be no peace in her kingdom?

Sometimes the queen was present during the loud quarrels that arose, and as always, she required that I stay close at hand to serve her. As a result I was often in the council chamber, and witnessed all that was said and done there.

"It must be King James, or no one," Cecil announced one morning to the others. "We cannot delay. He is the queen's nearest relation. He is a son of the true church, unlike his late Catholic mother Mary. He is of mature years, with a wife and children—"

"He loves boys," Rob interrupted. "He deserves to be burned."

Cecil went on unperturbed. "He has ruled Scotland for many years, and has kept order there. He is a learned man—"

"And a drunken sot, and a coward."

I could see the rage building in Rob's muscles beneath his

thin linen shirt. His jaw was set, his voice held an undertone of menace.

Cecil went on, not looking at Rob, who got up from the table and began pacing behind his overturned chair.

"Ah! The Wild Horse is loosed!" I heard the queen say with a chortle of pleasure.

"I have been in communication with King James," Cecil was saying. "He offers himself as our next king, in a spirit of service and godliness."

Rob snorted, loudly and rudely.

"Watch him! He's going to start pawing the ground, and neighing," was the queen's taunt. Louder, she called out, "Lettie! Bring me my cordial!"

I did as she asked. When I brought her the goblet she drank it off right away, her eyes shining with excitement. She watched Rob, who glared at Cecil.

"Why don't you ask our queen if she wants that prancing, puking sot to rule this kingdom? Go ahead, dwarf! Ask her!"

The others at the table stirred nervously. I was on the edge of my bench, wishing desperately that I could do something— anything—to distract my son.

"Perhaps further discussion—" offered the irresolute Lord Howard of Effingham, only to be squelched by the sound of Rob's large meaty hand slammed down on the polished oak table.

"Who is ruler here, our queen or this undersized upstart?"

"Or shall it be you, Wild Horse?" said Elizabeth, suddenly rising to her feet and approaching Rob with the agility of a woman half her age. "Aren't you just waiting for me to fall over into my grave, so that you can take my throne?" She grinned, hopping from one foot to the other, all but dancing with plea-sure.

Rob was confused. Was she making an accusation or toying

with him, as she so often did, in mock challenge. Frowning, he swayed on his muscular legs, unsure what to say or what to do.

"Rob—" I called out. "Rob—"

But it was too late.

"What? No answer?" Elizabeth demanded. "Cecil would have an answer! He knows!"

With a snarl Rob grabbed for Robert Cecil's neck, but before he could seize it the queen struck him, hard, across the cheek, her long nails breaking the skin and drawing blood.

Rob's hand flew to the hilt of his sword.

Immediately there were loud shouts for the guards, and a dozen armed men in the queen's livery rushed in to seize Rob and lift the queen and take her to safety, restraining the others around the council table while positioning themselves to safeguard the entrances to the room.

It was all over so quickly that I hardly had time to blink. I caught my breath. Rob was nowhere to be seen, but I heard the old queen call out, as she was being hurried into an antechamber, "Lock him away, the miscreant! The assassin! Lock him away and never let him out again!"

FORTY-NINE

IT was the beginning of the end.

Elizabeth eventually released Rob from his imprisonment, and he knelt to ask her forgiveness for his hasty and violent reaction to her blow. They resumed their uneasy comradeship, after a fashion, but I noticed that Elizabeth kept her rusty sword closer to her side than ever, and that she was never again entirely alone with Rob. And before long the risk of their volatile tempers clashing became moot, because the Spanish were again snapping at our heels, this time in Ireland.

The Irish, it seemed, were ever in rebellion, but now, with the grievously ill King Philip being told by his physicians that he could not possibly live much longer, he determined to make a final effort to strike a fatal blow at Elizabeth's realms. He sent soldiers, treasure and arms to support the Irish rebels, and according to Frank, the Spanish captains were actively searching for landing sites on the western coast.

Elizabeth sent Rob with an army of sixteen thousand men

culled from among the trained bands to engage and suppress the rebels and their Spanish allies. Chris went with him, as his deputy. Penelope's oldest boys wanted to go as well, but their father Lord Rich wisely refused to allow them to go, and I was relieved that he did.

For despite Rob's efforts, the Irish campaign was a disaster. Half the men in Rob's hastily assembled army came down with bog fever, and a quarter of them died. The Irish proved to be elusive—and lethal when found. Rob wrote me when he could, describing the horrors of bog fever (which he himself contracted), complaining of the constant bad weather and of the desertions among his men. I could not help remembering Robert's plangent letters from Flanders, for many of Rob's complaints were the same: the illnesses, the defections, the lack of sufficient funds and the waste of men and treasure. The English militiamen were not trained soldiers like the Spanish; they were not prepared to engage the enemy, merely to fight him off. As a result, the longer the skirmishing continued, the more the advantage went to the rebels and their foreign allies. It became clear from Rob's letters that he was losing the war—and losing hope.

In the end there was no choice but to make peace with the enemy—but not the peace of stalemate, rather the peace of virtual surrender. When informed of this, Elizabeth's wrath flared.

"I'll not have it! Not another Robin! Not another failure!" She called Cecil, and shouted loudly and long. In the end she shouted for me.

"Lettie! Write this! At once!"

I hurriedly gathered my writing implements and took down her words.

"To Robert Devereux, Earl of Essex, failed Lord Lieutenant of Ireland:

On no account are you to return to England
until you have subdued the traitorous Irish and
expelled their wicked Spanish confederates!

By order of Her Majesty the Queen."

I wrote the message, sealed it, and sent it by swift messenger who rode off into the night, headed for the West Country.

A scant month later Rob returned, ignoring the queen's command and rushing into the capital in full cry and with the few thousand soldiers he had left. He counted on crowds surging into the streets to follow him, their pied piper, on hordes of swaggering swordsmen idling in taverns pouring forth to join his ranks, on the London apprentices with their sharp knives and hatchets—in short, he counted on the people to rise up and follow him. His people. The folk of London, he felt sure, would sweep all opposition before them and put him into power.

But once he came among them, he soon found that Cecil had called out the London militias in full force, and all the royal soldiery, the men of the garrisons who had been too old to send to Ireland but were not too old to stand at the gates and fortresses of the capital with arquebuses at the ready. Cecil had even drained the treasury to hire paid troops, and to borrow from King James in Scotland what fighting men England could not supply.

From King James, who had been assured, in Rob's absence, that once the old queen died the throne of England would be his.

Word had been put about among the Londoners that Rob, the failed Lord Lieutenant of Ireland, had sent an Italian poisoner to kill the queen. The old, much derided, much criticized, yet ultimately very dear queen. The poisoner, so it was said, had been captured and sent back to Italy. Londoners rejoiced. Any chance Rob might have had to win their favor was lost.

He was soon arrested, and confined. There was no outcry. No one came to Rob's defense. The heavy iron doors of the dungeon were closed and locked, and soldiers guarded them, and my dear, reckless, foolish Rob was left to ponder his fate in darkness and alone.

FIFTY

At first they would not let me see him. My own son! I was refused entrance to his cell, they told me, even though I was his mother.

I demanded to speak to Cecil.

"No one may see him or speak with him," the secretary repeated curtly once he arrived at the prison. "He is a condemned traitor."

"You know well he is no traitor!" I fairly hissed at the hateful short man who stood between me and my son's prison door. "Open this door at once!"

But Cecil merely stood in front of the massive iron barrier, stubby arms crossed over his puny chest, staring straight ahead. No matter how loudly I shouted, or what foul words I used, he would not move. Soon a dozen armed guards came, and Cecil left.

Rob and Chris and a dozen others had been put on trial and all convicted and sentenced to execution. My hand shakes as I write these words: sentenced to execution.

What had they done, really? They had flouted a royal command to remain in a fever-ridden land and pursue a failing military venture. Instead of obeying, they had done the sensible thing and left Ireland. Had they not left when they did, thousands more men would have died.

I paced up and down in front of the prison door, beneath the impervious eyes of the guardsmen. I pounded on the old stone walls. I shouted Rob's name, again and again, and listened in vain for a reply.

Then, half mad with anguish and grief, I made my way to the palace. I was not admitted. I pretended to leave, but instead managed to enter the outer courtyard through a small gap in the old fence beside the water stairs, a place accessible only at low water and known only to those of us who had belonged to the royal household and knew the palace grounds well. Once inside, I took off my headdress and ruff and covered my head with a piece of stuff torn from my under-petticoat. Keeping my head down, and walking close beside a cart loaded with lumber and sacks of grain, at last I gained the inner courtyard, the courtyard I knew was overlooked by the queen's apartments.

I went to stand beneath the window of her bedchamber. I could see shapes passing back and forth in front of the high window. The curtains were open.

I stood where I was, directly below the window, unsure whether to call out—and risk summoning the guards—or wait until someone saw me from above.

Then I heard a familiar sound. The sound of screeching, and glass shattering. The queen was having one of her tantrums. Shouts and thuds. A muffled scream. Then, all at once, I saw a face at the window. Elizabeth's face, naked of paint, her thin scraggly white hair flying in all directions as the breeze caught it.

She was squinting down at me.

"Who is that!"

"Your cousin."

She peered down, unsure of what her eyes were showing her. "She-Wolf?"

Hardly knowing what words to use, yet certain that I had very little time to keep the angry queen's attention, I heard myself repeat the old formula from the creed.

"I am heartily sorry, Your Majesty, for all my offenses against you. I beg you, in your mercy, to release my son, and take me in his place."

"You!" I heard her shout, a shout of derision. "The forgotten widow of a failed soldier, a hated man! Take you?" She cackled.

"You did not hate him," I said. Suddenly we were talking of Robert, not my condemned son.

"He was a weakling. A coward!"

"He was no coward. He was a prudent commander."

"He was a coward!" she cried out, so loudly that the entire courtyard rang with her accusing clamor. "A brave man would have made me marry him!"

"And he would have lived to regret it!" Now it was my turn to shout, for her accusations against Robert infuriated me.

"God's wounds, She-Wolf! Get away, before I have you thrown into the dungeon with your rattlebrained son!"

She shut the window then with a loud clatter, and I knew there was nothing more that I could do. I sank to my knees in the dirt of the courtyard, beaten. She had won.

That night, as I lay in bed, at Leicester House, unable to sleep, I heard a loud banging on the door. I heard men's voices, and a servant releasing the bolts, and the tramp of boots on the stone floor.

"Lettie!" It was Marianna, my kind sister-in-law who had offered to stay with me while I awaited the outcome of Rob's trial and the carrying out of the cruel sentence against him.

"Lettie! It is a messenger from the queen!"

It was as if a bolt of lightning shot through me. Could it be? Was it possible? Did the messenger bring news of a reprieve?

I dressed as rapidly as I could and went out and down the stairs to the wide entranceway. A man stood there, someone I didn't recognize, wearing the queen's livery.

"Lady Leicester?" Although I was Chris's wife I did not use his name, but kept the title that had come to me as Robert's wife.

"Yes?"

He held out to me a small carved ivory box.

"From the queen," he said. "I am ready to accompany you. I will wait outside."

I opened the lid of the box. Inside was one of the blue and purple garters Robert had given Elizabeth years earlier, and a folded paper. I unfolded it and read the words written there in the queen's shaky handwriting.

"You may say goodbye to your son tonight. Forgive a poor, foolish old woman."

It was not a reprieve, but at least I was to be allowed to see Rob after all.

I was driven to the prison, and this time there was no officious royal councilor to try to prevent me from entering. The jailer admitted me to Rob's bare stone cell, lit only by a single torch burning low.

Rob sat on his wooden bed, running his hands through his hair. He wore his doublet and shirt, soft leather breeches and riding boots. He was prepared to leave, not to sleep.

"Mother!" he cried when he saw me approach. "Mother, have you come to take me home?"

The shock of his poignant words, the sight of him, anxious and eager, his face lit with a desperate hope, was too much for me. I collapsed, sobbing, into his strong arms.

FIFTY-ONE

"D EAR," I managed to say when my tears were spent. "My dearest boy." He looked into my face, and saw, without my having to say the words, that I had not come to take him away. To save him.

He kept his arms around me, comforting me. I had never before been so aware of his strength.

"There there now, mother. Don't take on so! All is not lost!"

"Ah, Rob, if only—if only I had been able to warn you, to make you listen, and Chris too—"

"You did try. You cautioned us. The gamble was mine, and mine alone."

"But now—" I could not go on. I had been told he would die the following morning. At first light. I thrust the thought from my mind. I could not bear it. Already I felt the weight of grief, pressing on me. Crushing me. Making it hard for me to breathe.

"Listen, mother. We must not give up, even now." He looked into my eyes. "Tell me, has the queen given you any sign, any message—even the slightest word or gesture could be important—"

I shook my head.

"Are you certain?" The intensity of his gaze was alarming.

"I—I went to see her. I begged her to take my life for yours. She was scathing. But then—"

"Yes?" He grabbed my shoulders, his hands almost cruel in their grip.

"She sent a message to me. To Leicester House. To say that I could come and see you. A man from the court brought me. Someone I don't know. He has a coach—"

"Ha!" Rob gave an explosive shout, a shout of triumph. "She is sparing me, mother."

"But—"

"I know her. She is devious. This way I can appear to escape. She means me to go with you, when you leave here."

"I don't think so, Rob," I said tentatively. Part of me wanted to believe what he was saying, but my intuition told me he was wrong. The queen's note was ambiguous. Forgive her, she had written. Forgive her for what she had to do, I thought it meant. Forgive her for condemning Rob. But could I have misread her words? Could there have been hope in that message?

My head spun.

"Don't you see, mother? There are still those who want to see me on the throne, and not the puking James."

I shook my head. No. It couldn't be.

"Rob! You must see reason!"

He was re-lacing his boots, smoothing down his tousled hair.

"Is there a guard in the corridor?"

I looked through the tiny opening in the heavy door.

"I cannot see any."

"Perhaps, after you go—"

I felt panic. "No! I don't want to leave you!"

"The longer you stay, the greater my danger."

He was convinced that my presence was itself a message. That he would be released—or allowed to escape. I wanted so to believe him, against all reason and common sense . . .

Impulsively I hugged him once more, holding him to my chest with all my strength. My heart told me that he was wrong, that he must accept the ghastly truth that there would be no safety for him, no way out. But part of me called out, from some unknown place, show mercy. Show him a mother's mercy, and let him hope.

And so I let go of his broad shoulders, his strong arms. I let go, and smiled—a genuine smile of joy—and called for the guard.

"Watch for me, mother. I may need you, once I am away."

I nodded, continuing to smile, to look at his beloved face, wanting to remember every curve, every line, even as I heard the heavy footsteps of the guard approaching the door, the jingle of keys, Rob's hasty words of farewell. For though my tears were falling, I knew that he was right. There would be release. His suffering would not last long. The dread end would come, and swiftly, with the dawn. And until it did, I would give my beloved son the only gift I could offer. The gift of hope.

Once I was outside, in the cold night wind, I wept, clinging on to the chill stones of the old prison in which he was being kept. I wept as never before or since. I was past thinking, I had no reason left. Only sorrow and dread.

Rob!

I looked up into the vast dark above me. Bright stars shone down on me, on the sleeping city. I cried to the unanswering stars, not caring who heard me or what I uttered.

I remembered what I used to say to Rob when I put him to bed, as a little boy, patting his head. Go to sleep, son, and may you dance with the angels! I said the words now, a dozen times, a hundred, until they blurred together and, feeling dizzy and lost, I let the queen's messenger gently guide me back into the coach.

EPILOGUE

IT has finally happened: I have become the oldest person I know.

I am in my ninety-fourth year, I rejoice to say, and that makes me a full two years older than Mistress Vaux in Bishop's Whittlewood and she is not likely to outlive me, not with her fainting spells and her two canes and her intemperate views on the king and his unruly Parliament.

I am old indeed, as my great-great-grandchildren would be quick to tell you, and proud, and some would say overly eager to make my voice heard. It is become a raspy voice, it quavers, and I cannot sing hymns properly any more, or Christmas carols. I leave that to the children, whose sweet voices reach me from St. Peter's even now, across the quiet churchyard cemetery, as I write these words.

I write them sitting at my father's old oak desk, with mementos of the past before me, surrounding me. Comforting me, like the heated bricks on which I rest my old feet in these wintry days.

Miniatures of my children, all long gone, my small painting of Frank's last ship, the *Gift of God*, a dried nosegay of roses and daisies brought to me last spring by one of the little girls—was it one of Dorothy's long line of girls? One of the ones with my red hair, that rare shade so like the red-gold of the late autumn leaves? One of the pretty ones?

I confess I cannot remember all their names, there are so many little girls and boys now, and I have watched so many be born, and grow up, and love, and fall ill, and die. I am the oldest tree in the forest. The oldest stone in the churchyard. Or soon will be.

There is a stuffed pheasant in one corner on my father's old desk, splendid in his fine red and gold feathers. A memento of Walter the great hunter. And Robert's dear old eyeglasses. And my locket with the bit of Rob's hair inside. Not his hair as a man, but his wispy blond hair as a baby. My child of the Evening Star.

Now to more vital things. It has seemed proper to me, as I embark on my ninety-fourth year, to bring to a close that record of my life begun so long ago and filled with my memories and my thoughts. I had meant to write an account of my entire life, but when I reached that ghastly day thirty-three years ago when my son Rob died I paused in my account—and until now, today, I have not been able to resume my story.

But today my great-grandson Gervase brought me a sobering reminder that time is not infinite—though if you are nearly ninety-four, it seems infinite—and that perhaps I ought to just write whatever I need to write in a few more pages ("if you can be so brief, dear," he says with a smile and a pat on my shoulder) and then end this account.

I must note here that Gervase, for all his well-meaning tolerance of me and my high pile of pages telling the story of my life, is not a very good poet, though he fancies himself one. His verses are stale, almost as stale as his breath. I despise men who condescend to women. I am not a poet, but if I were, I would at least attempt to be original.

Gervase has attempted to write my epitaph in verse. He takes undue pride in his few lines. Pray God that when the hour comes, and I am laid in my grave, someone will have the good sense to prevent those lines from coming to light. What mediocre poetry could ever capture my life? That elusive, rapturous chain of hours, a chain that continues, even as my pen scratches.

A tumult outside. I must record it. A search is being ordered for suspicious persons, a watch set along the roads and chief highways. There is trouble at the court again. That faroff place, the royal court. Where Her Rough Majesty Gloriana reigned, and I shadowed her, dogged her, for so many years. And where now the coward in chief, our prince, King Charles the Undecided, casts his short shadow.

The tumult has reached the churchyard. They are searching for dangerous men, enemies of the crown. Renegades. But I, with my old ears, can still hear echoes of the renegades of Queen Elizabeth's time, villains all. And among them, I am very sad to say, my own son. Of this I can write no more.

There is no memento of Queen Elizabeth on my father's old desk. One might say—Gervase would approve this sentiment— that I am a living memento of her reign, her life. I knew her as few others did, though she hated me with a great and enduring bitterness. If there is a heaven, and she is in it (blasphemy! I know), then she is still hating me, even there. For one thing is sure in this world, and that is that love breeds hate, and envy, and the overwhelming desire for revenge. Fortunately it also breeds loving children, and grandchildren, and on and on. I have a fancy that one day, far into the future (for the world will not end, no matter what anyone may say), some auburn-haired little girl will read these ancient words of mine, and reach out to me across time, and bless me for sharing my self with her.

Are you that little girl? If so, I wish you well, child. I heartily wish you well.

But I am wandering. I have only one more thing to write, a trivial thing. It is that I wear the queen's worn-out blue and purple garter still, strapped to my old leg. And I walk a brisk mile, and even dance a galliard or two of a morning, in her memory.

And now unto him whose birthday is at hand, whose carols the children are singing, whose enduring love embraces us all, I give these words, in hope and thankfulness.

—*Letitia Knollys, Countess of Leicester*
In this year of our Lord 1634